Sarah's heart broke into song.
Jake wanted to marry her.

"Is that a yes?" he gasped, breaking from the kiss and burying his face in her hair. "If we go into this with our eyes open, there won't be any disappointments. We can give Kylie the family she needs, and we can enjoy this chemistry between us forever."

But chemistry tended to blur reasonable thought.

Sarah paused to sift through Jake's entire speech, trying to recall something close to the words a woman needed to hear from the man she loved....

Yes, he loved their daughter...but Jake didn't love *her,* and the last thing she needed was another sham of a marriage....

Dear Reader,

As Silhouette Books' 20th anniversary continues, Intimate Moments continues to bring you six superb titles every month. And certainly this month—when we begin with Suzanne Brockmann's *Get Lucky*—is no exception. This latest entry in her TALL, DARK & DANGEROUS miniseries features ladies' man Lucky O'Donlon, a man who finally meets the woman who is his match—and more.

Linda Turner's *A Ranching Man* is the latest of THOSE MARRYING McBRIDES!, featuring Joe McBride and the damsel in distress who wins his heart. Monica McLean was a favorite with her very first book, and now she's back with *Just a Wedding Away*, an enthralling marriage-of-convenience story. Lauren Nichols introduces an *Accidental Father* who offers the heroine happiness in THE LOVING ARMS OF THE LAW. *Saving Grace* is the newest from prolific RaeAnne Thayne, who's rapidly making a name for herself with readers. And finally, welcome new author Wendy Rosnau. After you read *The Long Hot Summer,* you'll be eager for her to make a return appearance.

And, of course, we hope to see you next month when, once again, Silhouette Intimate Moments brings you six of the best and most exciting romance novels around.

Enjoy!

Leslie J. Wainger
Executive Senior Editor

Please address questions and book requests to:
Silhouette Reader Service
U.S.: 3010 Walden Ave., P.O. Box 1325, Buffalo, NY 14269
Canadian: P.O. Box 609, Fort Erie, Ont. L2A 5X3

ACCIDENTAL
FATHER
LAUREN NICHOLS

INTIMATE MOMENTS®

Published by Silhouette Books

America's Publisher of Contemporary Romance

This is a story about family,
and I've been blessed with the very best.
For my children, Mike, Colette and Laurie, and the wonderful people who love them. Stephanie, Matt and Bob.
And for the sweetest grandkids in the world,
Nicholas, Lexi and Lena.
And always, for Mike.
I love you all.

 SILHOUETTE BOOKS

ISBN 0-373-07994-X

ACCIDENTAL FATHER

Visit us at www.romance.net

Printed in U.S.A.

Books by Lauren Nichols

Silhouette Intimate Moments

Accidental Heiress #840
Accidental Hero #893
Accidental Father #994

LAUREN NICHOLS

fell in love with Montana nearly two decades ago when she and her husband took their three children out West to see "cattle country." Montana has owned a chunk of her heart ever since. In addition to writing novels, Lauren's romance and mystery short stories have appeared in several leading magazines. She counts her family and friends as her greatest treasures. When she's not with them, this Pennsylvania author is either writing, trying unsuccessfully to give up French vanilla cappuccino or traveling with her husband, Mike.

IT'S OUR 20th ANNIVERSARY!
We'll be celebrating all year,
continuing with these fabulous titles,
on sale in March 2000.

Special Edition

#1309 Dylan and the Baby Doctor
Sherryl Woods

#1310 Found: His Perfect Wife
Marie Ferrarella

#1311 Cowboy's Caress
Victoria Pade

#1312 Millionaire's Instant Baby
Allison Leigh

#1313 The Marriage Promise
Sharon De Vita

#1314 Good Morning, Stranger
Laurie Campbell

Intimate Moments

#991 Get Lucky
Suzanne Brockmann

#992 A Ranching Man
Linda Turner

#993 Just a Wedding Away
Monica McLean

#994 Accidental Father
Lauren Nichols

#995 Saving Grace
RaeAnne Thayne

#996 The Long Hot Summer
Wendy Rosnau

Romance

#1432 A Royal Masquerade
Arlene James

#1433 Oh, Babies!
Susan Meier

#1434 Just the Man She Needed
Karen Rose Smith

#1435 The Baby Magnet
Terry Essig

#1436 Callie, Get Your Groom
Julianna Morris

#1437 What the Cowboy Prescribes...
Mary Starleigh

Desire

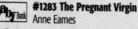
#1279 A Cowboy's Secret
Anne McAllister

#1280 The Doctor Wore Spurs
Leanne Banks

#1281 A Whole Lot of Love
Justine Davis

#1282 The Earl Takes a Bride
Kathryn Jensen

#1283 The Pregnant Virgin
Anne Eames

#1284 Marriage for Sale
Carol Devine

Chapter 1

"Be right there!" Sarah Harper gave up looking for her favorite spatula, then shoved the electric mixer to the back of the countertop, handed her two-year-old daughter an icing-covered beater and hurried to answer the doorbell.

If the caller wanted to sell her encyclopedias or a vacuum cleaner he was in big trouble. A hundred cookies sat on the kitchen's butcher-block work island waiting to be frosted, there were more in the oven, and Sarah was running behind. She'd been rushing ever since returning to town after spending two weeks caring for her aunt, who'd had surgery.

Dazzling Montana sunshine spilled through the screen as she opened the pretty Victorian's inside door and squinted up at the tall man on the porch. As her eyes adjusted to the morning's brightness, she got a quick impression of faded jeans, a blue plaid shirt and good shoulders on a lean, rangy frame.

Suddenly, shock razed Sarah's nerve endings, and all

thoughts of her catering business, wedding cookies, mini quiches and sherbet punch vanished in a rush of panic. Quickly, she schooled her expression—tried to pretend she didn't remember the cowboy on the porch. But as she watched his cordial smile fade and saw stunned recognition rise in his eyes, she knew pretending was a waste of time. He knew her too.

Sarah took a deep breath and swallowed. "Hello, Jake."

"Hello, Sarah," he said in the same hesitant tone. "It's been a long time."

"Yes," she replied nervously. "Yes, it has."

His voice was as deep as she remembered, yet the faint lines beside his dark blue eyes were a mystery, since she couldn't say if they'd been there before. But the moon over Cotton Creek had left her with a memory of high cheekbones, rugged features and collar-length dark hair. Now she could see that it wasn't just dark, but as black as the Stetson tugged low on his forehead.

Like those eyes, his hair color came as no surprise. She'd kissed those colors good morning every day for the past twenty-eight months...tucked those colors in every night.

"For-forgive me," she stammered, tugging the inside door nearly shut behind her. "I'm usually a little more together than this. It's just that...you're the last person I expected to see when I opened the door."

"Same here," he murmured, still assessing her uncertainly. "You said you were leaving Comfort."

She'd said a lot of things that night, none of which she wanted to remember. "Do you need directions?"

His gaze narrowed curiously. "Directions?"

Sarah nodded, praying that Kylie would stay in the kitchen with her tiny muffins and tea set. "Yes. If you didn't expect to see me, then that must mean you're looking for someone else.'' She drew a deep breath and released it on a tremble. ''Doesn't it?''

''I'm not sure. Why are you so nervous?''

''I'm not,'' she said, startled by his bluntness.

The last man she'd slept with glanced, frowning, into the front lawn where Sarah's fancy sign read Miss Lillian's Bed and Breakfast. When he faced her again, their past was in his eyes. Though, how could he *not* think about it? Beneath her apprehension and embarrassment, even she was having a hard time keeping her memories at bay. They'd been wild together.

''Sarah, I apologize if this makes you uneasy, but I really need a room. Just until I can find an apartment.''

Dear God.

''For now, I'm staying at the motel outside of town,'' he continued. ''But rooming here would be more convenient. It's closer to my office.''

She managed to find her voice. ''Your office?''

''Yes. In a nutshell, I've been hired to finish your ex-sheriff's term. I guess you haven't heard.''

''No. I—I've been away.''

''I see. Well, I'll be here until January. Longer if I like the town and the town likes me.'' He nodded at the door she guarded so resolutely. ''Would it be all right if I came in and looked around? I'd like to see your rooms.''

No! No, he couldn't! ''I'm sorry,'' she blurted, ''but I don't have any rooms available right now. And I don't think anyone else in town takes in boarders.''

''Then the vacancy sign out front is a mistake?'' His mouth thinned grimly. ''Maybe I should be talking to Miss Lillian.''

The second lie rushed out, even more desperate-sounding than the first. ''What I meant to say is, I'm closing.

This is my place. Miss Lillian passed away several years ago.''

Jake moved closer to the door, and Sarah took an uneasy step backward. A late-August breeze carried the earthy scent of his aftershave to her. She detected a marked difference in him from the man she remembered. This man was strong and confident—self-assured and determined. And suddenly she knew that his baring his soul to her that night had been an anomaly. He'd only shared his past because he was wounded and hurting, and he'd never expected to see her again.

''Look,'' he said. ''If you're worried about what happened between us before, I don't plan on repeating it. All I want is a warm bed and a roof over my head, preferably a little cleaner and a little closer to my office than the Twirling Spurs Motel. I wouldn't be here long, and I'm willing to pay whatever you want. Right now, I just need to find somewhere to—''

Suddenly his gaze shifted from her face to a spot somewhere behind and to the left of her, and his grave features gentled. ''Well, now,'' he said. ''Who do we have here?''

Miserable, Sarah turned around, already knowing who she'd see. As they'd talked, the inside door had drifted open and Kylie stood in the hall, silky black hair skimming her narrow shoulders, blue eyes peeking shyly from beneath her bangs. She was still wearing her pink eyelet nightie, and the beater in her hand was now frosting-free— which was more than Sarah could say for her daughter's hands and face. Kylie ran to her, and Sarah lifted her into her arms, praying that she would never know the fear her mother was experiencing at this moment.

''What's your name, cutie?'' Jake asked with a smile.

Kylie hid her face in Sarah's neck and whispered, ''More f'osting, Mommy?''

Frosting, Sarah thought gratefully. *Cookies.* An excuse to terminate the conversation. "In a minute, sweetheart," she answered, and faced Jake again. "I'm sorry, but I have cookies in the oven. I hope you find an apartment soon, Mr.—" *Oh, God, she didn't know his last name.* They'd been as intimate as a man and woman could be, yet they hadn't exchanged the simplest information.

"It's Russell," he supplied quietly, then added, "Sarah, relax. We didn't do anything wrong. We both needed a friend that night. I was glad you were there for me, and I think you felt the same. At least until—"

Sarah jerked away from the screen. "I have to go. You might want to check the paper for apartments. Our weekly comes out today." Then, before he could speak again, she shut the inside door and collapsed against it, tears filling her eyes.

She didn't have one-night stands! She didn't! Yet the child in her arms was proof positive that, once, she had done just that.

Sarah hugged Kylie close, kissed her hair, then put her down and watched her run into the kitchen. He couldn't know. This man who had always longed for family—this man she'd known for only *one hour*—would want to be part of his child's life. It was as certain as snow in winter. And Sarah would never share her daughter with a stranger.

She'd barely taken a step when she acknowledged the other reason for her anxiety. Beneath his questions and her fears, the electric attraction they'd encountered three years ago was still there. And if Jake learned that Kylie was his, they'd be thrown together again.

Maybe her life wasn't a thrill a minute, but it was stable, orderly and uncomplicated, and she liked it that way. She didn't know what would happen if hormones and memories tested her judgment...again.

* * *

Pulse pounding, Jake left the sparsely populated outskirts of town and drove back toward his office. On his left, towering mountain peaks rose out of thick, rich timberland to pierce the blue sky. But he was only half-aware of them.

He was thinking of Sarah. Pretty, honey-blond, brown-eyed Sarah. Pretty, frightened-to-the-bone Sarah.

He understood the awkwardness. They had intimate knowledge of each other—and they'd never expected to see each other again. Hell, he hadn't been sure of what to say at first, either. But why the anxiety? Why the rattled, frantic behavior? Unless…

Of course.

A child usually meant there was a husband in the picture. Was she afraid that if she rented Jake a room, her new husband would see the tension between them and start asking questions? Or, he wondered, scowling, had she gone back to the womanizing creep she'd divorced?

He plucked his sunglasses from the visor and slipped them on, his mind rolling back to that night in the tall grass—just as it had so many times after he'd returned home from his discouraging visit here. It all came back— all the heat, all the desperation, and all the guilt. Because it had been clear that any pleasure she'd derived from their lovemaking had disappeared when they were both able to breathe normally again and she'd faced what she'd done.

Jake sighed. He'd known she wasn't thinking straight that night; he shouldn't have let it go that far. But chemistry was chemistry, and he'd put nobility on the back burner and taken the comfort he'd needed, too.

Punching a few buttons, he found an upbeat country song on the radio and acknowledged the feeling in his gut that said the chemistry was still there. But he wouldn't bother her again. Even if she weren't already attached, she wasn't the kind of woman he looked for these days. She was too sweet, too wholesome—and despite the fevered way they'd come together—too principled. All he wanted from a woman these days was an occasional date and some no-strings sex. He'd given up the two-point-five kids and picket-fence myth. Dear, deceitful little Heather had set him straight on that score.

Although, if he had to be honest, his trust in women had been shaken a lot earlier than that. A boy couldn't grow up knowing he was an afterthought in his own mother's life without having a few hang-ups.

A horn blast jarred him, and Jake spiked the brake as a white truck bearing Idaho plates shot across the road in front of him. Quickly, he looked across the intersection to check for a stop sign, then swore when he spotted it— flattened at the side of the road. Obviously, the out-of-state driver hadn't seen it. Jake nearly gave chase, then decided against it. There was no point wasting time on an arrest that wouldn't hold up. The best he could do now was see that the sign was fixed before someone got hurt.

The midmorning sun glinted off the sheriff department's white Jeep as Jake pulled his tan Mountaineer in beside it. He got out and slammed the door. As he walked past the wide front window with its fancy gold seal, he waved at Maggie Dalton, who was just hanging up the phone.

"Hi, again," he said, coming inside.

"Hi." She finished scribbling a note, added it to a pile and sent him a friendly smile. "Didn't expect you back so soon."

"I'm fast. Anybody report a downed stop sign at the corner of Mountain and Prairie?"

"Yep. County maintenance is on it."

"Good."

The reception area was fairly large, with the dispatcher's desk in the middle of the room, and flanked on both sides by a low-railing fence with a swinging gate. To the right stood a row of straight-back chairs and the door to the lockup; to the left, Jake's private office. Above the waist-high wood paneling, the walls were pale municipal green and needed a fresh coat of paint.

Jake hung his hat on a peg by the door, then walked to the desk and nodded at the stack of messages that hadn't been there an hour ago. "Some of those for me?"

"Nope, all of them. Nothing too pressing. Judge Quinn wants you to stop by his office at the courthouse sometime this week—but not Friday, he's going fishing. And there's a town council meeting on Friday that you're required to attend. The list of topics to be discussed is in the computer. I'll print it out for you."

A teasing grin lit her eyes. "Oh. And the mayor wants you to join her for dinner before the meeting."

"What's the grin for?"

"Was I grinning? Gee, I didn't mean to." Still fighting a smile, she handed him his messages. "The rest are mostly well-wishes from businessmen. They'd like you to return their calls when you get time."

Jake sifted through them, deciding that whatever had tickled her fancy was destined to remain a secret. "Anything else?"

"Your uniforms arrived. I put them in your office."

"Thanks. I'll change before I start my shift."

His deputy was a pretty woman in her late twenties with a long black braid and brown eyes, and from the little he'd seen, organized, focused and good at her job. A jittery feeling pooled in his belly. *She was also Ross Dalton's brand-new wife.* He'd been stunned—and pleased—to receive an invitation to their wedding at the Brokenstraw Ranch when he'd toured the town a week ago. *Life was full of surprises.*

"So, did you get a room at Miss Lillian's?" Maggie asked. "Or did your male pride balk at living in a pink house?"

"The color was fine." In fact, he'd found it striking with all the curlicued white gingerbread and spindled railings on the wraparound porch. He even liked the lace curtains and tiny candle-lights in the front windows. "Unfortunately," he said, frowning, "the owners are closing it."

Maggie blinked in surprise. "After just having it painted? I spoke to Sarah yesterday, and she never mentioned it."

No surprise there. The way she'd acted, he'd bet a month's salary that she hadn't planned to do any such thing until he'd shown up. He'd also bet she'd reopen the instant he found a permanent residence.

"Did Sarah say why she was closing?"

"No, she just told me to check the want ads. Maybe she and her husband don't want strangers roaming the house with their daughter being so young."

Maggie clicked on the computer to her right and scanned a file list. "Interesting theory, but Sarah's not married."

Jake froze for several seconds, then tucked his messages in his breast pocket. His blood clipped along a little faster.

"In fact," Maggie added, "if she hadn't divorced Vince Harper a few years ago, technically she'd be a widow."

He was so startled, he couldn't keep his shock from showing. "Sar—the woman I just spoke to was married to *Vince Harper?*"

Maggie punched a key on the keyboard, and the printer

started spitting out data. "I take it you've heard the name?"

Headlines hyping Harper's notorious diamond theft blazed through Jake's mind, complete with a mug shot of a smirking man with a long blond ponytail. "Oh, yeah," he said, scowling. "I've heard it. Somehow, I can't imagine…"

"Sarah with him?"

Jake nodded. If he remembered correctly, Harper had been a bona fide loser for most of his adult life. No wonder Sarah had said the things she had the night they met. He pictured the three of them together—Harper, Sarah and that cute little girl—and held back another scowl. No way did *that* picture look right.

Maggie ripped a sheet from the printer. "Here's the topic list for Friday's meeting."

"Thanks. Now, if you can just find me a place to hang my hat…"

"Sorry, the best I can do is bring in the paper when it comes."

"Good enough." He grinned, then crossed the floor to his office, sank into his swivel chair and stared into space.

Sarah had been married to *Vince Harper?* The small-time hood who'd knocked over a Florida jeweler and gotten away with the gems? Unbelievable.

Jake had been working in Glacier County when it happened, but most lawmen in Montana knew the case well. The feds had put out an urgent APB, figuring that Harper would head for home. Agents had ended up apprehending the jerk while he was meeting his needs at a brothel a few miles outside of Comfort. After finding only a few diamonds on him, they'd searched the premises, without success. Then they'd learned that he'd spent time at his ex-wife's home the previous night, and they'd searched Sarah's house, too.

The remaining diamonds had never been recovered.

Jake eased back in his chair. Now that he remembered the time frame, the scandal had occurred right around when he'd found Sarah crying in that grassy overflow parking lot. But she hadn't mentioned the diamonds or feds that night. She'd only told him that her divorce had just become final, and she was through with marriage. Or anything close to it.

He'd understood. Fate, or karma or whatever power ruled the worlds of the romantically unlucky had handed him a big fat heartache only a week before.

The carnival aromas of cotton candy and French fries drifted in from Jake's memory, and suddenly he could smell them, and hear the music floating down from the Founder's Day celebration two streets away. He caught the faint perfume of the summer cottonwoods, too, and the stirring fragrance of the teary woman in his arms. They'd emptied their souls, and had danced. Because nothing comforted better than a human touch....

"Don't cry," he whispered, trying to keep his attraction under wraps as they moved together in the calf-high grass. "Believe me, you're better off without a cheat and a liar."

"I know," she answered in a ragged voice. "It's not that I still care about him—I don't. I don't ever want to see him again. But I'll miss being in love."

"You won't miss it for long. You're a beautiful woman. There'll be someone else."

Sarah shook her head. "No, I don't trust my judgment anymore. I was so sure he was good, and decent, and... And he was none of those things. I won't chance marriage again."

"You're prepared to be alone for the rest of your life?"

"It's better than hurting all the time."

Jake had to agree. Since Heather, he'd adopted a new philosophy. Don't expect too much from a relationship and you won't be disappointed. But God, he thought, shortening his steps to a gentle rock and sway, it still felt good to hold someone.

He'd thought he couldn't feel any lower when he'd found out Heather was sleeping around. He'd been wrong. On the heels of that, he'd learned that the father he'd never known—the father he'd imagined and hoped for as a child—had died. But his dad had sired two other sons. That's why Jake had traveled three hundred miles to Comfort, Montana. He'd come to meet his brothers.

"You should tell your brothers who you are," Sarah murmured, seeming to read his mind. "It's too late to do anything about your dad, but you do have other family."

"I tried. Walked right up to them tonight at the food booth and lost my nerve. I didn't want them thinking I was looking for money or a chunk of their ranch. I don't have any proof that we're related."

"Maybe your mother could talk to them."

"Nope," he said, and forced a smile. "Emily's gone, too. But considering that she never even told *me* who my father was, I doubt she'd get involved even if she were alive. If I hadn't run into a friend of hers last week, I still wouldn't know."

"Oh," she said softly. "Oh, I'm sorry."

"Yeah, me too," he said. "Would've been nice to know the guy responsible for my being here."

Sarah's compassionate gaze gentled on his. And suddenly, there was something so special and giving about her—something so good—that he needed to take a tiny bit of it for himself. Swallowing the lump in his throat, he cupped her face, lowered his head and kissed her. Softly. Briefly. Then, not so briefly.

Slowly, Jake eased away, feeling his blood pump harder, feeling the stirrings he'd been trying to ignore for the past hour finally surface.

Sarah touched his face.

He searched her eyes.

Then hungry lips found each other, and dancing became sweet, needy friction.

Maggie rapped sharply on the door, shattering his thoughts as she breezed inside. "Here's the paper. Hope there's something promising in there."

Jake almost stood, then realized with a start that he'd gotten far too involved in his memory. "Thanks." Taking the paper, he opened it to the want ads to cover his embarrassment. "Seems like that's all I ever say to you."

"No reason to. I haven't done anything."

"Right. You're only helping me find a place to live, and boarding Blackjack at your ranch."

"Not mine, my family's. And it doesn't take a lot of time to feed and water one more horse."

"I'm still grateful."

"And you're still welcome." Maggie paused for a moment, then spoke hesitantly. "Any chance you'll be here for a while?"

Jake glanced up from the disappointing listings. "I plan to be. Do you have errands to run?"

"No, but I need to talk to Ross. We have tentative plans to meet at Aunt Ruby's at eleven-thirty, but I can stay until Joe gets back if there's something in the paper that piques your interest."

"Go," he said. "Have lunch with your husband. From the looks of it, I'm out of luck unless I want to buy a used washer and dryer, or baby-sit from eight to four. If a crime wave hits, I'll phone you at the café."

"Great," she said with a bright smile. "See you later."

But as the door closed in the outer office, Jake's thoughts returned to Sarah.

Shoving the paper aside, he went to his office window, remembering again how extraordinary their lovemaking had been. An illogical stab of jealousy followed as he imagined her with Vince Harper.

Turning from the window, he started back to his desk. How could she have let Harper touch her, feeling the way she did about the pony-tailed creep? Worse, how could she have let herself get preg—

Jake froze in his tracks as that family picture he'd conjured earlier formed again in his mind and he realized why, aside from obvious reasons, it had looked all wrong.

Vince Harper had had blond hair.

Jake stopped breathing as his mind played a cautious game of connect the dots. First he ticked off the months since he'd made love with Sarah. Then he took a guess at her daughter's age.

Hair color didn't necessarily prove parentage, he told himself as his heart pounded. Eye color didn't, either, unless you had enough family history to factor in. But Sarah Harper was a brown-eyed blonde, and her ex-husband's hair had been light.

Kylie Harper had blue eyes, and her hair was black.

Every adrenaline-juiced nerve, muscle and cell in Jake's body sprang to life, and he damned Maggie's early lunch. He had to see Sarah again.

She's becoming a little person, Sarah thought, shooing Kylie into the single bed in the first-floor toy room. But she still had that precious baby voice. That sweet, trusting baby squeak that often replaced *L* and *R* sounds with *W*s, but managed to make herself understood very well, anyway. For a child who wasn't yet two and a half, Kylie had an amazing vocabulary.

"Mommy, I'n not tired yet."

Sarah kissed the tip of her nose and covered her with a thin blanket. Then she squeezed into the narrow bed with her daughter, dodging half a dozen stuffed animals, a green dinosaur and a naked Barbie doll with wild hair.

"I know you're not," Sarah murmured. "But Mommy and Pooh are, so we're all going to take a nap before we start supper. Now, you close your eyes and I'll close mine, and before you know it, it'll be time to wake up."

"Let's look at Kylie pictures!"

Sarah smiled. "Nope, we'll look at the photo album later. It's time to dream." In only a few minutes, dark-lashed lids closed over blue eyes like her daddy's, and Kylie was asleep.

Sarah felt her heart break.

Time to dream? If she ever slept again, her sleep would be filled with nightmares. One indiscretion. One terrible, wonderful mistake three years ago had given her the child she'd always wanted. But it had also given her the greatest fear she'd ever known. He would be living here now, seeing them at the market and church, bumping into them on the street.

He had a right to know. A man like Jake—who'd been raised by a rootless single mother then shuffled from foster home to foster home when she died—*deserved* to know he had a daughter. But if she told him, what then?

Even joint custody would be a horror, and it could happen, given the courts' near-manic sympathy for fathers' rights lately. Just last week, a friend of Sarah's had lost a custody battle that should never have been decided in the father's favor. If that happened, and Kylie was taken from her...

Sarah tried to contain her panic. Maybe they should leave—just pack up and move. It wouldn't be easy to establish her catering business in another town, and her dad would miss them, as they would miss him. But he had friends, didn't he? He and Judge Quinn were always doing something together.

Tears welled, and Sarah touched her forehead to her sleeping child's. No, she couldn't do that to her father. With her mother's death still a raw ache after nearly two years, he depended on Sarah for love and support. But Kylie was another matter. Kylie's laughter and kisses had become his lifeline. She couldn't take that from him, just as she couldn't deprive Kylie of the grandfather she adored.

Blinking back tears, Sarah slid her arm out from under Kylie's neck, backed out of the bed below the protective side rail, then moved silently into the hall and closed the door to within a crack.

She would not cry, she told herself. She would not be a weak, blubbering wreck ever again. The last time she'd allowed that to happen, a lonely deputy sheriff on holiday to meet the brothers he'd never known had found her by Cotton Creek, and Kylie had been conceived.

She would pull herself together and tell herself she was overreacting. She would make the meatballs and sauce for the Tully girl's nuptials and put some aside for tonight's supper. She would not let Jake Russell's threatening presence get to her. And she would *not* cry.

All right, she decided as her tears rolled, anyway, she would cry. But she would do it quietly.

Chapter 2

Keyed up and irked that he had to wait for oncoming traffic, Jake stopped the department's white Jeep opposite Sarah's house and waited for a battered red truck to go by. He was startled when the grizzled old man behind the wheel sent him a cold, hard look as he drove past.

"You have a nice day, too," Jake muttered, wondering what he'd done to tick the man off already. Was the driver a fan of Comfort's ousted ex-sheriff? Or had the official vehicle and Jake's uniform made him wonder what Sarah had done to earn a visit from a lawman?

Easy answer, he thought, hitting the gas pedal and making a squealing left turn. She just might have given birth to his daughter.

Much of her pink Victorian home was hidden from the road by a thick stand of pines. Jake's heart leapt as he left them behind and moved up the steep, paved driveway. Sarah was just descending the porch steps.

The instant she saw the car, her spine stiffened, and Jake

knew their meeting wasn't going to go well. But that knowledge didn't prevent him from admiring her long tanned legs and cutoff denim shorts as she strode to the middle of the yard. A length of wide black plastic fluttered from her right hand, and a roll of silver duct tape circled her wrist, bracelet-style.

He swore as he realized what she was about to do, then cut the engine, got out and quickly crossed the lawn. By the time he reached her, she'd already draped the plastic over her sign and was fighting the wind to secure it to the post.

"Why are you doing this?" he demanded.

"Why am I doing what?"

Damn, he hated it when people answered that way. He tried to count to ten—and made it to five. "If you're closing because you don't want to rent me a room, forget I even asked. I'm not going to make a big deal of your staying open. You have a child to support."

"I don't need the income from the bed-and-breakfast to support Kylie," she returned, ripping off another piece of tape and slapping it on her sign. "And my closing has nothing to do with you."

"After the talk I had with Maggie, that's a little hard to believe."

Sarah stopped moving, and her gaze widened accusingly. But there was hurt in her eyes, too. "You told Maggie about us?"

Sighing, Jake shook his head, feeling bad that he'd put her on the defensive. But if she thought that giving him attitude would scare him off, she was wrong. "I don't kiss and tell, Sarah. My conversation with Maggie concerned my finding a room to rent. When I told her you were closing, she was surprised. She said she'd spoken to you recently, and you hadn't mentioned it."

With a cool look, she gathered the plastic together at the base of her sign, then ripped off another length of tape and wrapped it tightly. "I didn't tell Maggie I'd just had my teeth cleaned, either, but that doesn't mean it didn't happen." Sliding the roll of tape back on her arm, she stared at him through wind-tossed bangs. "Why is my closing or *not* closing so important to you? We're strangers."

"If we were strangers, my showing up here this morning wouldn't have rattled you the way it did. You're not doing much better now. Why is that?"

"Why?" she repeated in an incredulous tone. "How can you even ask that question? Seeing you reminds me of something I did that I'm not very proud of, and I don't want to be reminded of it. Maybe what happened between us was just another roll in the hay for you—"

"I told you it wasn't."

"—but I don't sleep around." Her white knit top had a scooped neckline, and her pulse hammered at the base of her throat. Inappropriate or not, Jake remembered kissing her there.

"The truth is," she continued, "I've been thinking about closing for a while now. Your showing up just pushed my plans ahead a few months. I'm finding that I don't have time to make meals and change sheets for guests anymore. My catering business is doing very well, and—and Kylie's growing up fast. She deserves more time with me, and I need more time with her."

Something in Jake softened. Whether she was his child or not, he was glad Sarah could work out of her home and give Kylie the attention and support she needed. He'd loved his mother, and in her way, he supposed Emily had loved him. But he'd always known he was third in line behind the current boyfriend and the next party. He hadn't fared much better with the foster parents he'd stayed with after Emily had died. Kylie would never know that loneliness.

The low hum of an engine drew Jake's attention, and he turned to see a car come up the driveway, squeeze past his Jeep and continue on to the far side of the house. It stopped in the small parking area assigned to guests.

The color drained from Sarah's face as an older man got out of the car.

"We're back, Mommy!" he called with a broad smile. "Safe and sound." Then he opened the back door of his gray sedan and lifted Kylie out of her car seat.

Even as his heartbeat increased, Jake was startled to realize he'd been so involved with Sarah that he'd nearly forgotten Kylie was his main reason for coming back here. As she raced across the lawn to her mother, he fought to keep his features calm and controlled. Was Kylie his? Could she be?

"Hi, sweetheart," Sarah said warmly, her voice shaking a little as she scooped her daughter into her arms. "Did you and Grandpa have a nice lunch at Aunt Ruby's?"

"I had ice cweam!"

"I can see that," Sarah replied. "It's all over your shirt. We'll have to change it before your nap."

"Sorry," the older man said, chuckling as he walked to them. "I should've asked Ruby for a bib. And before you yell at me, she had macaroni and cheese before the ice cream—I promise."

"But more ice cream than macaroni, I'll bet," Sarah said, laughing. Her smile faded a little then, and after giving Jake a hesitant look, she put Kylie down. "Dad, this is Sheriff Russell. Sheriff, my father, Bill Malloy."

"Nice to meet you," Jake said, and they clasped hands. "Same here."

Sarah's father was a good-looking man in his late fifties, and aging well, despite the fair amount of gray in his dark hair and mustache. His choice of vehicles—a sedan—as well as his gray trousers and yellow knit shirt, suggested that he didn't ranch or farm.

"So what do you think of our little town, Sheriff?"

"I like it. Hope I have the chance to stay for a while."

"You're talking about the November election," Malloy guessed. "Well, just don't tick off Ed Cooper at the paper or any of our local busybodies in the next couple of months, and you shouldn't have a problem."

"Thanks for the advice," he answered, thinking about the old man in the red truck. "But it's hard to know what annoys people until you get to know them."

"In this town, it could be anything," Malloy returned wryly. "No matter what you do, you're bound to rub someone the wrong way." His devoted gaze fell to Kylie. "Except for Kylie, here. She loves everybody."

Malloy's statement seemed to invite a conversation with his pretty little granddaughter, and Jake crouched down and smiled. She wore black shorts and a gray knit shirt with black sleeves and Mickey Mouse ears stitched to the hood hanging against her back. Or maybe they were Minnie Mouse ears. Suddenly everything this tiny girl wore, every move she made, every silky black hair above her blue eyes and animated baby face were vitally important to him.

"Hi, honey," he said.

Lightning quick, Kylie speared his badge with her index finger. "That's a star!"

Jake's heart took off running, and he wondered how he'd lived this long without feeling this many emotions at once.

Sarah tugged Kylie back against her legs. "I'm sorry,"

she said hurriedly. ''She gets rambunctious when she has too much sugar.''

''No, no, she's fine,'' Jake said, pushing to his feet.

''Let's go to *your* house and pway!'' Kylie piped up, and Jake wasn't sure what to say. For starters, he didn't have a house. But, by God, if Kylie was his, he'd find one.

''Dad?'' Sarah said, looking pale again. ''Why don't you take Kylie inside? I'll be right in to change her shirt.''

For a second, Malloy stared curiously at his daughter. Then he shrugged, grinned and scooped Kylie into his arms. ''Sure. We'll have a cup of coffee while we wait, won't we, cupcake?''

''Dad—''

''Okay,'' he said, chuckling. ''We'll have milk.''

When they'd disappeared inside, Sarah mustered a wobbly grin and sighed. ''He spoils her rotten.''

''He probably can't help himself. She's wonderful.''

''Thank you.'' Sarah glanced toward the door, a troubled look still clouding her eyes. ''I'd better go. Dad can't say no to her, and if he's drinking coffee, she's stealing sips. Between the sugar and the caffeine…well, you know.''

But Jake wasn't thinking of sugar and caffeine; he was studying Sarah's classic features again—her wide brown eyes and lightly tanned skin. Her sideswept bangs and shoulder-length blond hair.

He realized that his suspicions were still only that. But none of Sarah's coloring had shown up in her daughter.

None of it.

Suddenly, every warning he'd given himself about taking his time and gaining her confidence deserted him. He had to know. His chest was on fire, and he had to know.

''Does her other grandfather spoil her, too?'' he asked as she turned toward the house.

"What?"

He fell into step beside her. "You said your father spoils her. I asked if her other—"

"No, her other Grandpa passed away."

"And by that, you mean your ex-husband's father?" he persisted. Or did she mean *his* father? He'd told her that night that his dad had died before Jake had a chance to meet him.

Sarah moved faster through the grass. "My late husband's father passed away, yes. Now, if you'll excuse me, I need to change my daughter."

No, dammit, he wouldn't excuse her. He'd come here looking for answers, and he wasn't leaving until he got them. Kylie waved from the screen door, and a small voice cautioned, *Don't press your luck.* But he couldn't listen. Just one question. Maybe two.

"How old is she, Sarah?"

She started up the steps. "She's two."

"When will she be three?"

On the porch now, Sarah whirled on him, her dark eyes full of fire and fear. But was she afraid because a lingering conversation might tip her father off that they had a past, or because she was keeping a secret she didn't want Jake to know?

"What is this?" she asked in a low, shaky voice. "An occupational hazard? Do you interrogate everyone you meet?"

Jake raised his hands and backed off. He'd pushed too hard. If Kylie *was* his daughter, he didn't want to antagonize Sarah, because he wanted to be part of her life. If she *wasn't*, he didn't want to look like a fool. He'd already shared too much of himself with this woman, and the last thing he wanted was to look weak in her eyes. Though why he cared, he didn't know.

The radio in the Jeep squawked loudly, and a distorted voice hailed him. Jake sent a frustrated look at the car. "No, I don't interrogate everyone I meet. I'm sorry if I gave you that impression. I'd just like for us to be friends."

The radio squawked again.

"Please..." he said, sidling away. "Just give me a minute to answer that, then we can finish talking. Okay?"

But by the time he'd reached through the window, grabbed the mike and looked up again, Sarah was gone and both front doors were closed. "Yeah, Maggie," he said through a sigh. "What's up?"

A cattle theft, that's what was up. Two auction-ready steers were missing from the Wilson ranch. Jake drove out there and checked the cut fence line, then listened to Hap Wilson's diatribe about shooting first and asking questions later if he found anyone near his stock again. Then Jake returned to the office without a shred of evidence, knowing that chances were, the people who'd taken Wilson's cattle would never be found—not unless they made a habit of it and got sloppy.

It was close to five-thirty when Jake parked the Jeep in Sarah's driveway again and got out. Three visits in one day made him feel more like a stalker than a man trying to get at the truth, but he couldn't help himself.

Until this afternoon, all he'd had were suppositions. Now he had more. It wasn't the most commendable thing he'd ever done, but a trip to the courthouse had told him that Kylie had been born on April 18.

April was nine months from July and the Founder's Day celebration.

Quickly ascending the steps to the wraparound porch, Jake rang the bell, waited a moment, then jabbed it again.

He could hear it chime inside the house, but there were no footsteps on their way to him, no high-pitched baby giggles and running feet. Still, he had a strong feeling that Sarah was inside.

For a second, he considered checking the garage in the back to see if her car was there. But he knew if Sarah saw him do it, it would make her even more wary and defensive.

He rang the bell again. And once more, all he got for his trouble was silence.

Frustrated, Jake pulled a hand over his face, then yanked off the Stetson that matched his uniform and tugged it back on. All right, he thought, descending the steps again. She'd won this round. But she couldn't avoid him forever.

"Jus' whisper?" Kylie murmured again.

Sarah nodded and kept her voice low. "Yes, baby, this is a funny game. We just whisper." She was holding Kylie again and trying to keep her still, two rooms away from the long panes of glass fronting the porch. Sarah peered through the dining room's slightly open French doors, into the parlor and finally through the lace shades and curtains. She exhaled in relief when the white Jeep did a two-point turn in her driveway, coasted down to the road and disappeared. Thank heaven she'd seen him pull in and had time to shut off the TV.

Three visits in one day? She didn't know how, but somehow, Jake suspected that Kylie was his child. That second visit he'd paid on them had had nothing to do with his wanting them to be friends. Worse, his showing up here had drawn curious looks from her father, and she wasn't ready to make explanations to him yet.

"Oh, sweetie," she murmured. "What are we going to do?"

Feathery eyebrows dipped as Kylie seemed to consider her answer for a moment. Then she ventured, "Have cake?"

Despite the conflicting feelings of fear and attraction that still shivered through her, Sarah had to smile. "Good idea. We could both use some chocolate. But let's have supper first."

Only one person knew that Kylie's father was a deputy sheriff from one of Montana's northern counties—Sarah herself. She hadn't even told her parents because she'd feared they'd track him down and demand that he "do the right thing." Now, two nerve-racking days after Jake's last visit, she was about to add another name to the list.

The bell over the door jangled as Sarah carried Kylie and a small tote bag full of toys into the noise and bustle of Aunt Ruby's Café. As usual, the restaurant rang with country music, clanking silverware and the buzz of lunchtime diners. Sarah scanned the crowded tables and bright red booths, then moved forward.

Ruby Cayhill hadn't been hard to spot. The elderly proprietress was the only person in the café under five feet, over seventy-five and wearing red high-top sneakers. The red cardigan topping her white uniform dress flapped around her skinny frame as she approached them. Though the tiny woman insisted that everyone call her *Aunt* Ruby, her only blood kin were the Dalton brothers who owned the Brokenstraw Ranch.

"Afternoon, Sarah," she sang out, carrying two empty coffeepots toward the lunch counter. She grinned at Kylie. "Hi there, sweet pea. You look like a gal who'd like some French fries."

Sarah managed a smile. "She sure would. It's all she's talked about since I told her where we were headed." Falling into step with Ruby, Sarah glanced down at the hairnet capping the woman's frizz of gray curls. "So how's business?"

"Fine as frog hair." Ruby cackled. Pale blue eyes twinkled behind her wire-rimmed spectacles. "Cash register's been ringin' since sunup." Moving behind the counter, she rinsed the empty pots, then rigged the coffeemakers with fresh grounds and water.

"How's everything on yer end of town?" she called over her shoulder.

Sarah sat on one of the red vinyl stools, then settled Kylie on her lap. "Not as fine as frog hair, but things are coming along."

"Heard you shut down the bed-and-breakfast."

Sarah smiled wryly. Why was she not surprised that Ruby already knew? "Who told you?"

"Who didn't?" Ruby harrumphed. "You know this town better'n most."

Yes, she did. Marrying Vince had made her the target of gossips for years. Kylie's birth had given them even more to talk about. Sarah glanced around the room where rotating ceiling fans cooled too many customers who might overhear. "Actually," she said, softening her voice, "that's what I'd like to talk about. When you have time."

Ruby paused for an instant, then clicked on the coffeemakers and turned from her task. "Got time right now. Will you be wantin' lunch?"

Sarah shook her head. "Just French fries and apple juice for Kylie."

Motioning for Sarah to follow, Ruby grabbed a booster seat and strode to a back booth, calling the order to one of her waitresses. "And bring us two cups of regular," she added.

But once there, Sarah put Kylie in the booth with her

toys, and she and Ruby took seats at the adjacent table. Sarah didn't want Kylie overhearing their conversation.

When Kylie was engrossed in her French fries and happily humming along to the nursery rhymes coming from her "boom box," Sarah met Ruby's gaze over their coffee cups.

Some days, Ruby Cayhill was as no-nonsense and brittle as a pan of rock candy. But she had one of the warmest hearts and truest stares Sarah had ever known. She'd always been a good friend. Since her mother's death, Sarah had come to depend on Ruby's counsel even more.

"Thank you, Aunt Ruby."

"Ain't done nothin' yet, honey. What's the trouble?"

Sarah drew a fortifying breath. Whoever said that confession was good for the soul had exaggerated badly. "It's the new sheriff."

"The sheriff?" Ruby chuckled, and her pale eyes lit with mischief. "From what I've seen, he's no trouble a-tall. Takes all his meals here, and the women can't keep their eyes off him. That young fella's been dang good fer business."

"Has...has he been in today?"

"Not thirty minutes ago."

Good. Then he wouldn't be walking in while she and Kylie were here. Sarah stirred cream into her coffee and watched Ruby bring her cup to her lips. There was no point in sugarcoating the announcement. She might just as well spit it out. "I slept with him, Aunt Ruby."

Coffee sloshed over the rim as Ruby clattered her cup back into her saucer. After a moment, she took several napkins from the chrome dispenser and mopped up the spill. "Well, I'm no expert on such things, but if that's what you call trouble—"

"It was three years ago," Sarah continued quietly.

"Right after that horrible mess with Vince. Jake is Kylie's father."

Periodically checking on Kylie, she told Ruby all of it—how she'd been crying, tired of people whispering behind their hands about her, hating their pitying looks. Then how Jake had found her like that, and he'd been just as low as she was.

"So, mutual commiserating became something else," Sarah concluded. "Now..." She smiled tightly, but with love, as she watched Kylie triple-dip a mangled French fry in the puddle of ketchup on her plate. "Now I have a precious little daughter."

"Does he know?"

"He suspects. And he deserves to know, but I'm afraid to tell him. You remember Betsy Chappell, don't you?"

"Moved up to Helena a while back."

Sarah nodded. "I saw her last week when I was there helping my aunt Vera after her back surgery. Betsy just lost a custody battle with her baby's father. He was married, and when he went back to his wife, Betsy had some emotional problems. Unfortunately, the man's a respected doctor with influential friends. Now he and his wife are raising Betsy's son."

Ruby's sober gaze studied Kylie. "Afraid the sheriff'll git himself a lawyer?"

Sarah nodded again. "He never knew his father, and he was raised by a single mother with a gypsy life-style. After she died, he spent some time in foster homes. Aunt Ruby, this man has wanted a real family all of his life. Yes, I'm afraid he'll get a lawyer."

"More dip-its, Mommy?"

Sarah rose to squirt more ketchup on Kylie's plate, then returned to her seat. "I can't lose her. Even joint custody would be a horror." Tears stung her eyes, but she refused to let them fall. "He's a stranger," she murmured. "How can I tell him he has a daughter when I don't know anything about him?"

Ruby chewed her lower lip for a time, then settled her gaze on Sarah's. "First off, I don't think you'll lose her. But Lord knows I been wrong before. Once when I voted fer Cy Farrell, who turned out to be a low-down skunk, and once when I swore up and down I could raise watermelons.

"That said, I think he's a decent sort. No fella without a conscience woulda stopped to make sure you were okay that night. Plus, he's been here twice a day since he arrived, and I've watched him close. After the last fool we had wearin' a badge in this town, I need t' be sure this fella deserves my vote come November. If he keeps up the way he's goin', he's got it."

"So what do I do?" Sarah asked. "What would *you* do?"

"Think on it some, I reckon. Trust that the Lord knows what He's doin', bringin' Jake Russell to this town. I'm fresh out of magic wands, Sarah. If I'd had any years ago, I'da zapped that cheatin' husband of yers clear to Jupiter. Best I kin do fer you right now is offer you a piece of apple pie and freshen that cold coffee in front of you."

"Thanks," she said through a sigh. "But I—" Sarah stopped abruptly as the door opened, and Jake walked inside. To her shock and mortification, her skin began to tingle and warm, and a disconcerting airiness wafted through her stomach.

He was a light that dimmed every other man in the room—ruggedly handsome and well-built in a tan uniform that fit nearly as well as his jeans did. Removing his Stetson, he crossed to the lunch counter to speak to Jeannie Baker, the waitress who'd brought their order. Instantly, the girl's posture was better, her smile brighter and her attention rapt.

"I thought you said the sheriff had already been here," Sarah said nervously, irrationally bothered by Jeannie's interest.

Ruby turned to peek toward the front of the café. "Could be he changed his mind about dessert."

Oh, please, don't let it be that, Sarah prayed, staring into her coffee cup.

"Nope," Ruby continued. "He ain't sittin' down. Looks like he's handin' Jeannie one of them lunch vouchers. Must be holdin' somebody over at the jail."

Slowly, Sarah ventured a look. But Jake chose the same moment to scan the room, and Sarah felt her face flood with heat as their gazes met and locked.

At the front of the café, Jake frowned thoughtfully as Sarah jerked her gaze from his. He'd been racking his brain for two days trying to think of a way to reestablish some sort of friendship with her. He'd really screwed up, pressuring her the way he had.

Now, as he considered his next stop, he wondered if a partial solution to his problem might be in his shirt pocket. He'd planned to ask a salesclerk for help. But talking to Sarah about something that had nothing to do with Kylie might just ease some of her insecurities where he was concerned, and pave the way to some honest conversation.

He didn't want to resort to demanding a paternity test.

"I'll be back in a few minutes, Jeannie," he told the waitress. Then he walked back to Sarah's table with a smile for all three of them.

"Afternoon, ladies," he said. He tried not to focus on Kylie, but it was difficult. His heart wanted to look.

"Sheriff," Sarah murmured.

"My name is Jake, Sarah," he said pointedly.

With a smile that lit her whole face, Kylie scrambled to her feet in the booster chair and teetered precariously. "Hi, Jake! Want a fench fwy?"

Adrenaline shot through him. Before Jake could lunge for Kylie, Sarah sprang from her chair and sat Kylie back down. He blew out a relieved breath as she scolded her daughter softly, then shook his head at Ruby.

"Kids," Ruby chuckled, levering herself out of her seat. "As fer them fries, from the looks of 'em, you'd be happier with pie."

Jake chuckled, too. "Thanks, but I'm still full of stuffed peppers."

"Then I'll git you some pie to take along. Yer too skinny. Wouldn't take a good wind long to blow you clear to Livingston." She started away at a brisk clip. "While I'm at it, I'll git a washcloth for our little honey-girl."

"That's okay," Sarah called, and Jake could hear a hint of alarm in her voice. "I'll just take her to the ladies' room. Aunt Ruby? I think the sheriff wants to talk to you." But Ruby was too far away to hear.

"Actually," Jake said, sliding into the booth across from her and setting his hat beside him. "It's you I want to talk to, Sarah."

Chapter 3

With her nerves bouncing around like jumping beans, it was difficult for Sarah to keep her features composed. The last time this man said he wanted to talk, she'd had a home she could escape to. Now she was trapped.

Lifting Kylie out of the booster seat, she grabbed a napkin and mopped the worst of the ketchup from her daughter's hands and face. Then she sent Kylie running to Aunt Ruby so she could finish the job with a washcloth.

Sarah brought her gaze back to Jake. He looked disappointed that she'd sent their daughter away, but that's the way it had to be. She wanted to know him a lot better before he spent more time with Kylie.

"You wanted to talk?" she reminded him. Scooping up Kylie's toys, Sarah stuffed them into the tote bag, glad to have something to do with her hands.

"Yes," he said, adding building blocks to her tote. "I need a favor."

Sarah glanced up in surprise.

"I didn't plan on asking you until I saw you sitting back here," he added.

"What kind of favor?" she asked warily.

"I picked up a young runaway a few minutes ago—barely fifteen. Her idiot boyfriend dumped her outside of town. Jeannie's putting together a lunch for her, but all the girl has are the clothes on her back, and they're in bad shape. She needs something decent to wear."

Then…this conversation wasn't about Kylie? Were all of his questions the other day idle curiosity, and not the threat she'd thought them to be? Had she overreacted?

"Maggie's helping her get cleaned up and giving her the standard orange jumpsuit for now, but the girl's parents are on their way. She shouldn't have to face her folks dressed like a criminal."

Finally seeing where this conversation was headed, Sarah hid an enormous sigh of relief and nodded in complete agreement. "No. No, she shouldn't. If we're about the same size, I'm sure there's something in my closet—"

"Thanks, but all I'm asking for is a few minutes of your time. I need someone to shop for her."

He took a sheet of paper from his breast pocket and unfolded it on the table. And without warning, the detailed signet ring he wore on his strong, capable right hand sparked a memory that brought a flush to Sarah's face. In his haste to be rid of her panties that night, his ring had caught on them and they'd torn. But she hadn't cared…and Jake hadn't known.

Sarah pushed away the image and jerked her attention back to his face. But in glancing up so quickly, she caught a flash of heat in his eyes—something he obviously hadn't intended her to see—and she swallowed. Was this the way chemistry worked? she wondered. One lover had a thought…and the other automatically received it?

Clearing his throat, Jake got back to business. "Maggie listed the sizes for me, but shopping for a young girl isn't my strong suit. Would you mind? Maggie's not feeling well today, or she'd do it."

Nerves still thrumming, Sarah nodded. Like Kylie, this young girl had once been some mother's toddler, some mother's joy. Sarah hoped that if Kylie ever needed help someone would step in for her. But after buying the clothing, she'd have to deliver them, and that made her uneasy. They didn't need more contact with these disturbing undercurrents between them.

Jake stood and pulled several bills from his wallet.

"You're taking care of this?" she asked. "You personally?"

"Yep."

"May I ask why?"

"Because she's a nice girl beneath the attitude, and she needs them." He handed her the money. "Try to find her something soft-looking."

Sarah tingled as his gaze fell to the light pink sweater that topped her jeans, then lingered a bit longer than necessary.

"Something like you're wearing," he continued. "It has to dull the impact of a dyed-black Mohawk and a dozen earrings."

Jeannie called to him from the lunch counter and raised a take-out bag, and Jake called back that he'd be right there.

He swept back his hair and tugged his hat on. "Thank you," he said quietly, and Sarah felt that tingle again.

"Glad to help."

Just then, Kylie raced back to them and hurled herself onto Sarah's lap. Her face was clean and glowing, and looking at her brought back the anxiety Sarah had momentarily forgotten. Who wouldn't want this child for his own?

"We won't be long," she said, standing and taking Kylie's hand. "We'll drop the clothes off at your office."

"Great," he said, then bent down to grin at Kylie and tap her nose with his fingertip. "Bye-bye, funny face."

Giggling, she jabbed a tiny finger right back at him. "*You're* a funny face!"

Sarah's heart nearly stopped. Then to her relief, Kylie's father waved, collected his order and left.

She didn't move again until she was sure he'd stepped off the wooden boardwalk outside and headed for his office. Then she reclaimed Kylie's hand, paid her bill and left, conflicting emotions stirring her up again.

On one hand, that silly, nose-tapping moment was a frightening thing. On the other, she'd just watched Kylie interact with her daddy, and it had evoked feelings of tenderness and warmth she'd never expected.

She would tell him. As soon as she was absolutely certain that Jake Russell was father material, she would tell him.

But what would he do with that knowledge? she wondered.

She wondered something else, too, as they walked the boardwalk, passing restored 1890s storefronts and stone buildings that recalled Comfort's early days as a booming gold and cattle town.

She wondered about his generosity in paying for the girl's clothes. She'd learned some things about him the night he'd let his guard down…the night they'd made love. In some respects, she knew more about Jake than she'd known about her own husband. Certainly, Vince had never opened up to her emotionally. Was helping a young girl

Jake's way of repaying a kindness done to him when Jake was the young runaway?

Or had there been no one there for Jake...and he wouldn't see another child do without the things he'd needed?

When she arrived at the jail thirty minutes later, Sarah hoped that Maggie Dalton would be the one to greet her. Just approaching the door had made her anxious again. But it was Jake who stepped out from his private office as she entered. And Sarah was helpless to stop the shivery attraction that raced through her. He wasn't just goodlooking. Jake Russell was everything it meant to be heartstoppingly, breathtakingly male.

"Did you lose your little helper?" he asked, taking the package she offered.

"Just for a while," Sarah replied, faintly guarded again. "She ate most of her lunch, so I told Ruby she could have ice cream." It wasn't a lie, exactly—just more recently accomplished than he had to know. The closer they'd come to the sheriff's office, the less inclined Sarah was to bring Kylie with her. "Your change is in an envelope inside the bag."

"Thanks." Jake fished out the envelope. "Can I ask one more favor?"

"I guess."

"Would you mind delivering the clothes? Maggie's in the lockup with her, and I think there's some girl talk going on. They're in the last cell."

Sarah felt her jaw drop. "You locked up a fifteen-year-old girl?"

"No," he answered, his brow creasing in annoyance. "She needed some privacy, and I gave it to her. Why are you always so quick to believe the worst of me?"

Shamed, Sarah met his eyes in apology. Before she could make amends, the door to the lockup flew open and crashed against the wall. Maggie rushed out, holding a hand over her mouth and heading for the rear of the office. A second later, a thin teenager with a terrified expression came out after her.

The girl's defiant green eyes shot to Jake. "I didn't do anything! We were talking, and she just jumped up and ran!"

Sighing, Jake shook his head and went to her, his rangy frame dwarfing hers. She looked waif-thin in the baggy orange jumpsuit. "I know you didn't do anything. Maggie's just a little under the weather today. Come on, I want you to meet someone."

The girl obviously had no interest in being cordial. Nevertheless, she let Jake nudge her to the dispatcher's desk where Sarah waited. "Lisa, this is Sarah Harper. Sarah picked up some clothes for you. Sarah, Lisa Sheldon."

The girl's belligerent gaze never left Sarah's face, though she spoke only to Jake. "Why would she want to buy me clothes? She doesn't know me."

Sarah extended the bag. "The sheriff paid for them, Lisa. I just picked them out. Maggie gave him your sizes."

She cut a look at Jake. "Yeah, well I can't pay you back. Bryan took all of my money."

"I'm not asking you to repay me." Sarah didn't miss the brief chill in his eyes that said "Bryan" wasn't one of his favorite people. "I just want you to look nice when your mom and dad get here."

"Oh, I'll look lovely." Without mousse or gel, her hair parted in the center and hung on either side of her shaved scalp. "They'll kill me when they see this."

"I doubt that," Jake replied.

"You don't know them."

"I know your mom cried when I told her you were safe. Give them a break. These past two months haven't been a cakewalk for them, either."

The girl was silent for a moment, then she said, "My mom cried? Really?"

"Yes, really. Now, how about trying on your new duds?"

When Lisa had disappeared into the lockup, Sarah's gaze returned to Jake. His treatment of the young girl had touched her. There'd been no coddling or threats—just kind, straight talk. Now, more than ever, she owed him that apology.

"I'm sorry about what I said before. I had no right to make assumptions like that."

Jake nodded grimly. "We only know each other in one way, Sarah. I'm more than what you see."

More? If he were any more than what she saw, she'd be running right now. Without his hat to keep them back, a few strands of black hair fell over his forehead, softening his craggy good looks and calling her attention to his deep blue eyes and tanned cheekbones. Below that was a perfect mouth and teeth, and just enough beard shadow to make her remember its sexy scratch against her skin. The man was a mating song in boots.

"Have coffee with me sometime," he persisted, keeping his voice low. "Let me prove it. I'm not looking for anything more than friendship and conversation." But the memories swirling through his eyes seemed to belie his words.

"I don't think so."

"Why not?

"Because it was friendship and conversation that got us into trouble three years ago," she returned.

"That was different. That was comfort and support."

"No, it was sex. And you and I both know that once you cross a line, it's too easy to cross it again. I don't want that."

The toilet flushed, reminding them that they weren't alone, and though Jake's gaze hardened, he didn't reply. Possibly because he knew the conversation had gone as far as it could go. A second later, Maggie came out of the rest room looking pale.

Some friend she was, Sarah thought. Just looking at Jake had blown everything out of her mind except him, including Maggie's illness.

His voice lowered in concern when she joined them. "You all right, Maggie?"

"No, but I'm better."

"Sure you don't want to go home?"

"Not yet," she said, working up a smile. "Let's see if it gets better." She turned to Sarah. "Hi. What brings you in?"

"Shopping," Sarah answered, smiling. "I bought the clothes for your young guest."

"Oh?" Maggie looked at Jake. "I thought you were giving the list to one of the salesclerks."

His features froze for a moment, then he answered. "I was, until I ran into Sarah. The salesclerks at Hardy's are nice, but they're all older. I figured a younger woman would pick out something more appropriate." He frowned and glanced at his watch. "Excuse me? I need to make a phone call." A moment later, he was gone.

Sarah held back a sigh. She didn't know if she should feel relieved or disappointed. But she couldn't have answered him any other way.

She spoke to Maggie, who'd taken a seat at the dispatcher's desk. "Are you okay?"

With a humorous twist of her mouth, Maggie reached into a low drawer and produced a long tube of crackers. "Actually, I think I might be a whole lot better than okay."

"How nice!" Sarah said with a smile, recognizing the signs.

"I haven't seen a doctor yet, but I'm pretty sure. Got any room left in your quilting class at the Grange hall? I think it's time I learned which end of a needle to thread."

"You bet. When's the baby due?"

"March, I think." Maggie's grin spread. "Ross and I were planning to wait to start a family, but it looks like we had a head start on this little one before the wedding."

"Does the sheriff know?"

"Not yet, but I have to tell him. I hate leaving him high and dry, but I can't stay on. Ross and I talked. Comfort's hardly crime-ridden, but things do happen occasionally, and I won't risk my pregnancy."

"I'd feel the same way," Sarah agreed. "Have you picked out names yet, or is it still too early?"

"It's still too—" With a frantic look, Maggie shot to her feet again. Seconds later, she was back in the rest room, leaving Sarah to sympathize and remember her own morning sickness. The morning sickness she'd gone through alone.

When she picked up Kylie several minutes later, she felt good about Lisa Sheldon's future, yet faintly uneasy about Jake's distant behavior. Which made no sense to her at all, since she'd practically *asked* him to keep his distance.

Why did she feel she'd let him down? Was it reflected guilt? Did she subconsciously feel that withholding the truth about Kylie from him entitled Jake to something else?

Sarah put Kylie into her car seat and climbed behind

the wheel. The man scrambled her mind and made every nerve in her body vibrate. If she slept tonight, it would be a miracle.

Tossing and turning, kicking the covers to the foot of the bed, Jake cursed a blue streak and tried to find a comfortable position on the lumpy mattress. He couldn't believe he was *paying* someone to stay here. A bedroll on concrete would've been more humane. Every few seconds, the Twirling Spur's neon cowboy boot flashed under the too-short drapes, striping the carpet with fluorescent orange, and adding to his misery.

Vaulting from the bed, he snatched the alarm clock from the nightstand. *Three-forty? Could that be right?* He plunked it back down and pulled his hands over his whiskery face. Between the bed, the boot and fantasies about Sarah Harper, he didn't have a prayer of getting any more sleep tonight. Not a prayer.

But, he thought hopefully after a moment, there was a foldaway cot in his office, and if Deputy Joe Talbot wasn't in it, he might be able to sleep for an hour or two before his shift started at seven. If not…well, he could review applications for a deputy to replace Maggie. She'd phoned him earlier in the evening to tell him about her pregnancy.

Orange light flashed across his bare feet.

And flashed.

And flashed.

And flashed.

Jake clenched his teeth and headed for the shower, masochistically picturing the comfortable beds Sarah had to have in her pink house.

By the time he'd swung his Mountaineer into his parking space, doused his headlights and hailed Joe Talbot, who was just pulling away from the office, Jake's mood hadn't improved much. Probably because he'd had to drive past Sarah's home with its welcoming glow and pretty candle-lights in the windows.

His burly blond deputy called to him through the Jeep's open window. "Something going on?"

"No," Jake returned with a rueful smile. "Just can't sleep."

"Still no rooms in the paper?"

"A few houses for sale, but I'm not ready for that yet."

"Well, the cot's free," Joe called with a sympathetic grin, and eased off the brake. "I'm just making rounds. I'll be back in an hour or so."

"See you then." With a wave to Joe, Jake got out, unlocked the door and let himself inside. He wasn't on the cot long when a ridiculous thought that wouldn't go away had him calling himself an idiot and rolling to his feet again.

Jake tore through the files behind the desk out front, found nothing, then berating himself even more, went to the back room where old files were stored. He'd *never* done anything like this before. It was stupid, and sappy and sophomoric. But he couldn't stop himself.

A few minutes later, he was staring hard at the police photo in his hand. What in hell had Sarah ever seen in this guy?

The cocky grin and pretty-boy features that stared back at him reminded Jake of the young studs the girls from his old high school used to go nuts over. Lots of rock-band hair and more brass than the New York Philharmonic.

He scanned the accompanying description. Vincent Charles Harper had been a white male, five foot eleven, with sandy brown hair, no distinguishing marks and...

And information he hadn't even been looking for jumped out at him. *Brown eyes.*

Jake's heart broke into a full gallop. Slowly, he slid the file back into the cabinet.

He remembered enough about a genetics class he'd taken in college to know that two brown-eyed parents could still have a blue-eyed child. But at the same time, Kylie had *his* coloring and had been born nine months after he'd been with Sarah. That was just too much of a coincidence to *be* a coincidence.

Kylie Harper was his daughter.

The wind kicked him full in the face that evening as Jake took Blackjack on a flat-out run across the long, pale pasture, inhaling the energy around him and letting the stallion's hoofbeats drum out the nagging thoughts in his head. Chokecherries, pines and golden aspens blurred in his side vision. The cloudless blue sky above all but disappeared. They didn't slow down until they'd gone nearly as far as wooden posts and barbed wire would permit. Then Jake reined the horse in and eased him into a blowing, cooling-down walk.

He couldn't yet see the big white main house where Jess and Casey Dalton lived with their little daughter. But corrals and outbuildings lay ahead, and to his far right, a row of pines marked the long access road to the ranch.

Jake frowned as he pointed Blackjack toward it and the barn beyond, realizing that the ride had given him only a temporary respite from his tension. He was as churned up now as he'd been this morning when he'd read Vince Harper's description.

He was almost to the road when two riders cut through the trees on horseback.

With a jolt, Jake recognized Sarah and Maggie Dalton, both astride chestnut mounts with white blazes.

"Jake! Hi!" Maggie called as they rode toward him. Both women were dressed in jeans and boots, but while Maggie wore a navy blue sweatshirt, Sarah wore a faded denim jacket over her white blouse. Both collars were up and her top two buttons were undone, creating a deep V from her long, smooth neck to the top of her chest. She rode well.

"Hello," Sarah said with a cautious smile.

Jake smiled back and returned the greeting, thinking that she was probably wondering if he was still irritated because she'd refused his invitation to have coffee. Well, yes, he was. He was also irritated because he was sleeping on a medieval rack, acting like a jealous kid because of her, and being kept in the dark about the daughter he knew was his.

But this was another opportunity to smooth the friction between them and gain her trust, and he wasn't going to get impatient this time and blow it.

"Starting your ride or finishing?" Maggie asked.

"Finishing. I was just heading back." He relaxed in the saddle, looping his reins around the saddle horn. Underneath, his blood pumped hard. "Nice day."

"And if you believe the forecasters," Maggie said, "tomorrow could be even better. I was supposed to ride with Ross, but he apparently got busy so I invited Sarah to join me." She laughed. "She brought me an instruction sheet. I'm going to *attempt* to make a quilt."

"You'll do fine," Jake said, then remembered their phone conversation last night. "Should you be riding?"

"According to Doc, I can do anything I normally did."

She shrugged. "I've always ridden. Now that I know about the baby, I'll take it a lot easier, though."

"That's good." A flock of noisy blackbirds sailed past them and landed some distance away in a field of winter oats. Jake gave them a cursory glance before continuing. "How would you feel about staying on for a while?" he asked. "Not as a deputy, but as the office manager. I never did get around to considering anyone for the position. Joe's agreed to work full-time, and I'll hire a part-timer to take his place."

Maggie broke into a beaming smile. "I'd love it. Until the baby comes, there really isn't much to keep me occupied." She turned to include Sarah in the conversation. "Except quilting, if I can get the hang of it."

"You will," Sarah assured her.

"Wait, now," Jake said. "Before you accept, see what Ross thinks."

"Ross thinks I should be in a wheelchair with nurses attending me twenty-four hours a day. In fact, he doesn't even want me riding. Which could be why he's been 'detained.' He probably thought if he stayed away, I wouldn't go."

"Then maybe your staying on isn't a good idea. I don't want any trouble with your husband." *For a variety of reasons,* Jake thought.

"Don't worry. He'll get used to the idea."

Almost as though he'd been summoned, Ross cantered his buckskin-colored horse through the same section of lodgepole pines the women had emerged from, and rode toward them.

A feeling that was half-eagerness and half-vulnerability moved through Jake—the same knotted feeling he had whenever his path crossed Ross's. It seemed to intensify out here with the Dalton homestead so near, and Broken-straw cattle grazing in the distance.

Ross reined his horse in. He was a lean, fit, sandy-haired man, and sat tall in the saddle. Beneath his tan Stetson, his deep blue eyes were worried as he addressed his wife, but he tried to hide his disapproval behind a smile.

"Thought you were going to wait for me," he said.

"Sorry, but it got late, and I didn't want to waste the sunshine. We won't have many more seventy-degree days."

"I know, but…" Ross seemed to remember his manners then, and glanced at Sarah. "Nice to see you, Sarah." His gaze slid to Jake, the smile flagging a little. "Afternoon, Sheriff."

"Ross." Jake couldn't say if Ross's reaction was personal, or if the man's long history with the former sheriff had turned him off law enforcement in general. But there was always a hint of dislike in Ross's eyes when they met. If it *was* personal, their relationship was destined to get even more strained when Ross learned who Jake was.

"Excuse us for a minute?" Ross asked. "Maggie and I need to talk about something."

"Sure," Sarah said.

"No problem," Jake returned at the same time. He didn't mind at all. He'd been looking forward to getting Sarah alone.

Still, Jake's gaze followed the newlyweds as they rode their horses to a dying willow tree, as if some genetic link made it impossible for him to look away. Then Ross brought his horse alongside Maggie's to kiss her, and common decency made Jake turn away.

He was shocked to see what could only be called longing in Sarah's eyes when she, too, glanced away from the intimate scene.

Jealousy cut through him, stark and powerful. Was that yearning he'd seen in her eyes for Ross? Did Sarah have a thing for Maggie's husband?

Without thinking it through, without weighing the consequences of his actions, Jake walked his horse closer to Sarah's and stared into her expectant brown eyes. Then he asked, point-blank, "Is Kylie my daughter, Sarah?"

Chapter 4

Sarah's eyes widened in shock, but Jake could see fear there as well. She sent an anxious glance toward Maggie and Ross. "What are you talking about?"

"I'm talking about paternity. You, me—getting it on beside that little creek the night—"

In a heartbeat, fear and surprise became outrage. *"Getting it on?"* she repeated, her dark eyes flashing. "Well, thank you very much. If I didn't feel cheap before, I certainly do now." With a click of her tongue and a quick nudge to the mare's ribs, the horse broke into a gallop.

Snapping Blackjack's reins, Jake galloped across the pasture after her, damning himself for letting his control slip again. He came up alongside her, talking to her frozen profile since she refused to look at him. "Sarah, I'm sorry. That was frustration talking. I didn't mean to imply that our being together was anything— *Will you just hold up a minute?"*

"No!"

"She has black hair and blue eyes, Sarah," Jake persisted. "She didn't get that coloring from you or your ex-husband. And she was born in April."

Sarah yanked back on the reins, and her mount came to a skidding halt. Jake halted his horse, too. *"How could you know that?"*

"It doesn't matter. I know."

Calling from across the field, Maggie rode back to them. "Hey! No fair taking off without the trail boss!"

Frustrated all over again, Jake blew out a long blast of air. Dammit, why did she have to come back *now,* just when he was finally getting somewhere?

Maggie smiled as she came up to them, politely ignoring the tension in the air, though her eyes said she'd seen everything. "Guess what? I was wrong about Ross's motives. He has a project to finish that can't wait."

With enormous difficulty, Jake forced his face into amiable lines. "Did you ask him about the dispatcher's job?"

"Not yet. I thought I'd let him get used to my riding before I sprang anything else on him."

Sarah reined her horse away and spoke stiffly to Maggie. "Ready to go?"

"Yep. Jake? You're welcome to join us."

"Thanks, but I'm finished here." Boy, was he ever. "See you tomorrow." Then, with another tight smile, he nudged Blackjack into a tail-swishing walk and headed for the barns.

Sarah released a trembling sigh and thanked God that Maggie had returned before Jake could ask about Kylie again—and that he hadn't insisted upon an answer in Maggie's presence. She didn't know what she would have said.

She *would* tell him. But only when there was no chance of anyone overhearing them and they had plenty of time.

"Feel like talking about it?" Maggie asked as they rode along.

Startled, Sarah met her eyes. "Talking about what?"

"Whatever's going on between you and Jake. That was a tense little scene I rode up on."

"Tense?" Sarah repeated, stalling for time.

"Tense. There were enough sparks flying between the two of you to burn this pasture to the ground. What's going on?"

With a laugh and a shrug, Sarah eased her horse into a faster walk. "I don't know. We just rub each other the wrong way. Maybe we were enemies in another life."

"Or lovers," Maggie joked.

Sarah gripped the reins in a stranglehold and changed the subject. Soon she had Maggie excited about choosing patterns, fabrics and trims for the quilt she wanted to make for her baby, and the conversation was as far removed from Jake Russell as it could get. But beneath it all, Sarah was ashamed because she'd finally told an out-and-out lie.

How many others would she be forced to tell before this was over?

A few minutes later, still battling his frustration, Jake led his horse past the tack room and into the barn, blinking as his eyes adjusted from bright sunlight to the comforting dimness of dark, sturdy beams. His mood began to level out. He'd been here twice since he'd relocated, and the same observations he'd made the first time occurred to him again. There was no new wood in sight. The barn was old, silent—almost churchlike if you could get past the earthy smells of hay, leather and manure. Sunlight streamed through windows speckled with hay chaff.

He doubted it had changed much since Ross Senior had been alive.

Frowning at the uselessness of his thoughts, Jake led the stallion into his stall, unsaddled him, then closed the stall door and carried his gear to the tack room.

He was startled to see Jess adding liniment bottles to the shelves near the medicine cabinet. He'd been so pre-occupied, he'd passed Ross's older brother without seeing him. Not good for a lawman whose instincts needed to be needle sharp.

Jake hung his saddle on a peg, then smiled and walked over to the Brokenstraw Ranch's co-owner. "Hi. Didn't see you in here when I went by."

"Figured you didn't," Jess said over his shoulder. "How was your ride?"

"Great. We kicked out a few nice mule deer. Horse picked up some major burrs, though."

"That's not the horse's fault." Jess chuckled. "You were the guy holding the reins."

Jake chuckled, too, as he took a currycomb and brush from a shelf. "True enough. Maybe next time I'll let the horse steer." For a moment, he almost asked Jess if the area he'd ridden through today held any special meaning for the Daltons, then changed his mind. If it did, maybe they wouldn't want him riding there anymore.

"Well," Jake said, unable to extend the conversation, "guess I'd better get to it, or it'll be midnight till I get back to town. See you."

"Yeah," Jess called back. "See you."

Heart thumping, Jake returned to Blackjack's stall, Jess Dalton's face frozen in his mind. Their similarities were staggering. But maybe that's because he was looking for similarities. They were both about the same height, same black hair, same build—same black Stetson. But Jess's eyes were brown, probably like his mother's, and he car-ried himself loosely, the mark of a man at peace with himself. Jake envied him that. He had too many unresolved issues in his life for that kind of peace.

He'd just started grooming his horse when Jess walked in and dumped a scoop of grain into Blackjack's bin. The animal nosed into it.

"Hear you're looking for a new deputy," he said.

Jake grinned, trying to act nonchalant. "A part-timer, anyway. You looking for work?"

"Me?" Smiling, Jess put his shoulder against the stall. "No, there's more than enough around here to keep me busy. At the moment, just keeping Ross settled is a full-time job. His boots haven't touched the ground since Maggie told him about the baby."

Jake fought to calm his nerves. "How about you? Looking forward to the new addition to your family?"

"We all are. The Dalton clan's pretty small as most families go."

Not as small as you think. "I see a lot of your aunt Ruby."

With a low laugh, Jess stroked Blackjack's neck as the horse continued to feed. "Aunt Ruby's a handful. Stay on her good side, and she'll give you the key to her heart. Tick her off, and she'll find you a first-class room in hell."

"I'll keep it in mind."

"If you want to eat, you'd better. Around here we've got Ruby's for food and Dusty's for drinks. There's not much else but grass, trees and mountains."

"Grass, trees and mountains work for me," Jake returned. "Speaking of which, you've got a nice spread."

"Thanks. But that was our dad's doing—and his father before him."

"Your dad's gone?" Jake asked, hiding a guilty twinge because he already knew the answer.

"For a while now. He and Ross's mom died when Ross was in high school. Small plane accident."

"Oh. I'm sorry."

"Me, too. I still miss them both. But, as I said, it was a long time ago." Jess glanced at his pocket watch, then tapped the side of the stall with the grain scoop. "Well, I'd better shove off. Casey'll be putting supper on the table."

Jake hid his regret behind a smile. "Nice talking to you."

"Same here."

But a moment later, Jess called from the doorway, "Care to join us? I think it's fried chicken tonight."

Jake didn't move for a long second. Then slowly, he ambled into the hay-strewn aisle between the rows of stalls to meet Jess's eyes. "Thanks, but I have a pile of paperwork waiting on my desk. I just came out for a little breather."

"Maybe another time, then."

"Yeah, maybe," Jake said. "Thanks again."

Stifling the gut-gnawing urge to follow Jess up to the ranch house, Jake wandered back to Blackjack's stall and grabbed the currycomb. For years, he'd wondered how it would feel to walk the same rooms his father had walked, wondered if—given the opportunity—he would feel a familial connection, a sense of belonging that had always been missing from his life. Now he'd passed up the chance. But much as he'd wanted to say yes, there was no way he could sit across the supper table from Jess Dalton without telling him they were brothers.

Sarah put the teakettle on to heat, still rattled over her unexpected meeting with Jake. She'd worried about his looking too closely at Kylie's coloring and wondering about it. But the current situation was worse. He knew her birth date. And the most logical place to get that information was at the courthouse.

If that's what he'd done, she prayed he'd done so under the guise of investigating someone else. Because if the courthouse clerks—especially Elvira Parsons—realized that Jake was looking into Kylie's parentage, Sarah's name would be on everyone's lips again.

Suddenly chilled, she tugged her white cardigan more closely around her. She could almost hear Elvira's voice....

I've always wondered who that child's father was. She doesn't look a thing like any of the family—including that thieving, no-account husband of Sarah's.

The kettle whistled. Sarah turned off the gas, then took a tea bag from the white-and-yellow ceramic canister on the countertop and dropped it into her mug. But something pulled her attention back to the canister set.

She frowned curiously. The sugar canister was turned around backward; instead of big, full sunflowers, it showed a cluster of small, barely open buds. And there was a trace of sugar spilled on the countertop.

Funny...she hadn't used sugar from the canister in the last few days. And she took pride in having a neat, clean kitchen. She wouldn't have left...

Kylie.

With a wry grin, Sarah wiped up the sugar with a damp sponge, then turned the canister around so that all four matched again. Obviously, her precocious little daughter was developing a sweet tooth, and was smart enough to move the kitchen chair back where it belonged after sneaking a treat. Still, what Kylie had done was dangerous. Tomorrow morning, Sarah would gently reinforce the rules about climbing.

Half an hour later, Sarah climbed the stairs, stepped over

the child-safety gate across the top, then showered and settled into bed to read for a while. But when she'd read the same two paragraphs three times without comprehending any of it, she returned the book to her nightstand and clicked off her lamp.

Why couldn't she get Jake Russell out of her mind?

She was through with men who sent her hormones spinning out of control. Sarah shook her head in the darkness, remembering Vince. Her teenage heart had fallen for him so hard, loved him so desperately and believed in him so fiercely, that she would have staked her life on their marriage lasting forever.

But behind his teasing smiles and charming compliments had beat the heart of a callous user who didn't care about anyone but himself. In the three years they were together he'd lied, bedded other women indiscriminately and stolen from his own grandmother. He'd hurt a man with his fists and held up a liquor store. But he'd given Sarah a valuable gift—one that nearly canceled out all the heartache and shame. He'd shown her how brutally flawed her judgment was.

She was *afraid* to feel something for another man. Especially a handsome, sexy, charismatic man. Especially one who guarded his heart as tenaciously as Sarah guarded hers.

A loud crash outside scattered her thoughts, and Sarah leapt out of bed and hurried to the window. Her view was of the garage and storage shed behind the house, and beyond that, thick pines.

Unnerved, she scanned the yard, straining to hear the next sound. Then, just as she was about to pull a robe over her nightgown and take a closer look, a big yellow cat shot out of the shadows beside the shed and raced across the moonlit lawn.

With a self-deprecating grin, she shook her head and climbed back into bed. For a moment, she'd feared she was being vandalized again. But it was only Goldie, the friendly tabby from down the road. Probably just looking for mice in the stack of old spouting the painters hadn't yet hauled away.

More power to her, Sarah thought, yawning. Minutes later, she was drifting off to sleep…dreaming of a strong, lean man with black hair and shadowy features who held her close, and told her everything would be all right.

She and Kylie were making Sarah's bed the next morning when a familiar knock rattled the screen door. "Grampa!" Kylie squealed, and broke for the hall.

"Oh, no you don't," Sarah laughed, catching her before she could get farther than the foot of the brass bed. "You stay right here. Grandpa can come to you." She lifted her voice to be heard downstairs. "We're making beds! Come on up!"

They'd been expecting Sarah's father momentarily, and Kylie was dressed and ready to go on their "field trip"— a huge help since Sarah still had food to prepare for the Tully wedding.

But as she finished smoothing her rose-printed comforter and replaced the lacy, pillow-stuffed shams, the fine hairs at the back of her neck prickled.

The footsteps she heard coming down the hall weren't her father's.

Sarah jerked a look at the doorway, just as Jake's rangy form filled it. The set of his jaw and the purposeful look in his eyes told her this was no random visit.

"You said to come up," he reminded her soberly.

Sarah's mind whirred like a hummingbird on straight caffeine. She'd expected him to show up eventually—another reason she wanted Kylie out of the house. But not at eight-thirty in the morning. "Y-yes, I did, but I thought you were my father. He's taking Kylie for the day."

"Hi, Jake!" Kylie piped up.

"Not Jake, Kylie. His name is *Mr. Russell,* remember?"

Jake's expression softened, and his voice grew warm. "She can call me Jake if she wants to. That's easier to say. Hi there, half-pint. Don't you look pretty today."

Sarah jumped into the conversation before it could get started. "Did you need something? I mean, if you're still looking for a room—" She had no idea what she was saying. No idea what she *wanted* to say. She'd never been good at mindless chatter, she was all out of diversionary rhetoric, and Maggie wouldn't be riding in to save the day again. To make matters worse, he looked bigger, taller and more blatantly male than ever before. Dressed in snug jeans, a black shirt and black Stetson, and with a faint beard shadow, he was a startling contrast to the frilly pinks and creams that surrounded him.

And why, oh why couldn't she be in the same room with him without experiencing those belly-tugging signals of arousal?

"I want an answer to my question, Sarah," he said flatly. "A simple yes or no. Is she or isn't she?"

"I—I don't want Kylie upset by this conversation." She also didn't want her father walking in on them. He would be hurt if he learned the truth this way.

"All I need is a one-word answer, and she's heard both of those words before."

She wanted to answer him truthfully. She really did—if for no other reason than to finally be able to look at her own reflection again without cringing. She wanted to say, *Yes, Kylie's yours, but we can't talk now. Let's meet somewhere later, and we can discuss everything.*

But she couldn't make herself form the words. Instead, an overpowering rush of doubt, insecurity and fear splintered through her, and once again, she backed away from the truth. *She'd only known this man for a few days. She needed more time.*

"Sarah?"

"I know how badly you've always wanted a real family," she murmured, thinking her way through her reply and wishing she could trust him. "That is, I remember your saying it. But the way to do that is to fall in love with someone and start one of your own."

Sarah held his narrowed gaze and swallowed. She kept her voice low. "I'm sorry. But having dark hair and an April birth date doesn't automatically make Kylie your child."

Slowly, the light in his blue eyes dimmed, but more than a little disbelief lingered there. His voice hardened. "Then why all the stalling? Why didn't you tell me this yesterday in the pasture?"

"Mommy?" Kylie said in a barely audible voice.

Sarah lifted her into her arms, then grinned and kissed her nose—once, twice, three times. "This discussion is over," she said, wrapping Kylie securely. "We're making her uneasy."

Jake blew out a ragged breath. "I'm sorry, I didn't mean to raise my voice. And I can't tell you how stupid I feel for thinking— It's just that, when I saw her..." He stopped, shook his head, then sent her a disappointed smile. "Never mind. Thank you for your patience."

Sarah's heart fell to her feet. Why did he have to say that? Unable to meet Jake's eyes anymore, Sarah spoke softly to Kylie. "What do you think?" she murmured. "Should we go downstairs and wait for Grandpa? I'm not sure where he's taking you today, but I bet it'll be fun."

Kylie nodded, happy again. "Want to cawy me, Jake?"

Sarah was at a complete loss for words.

Jake wasn't. "I sure would," he said, smiling. "Come here, honey."

Sarah's heart squeezed as he took their little girl from her arms and carried her into the hall. Was this an omen? she wondered, hurrying ahead to unlatch the safety gate and let them precede her down the stairs. Was it a harbinger of things to come?

Oh, please, she prayed, guilt and fear mingling. *Don't let it be.*

Jake took the stairs slowly. He felt lousy, but at the same time, he was captivated by the feel of baby arms around his neck and the sweet smells of talcum powder and shampoo. He'd brought this on himself. He knew that all the evidence at his disposal was inconclusive. But he'd wanted Kylie to be his so badly, he'd talked himself right into it.

The instant he put her down, she sailed through the screen door, ran out on the porch and took the steps down into the yard. "Kylie, wait!" he shouted, and followed her down, afraid she'd go too far.

The screen door banged shut, and a moment later, Sarah's calm voice came from directly behind him. "She won't go farther than the trees. She knows it's dangerous."

"Good," he said, but he continued to monitor her progress, anyway. Abruptly changing directions, she scampered to the backyard, dumped a basket of clothespins, then proceeded to toss them back into the basket. Jake turned back to Sarah.

"Well," he said. "Again, I'm sorry. I don't expect you to forgive me for barging into your home and demanding answers to questions I had no right to ask—"

"There's nothing to forgive," she returned, knowing

he'd had every right to ask those questions. She almost said that given their past and Kylie's coloring, he was bound to wonder. But that would have been closer to a blatant lie, and she was having enough trouble with half-truths. "I'm not angry with you," she added quietly.

Sarah held her breath as his gaze slid over her hair and face, then dropped briefly to the green plaid shirt she wore with her jeans before meeting her eyes again. "I'm glad. You're the only person in this town I actually know, and I'd like it if we could be friends."

"I'd like that, too," she said, meaning it and wishing she wasn't such a coward. He deserved a lot more than friendship for the wonderful gift he'd given her. But for now, an hour in his arms and a few tense visits weren't enough to know this man's soul.

"Who's that?" Jake asked as his attention shifted to the base of her driveway.

Sarah looked, too. Half-hidden by the tall pines, an old red truck idled on the left shoulder of the road, only its hood and windshield visible. In the next second, it rolled into the open, and the grizzled driver behind the wheel waved and moved on.

Sarah smiled and waved back. "That's my neighbor, Pete Jessup. He lives down the road."

"Does he make a habit of watching your home?"

Sarah blinked in surprise. "He wasn't watching my home."

"Then why was he sitting on the left side of the highway?"

Sarah stared at him curiously. "He probably planned to stop for a visit, saw that I had company and changed his mind." She paused. "I don't know how things were in your old jurisdiction, but this is a nice little town. We don't have bogeymen behind every tree." *Well, they didn't now that Vince was gone.*

"That's comforting to know."

"But you don't believe it."

"Let's just say that I've seen my share of bogeymen, so I never discount them." Tugging his keys from the front pocket of his jeans, Jake met her eyes sincerely. "No hard feelings?"

Sarah shook her head, nearly gagging on her guilt. "No hard feelings." Then she watched him drive off, sick at heart for misleading him and hoping she didn't have to keep the truth from him much longer.

Jake tried to chase the sinking feeling in his chest as he drove along, but his disappointment had nowhere else to go. She wasn't his. After all his snooping around, little black-haired, blue-eyed Kylie Harper was another man's child. For just an instant, he felt irrationally betrayed because he didn't like imagining Sarah with someone else. Then he blew out a self-deprecating sigh. He'd had other lovers after their meeting beside that small creek, so she'd certainly had the same option. It just bothered him that it had been so soon afterward. Months had gone by before he'd wanted to touch another woman.

Jake returned the wave of a local businessman as he wheeled onto Prairie Street, then swung his Mountaineer in beside the department's Jeep and cut the engine. At least now that he'd given up his illusions about her daughter, Sarah seemed willing to be friendly.

Friendly enough to have coffee with him after this uneasiness between them wore off?

The answer came quickly. Probably not. The air still vibrated with awareness whenever they got within ten feet of each other, and she felt it, too. He could see it in her eyes. But he saw something else in her eyes, too. Wariness and uncertainty. Clearly, she didn't want to get caught up in chemistry again. He knew he shouldn't want that, either. Not with Sarah. Because chemistry was all he was prepared to offer her, and she deserved better.

Chapter 5

The phone rang in the outer office on Friday morning as Jake sat at his desk reviewing the proposed topics for the evening's council meeting. A moment later, Maggie called for him to pick up. He was surprised to hear Lisa Sheldon's voice on the line.

"How are things with you and your parents?" he asked after the young runaway had repeatedly gushed her thanks to him. He marveled that there was no sign of the frightened young girl who'd hidden behind defiance a few short days ago in his office. This girl was obviously grateful to be back home.

"They're being pretty cool about everything," she said offhandedly, and popped her gum. "Well, everything but the hair. My mom made an appointment with her stylist as soon as we got back, and now I'm blond again."

Thank God. "How about school?"

A put-upon sigh flowed through the receiver. "Okay, I guess. Some of the kids think I'm a celebrity because of what Bryan and I did. But if they would've seen the crummy cabin where we stayed, they wouldn't think it was such a big deal.''

Jake stilled, then asked, ''What crummy cabin? You told me you'd been living in Bryan's truck.'' It was bad enough to imagine a kid her age living in a vehicle...but a derelict building? Shadowy images from his own past rose in Jake's mind.

There was a moment of dead silence, then Lisa spoke hesitantly. ''Oh. Well... Bryan told me not to say anything about that. He said if anybody found out we were down there, they'd think we were the ones who trashed the place, and we'd get in trouble.''

''Down where?''

Again, there was a long pause. ''Will I get in trouble if I tell?''

''Not if you tell me the truth.''

''Okay, then it's this place in the woods a couple of miles outside of town.''

Jake listened intently as Lisa described a small settlement that rang a bell in his memory. It sounded like the notorious lodge that had been in the news three years ago.

''When we saw someone shining a flashlight around in the cabin across from us, we got scared and left. That's why we were fighting the day you picked me up. It was really creepy down there, but Bryan still wanted to go back after the guy drove away. He said it was too crowded sleeping in his truck, and if I didn't like it, I could leave.''

So they'd slept in an abandoned brothel, Jake thought, grimacing. And someone else had been there as well. ''You said the person with the flashlight was a guy. Did you get a good look at him?''

''No.''

''How about his vehicle?''

"I didn't see that real good, either. It was some kind of a truck, though."

Some kind of truck, Jake thought when he'd hung up. Half the state had some kind of truck. Needing to verify his suspicions with Maggie, he went into the outer office. For just an instant, Jake saw his new dispatcher and office manager in a warmer, different light, saw the woman who would give birth to his niece or nephew. But of course, she didn't know that.

"Any chance you know of an abandoned settlement outside of town? A lodge—some cabins in the woods?"

Maggie scowled as she glanced up from the computer. "That would be Babylon. It used to be a poker parlor and brothel, but it's been boarded up for a long time now. Why do you ask?"

"Apparently, Lisa and her boyfriend stayed there while they were on the run."

Maggie made a face.

"I know. They said they saw lights on in one of the other cabins one night." He glanced at his watch. He had plenty of time to check it out and still make dinner at the mayor's. "Think I'll take a look. I don't want it turning into a teenage hangout. Can you give me directions?"

Maggie's directions were right on target. Thirty minutes later, with the fresh scents of pine and sage flowing through his open window, Jake drove the department's Jeep down the wooded dirt road, bouncing in and out of potholes. Grass grew up between the tire ruts, but it wasn't three-years-high, testifying that Babylon had seen some traffic lately.

A hundred yards from the main road, Jake passed a rusted gate hanging at a forty-five-degree angle from its post. Then the woods opened onto a wide, sun-bleached clearing.

Jake parked in the deserted gravel lot and walked toward the stone-and-log building. Funny...he'd expected it to be bigger. According to Maggie, Babylon had once been the place where cowboys and legislators alike came to sip from the cups of wickedness and temptation. Now it was just another abandoned building.

He went to a window and peeked in, then tried the door. The knob turned easily, and he stepped inside.

Though electric service had been cut, daylight through the dirty windows allowed him a brief look around. There wasn't much to see. Vandals had taken or smashed most of the furniture. There was nothing in the lodge that suggested creature comforts, which might have tempted partyers, so he moved to the cottages in the woods behind the building.

There were six cabins, appropriately spaced for privacy. His search of the first one revealed a forced door and a ransacked interior, the ransacking long past, if the undisturbed dust on beer bottles and the rickety tabletops were any indication. Then he left it and walked to the second cabin.

Suddenly the hairs on the back of his neck stood on end, but Jake didn't know why.

Cautiously unsnapping his holster, he pushed open the door, entered slowly and looked around. Red velveteen drapes and gold blinds still hung from the windows, but like the lodge, the rest of the place had been trashed. A gilt-framed print of chesty saloon girls lay in a corner beyond the white iron bedstead. There was no mattress atop the broken springs. Across the room, a cheap vanity with a cracked mirror hadn't fared much better.

The pungent aroma of coffee hit him at the same instant an engine roared to life outside.

Whirling, Jake ran from the cabin, listened for a split

second, then crashed through the low underbrush out back, following the sound of the retreating vehicle. His twenty-yard scramble ended at what looked like an overgrown logging road that cut through the pines and probably connected to the main road above. As the high whine of the engine faded, Jake swore softly. Then, after a frozen moment, he returned to check the area behind the second cabin.

Flattened grass showed the place where the vehicle had been parked. But there were no tire imprints on the hard ground, no fluid spots to help with identification. At the rear of the cabin, a rough-cut door that looked like an afterthought hung open. Jake stepped inside—into a dingy bathroom, then the cabin's main room again. The coffee he'd smelled was on the nightstand in a plastic travel mug, a quarter of the way full and still warm.

Careful not to smear any prints, he closed the spout on the thermal mug, lifted it gingerly by the sides of the lid and carried it back to the Jeep. A minute later, it was in an evidence bag and Jake was driving through tree-lined ruts again.

Trespassing wasn't a big thing if they were dealing with kids, he decided, staring through the windshield. Sometimes, teenagers just wanted a place to be alone. But the presence of black coffee, not some other beverage, suggested that the intruder had been an adult—as did having a fast, well-tuned vehicle at his disposal. One more thing: considering the condition of the cabins he'd seen—he still had four to search—the intruder wasn't a drifter looking for a place to crash.

Which was just as well, Jake thought, turning onto the main road and heading toward town again. There was a lingering feeling of depravity in those cabins. It bothered him to think of Lisa and her loser boyfriend spending time there.

But God knew he'd stayed in his share of hellholes, too. That was back when he was young and running from well-meaning social workers, and foster parents who didn't really give a damn. Tomorrow he'd return with new padlocks, plywood and No Trespassing signs—and he'd lock that gate again. In the meantime, he needed to find out whose coffee was in that evidence bag. He hoped there were a lot of latent answers on that travel mug.

It was nearly three o'clock when Jake reached the outskirts of town and saw a familiar row of pines. Nerves spiking, he eased his boot off the accelerator and cruised slowly past Sarah's driveway.

He did a quick double take. Pete Jessup was just slipping inside the gray-shingled shed behind and to the left of Sarah's house. Checking his rearview mirror, Jake made a U-turn in the middle of the road, roared up the driveway, then shut off the engine. He got out and stood beside the door. For the second time in two days, Jessup was triggering alarms in Jake's lawman's mind.

Pete emerged. And the scowl on his thick, jowly features deepened with every step as he lumbered across the grass toward Jake.

"You watchin' me?"

"Should I be?" Jake asked.

Jessup was a big, potbellied man with bristly salt-and-pepper hair, and could've used a shower and shave. But obviously, pride wasn't a priority with him. Even the red flannel shirt he wore over a stained T-shirt and gray utility pants had only a nodding acquaintance with soap and water.

"What's that? Sheriff talk? Answerin' a question with

a question?'' Jessup's bloodshot gaze rested coldly on Jake's. "I was puttin' back her hedge shears, if you got to know. Borrowed 'em a while ago.''

"I didn't accuse you of anything.''

"Didn't have to. I got eyes.''

Jake searched those eyes, wondering where all this hostility was coming from. True, he didn't trust the old man—and Jessup wasn't as old as Jake had originally thought. Late fifties, maybe. But Jake hadn't acted in a threatening way. "You don't like me much, do you?''

"Jury's still out on you,'' Jessup muttered, and walked past him. He was halfway down the driveway when he turned and called, "You want some advice?''

"Always.''

"Just do your job 'stead of sniffin' around here day in and day out, and folks'll like it a lot better. This town just got rid of a no-account sheriff. We don't need another one.''

Grimly digesting Jessup's words, Jake stared after him as he crossed the road, then disappeared behind the thick pines.

What was that all about? Were people monitoring his every move? Or was Jessup speaking for himself when he said that the citizens of Comfort preferred he kept his distance from Sarah?

Pushing away from the Jeep, Jake walked up the porch steps and rang the bell. As long as he was here, he'd find out if Jessup actually *had* been returning her hedge shears. The man's defensive attitude was really beginning to bug him. Checking in with Sarah wasn't just a flimsy excuse to see her again.

He knew that was a lie the instant she came to the screen door and his blood began to heat.

The fresh, wholesome look of her was a welcome

change after spending the last two hours at Babylon. Once again, she wore a light blue denim jacket, but this time, over a black tank top. Her honey blond hair lifted in the light breeze coming through the screen. Uncurled and unsprayed, it looked as silky as a child's.

Clearing his throat, Jake touched his hat brim deferentially and called up a professional manner. "Sorry to bother you, but I saw Pete coming out of your shed a minute ago, and I wondered if he had a reason to be there."

"Coming out of my shed?" Sarah repeated, obviously not seeing a problem.

"He said he was returning hedge shears that he'd—"

"—borrowed a few weeks ago," she confirmed, nodding. "Yes, that's right. Pete does my yard work. He's welcome to use anything in the shed that he needs." Abruptly, Sarah's gaze narrowed. "Did you stop him for that?"

Jake hesitated, hiding his discomfort. "I didn't stop him, exactly. But after seeing him at the bottom of your driveway the other morning, I thought we should talk. I wanted to be sure he wasn't doing something that he shouldn't."

"And he got defensive," Sarah guessed.

"He doesn't like me much."

Sarah stepped outside, folded her arms across her chest and studied her sneakers for a moment. She met his eyes again. "Maybe what you saw wasn't defensiveness or dislike. Pete's... Pete's different."

"How so?"

"First of all, he's not good in social situations. You were probably seeing uneasiness because he spends so much time alone, or even jealousy."

"Because?" Jake prompted when she didn't go on.

Her look softened. "Because of me. I think he considers

me his only friend, and maybe he's a little possessive."
She almost didn't continue, then did. "You *have* been here
a lot lately."

True enough, he thought sheepishly, but that's not what
concerned him at the present. "What's the other reason
he's different?"

"I'm sorry?"

"You said 'first of all, he's not good in social situations.' What's the rest of it? Should I be running a check
on him?"

"Please don't do that. Life hasn't been easy for him
since he came here." After another pause, she continued
reluctantly. "Pete has a drinking problem. Most of the
town avoids him like the plague, so he doesn't bother with
them, either. In fact, for a long time, even I cut him a wide
berth. Then, I…well, I had some trouble, and he was very
kind to me when others weren't."

She'd had some trouble all right, Jake thought. Her ex-
husband had helped himself to enough diamonds to run a
small country, and FBI agents had swarmed her home.

"He's a little scary-looking," she admitted. "But he's
a decent man underneath. We're friends now. I don't judge
him, and he doesn't judge me."

Kylie ran to the screen door, her face wreathed in
smiles. "Hi, Jake! Want to go wif me and Mommy?"

Jake watched a flush rise in Sarah's cheeks as she smiled
and opened the door for her daughter. Suddenly he felt a
little flushed, too.

"We just got back from delivering food to the Grange
hall for tomorrow's wedding reception," she told him. "I
promised if she was good, we'd take a drive for ice cream
after we brought the van back home and grabbed our jackets."

"She likes ice cream, huh?"

"No, she loves ice cream," Sarah said, laughing.

Jake hid a new stab of emotion, a new twinge of loss as Kylie repeated her invitation. "Sorry, honey, I can't, but thank you. I have a date with the mayor tonight."

"Okay." Then she raced across the porch and hopped on the swing.

Jake stared after her, grinning. "She's really upset, isn't she?"

"Crushed." Sarah's smile lingered, and a teasing quality entered her eyes. "You're having dinner with the mayor?"

He studied that smile, reminded of Maggie's reaction on Monday when she'd told him about the invitation. "Yes, she wanted to go over a few things before the town council meeting, so I guess I should get cleaned up. I was at Babylon longer than I'd planned."

After that smile, the sudden chill in her eyes startled Jake. Then he remembered that Vince had been entertaining a woman in one of those backwoods cabins when he was apprehended—and from what Sarah had told him the night they met, it probably wasn't the first time.

Unbelievable. What man in his right mind would want anyone else when he had Sarah?

Reaching behind the door, Sarah set the lock, then pulled the door shut and seemed to put her annoyance behind her. Her smile returned as she held her hand out to Kylie and the toddler ran to take it.

"Have a nice evening," she said, that light back in her eyes. "Eve's a good cook, so dinner won't be a disappointment. Just be careful that you don't wind up being—" She stopped abruptly, laughed and shook her head.

"What?"

"Nothing."

"Then why the silly smile?"

"No reason," she said, leading Kylie down the steps. "Just have a good time."

"You, too," he answered curiously, enjoying the view from behind her as he followed her down the steps. Eve Markham hadn't seemed strange when he met her two weeks ago. Was she a powermonger? One of those women in traditionally male roles who liked to call all the shots?

Jake climbed into the Jeep and watched Sarah and Kylie enter the garage behind the house where a burgundy Blazer shared space with her catering van. Then he preceded them out of the drive, still wondering how Sarah would've finished that odd sentence.

He and his libido both knew the answer to that question when he returned to the Twirling Spur that night. Jake unlocked the door to his room, turned on the light, closed the door and walked straight to the telephone book on the chipped nightstand. A moment later, he was dialing.

"Just be careful I don't wind up being dessert?" he said without preamble when she answered the phone.

Sarah's soft laughter spilled through the earpiece, and for some reason, a contented warmth filled Jake's chest—then promptly spread lower.

"And were you?"

"Nope," he said with a cheeky grin. "My honor's still intact. We had cherries jubilee."

There was more laughter on Sarah's side of the line, more tingles on his. "Then you had a nice time."

"No, I had an interesting time." Jake sank to his bed, carrying the phone along with him as he leaned back against the cheap headboard. Springs squeaked and pinged as they took his weight.

Suddenly, he wanted to talk, a real departure for a man

who hated phone conversations the way he did. "You weren't asleep, were you?"

"No, I'm in bed, but I—" She stopped, and Jake wondered if she was afraid of creating the wrong kind of images, of bringing too much intimacy to the conversation. If so, it was too late. He was already there. He could see her propped against pillows with lace-trimmed cases, a puffy satin comforter with pink and burgundy roses pulled up to her waist. And he saw a soft, pretty nightie on soft, pretty Sarah.

"I was reading," she said. "It helps me doze off."

Slowly, Jake kicked off his boots and matched the subdued pitch of her voice. "That really helps?"

"Sometimes. If not, it's a nice distraction if I have a lot on my mind."

He smiled against the receiver. "Maybe I should try that. I'm feeling extremely distracted tonight."

"Because of someone's cherries jubilee?"

What was it about a faint wine buzz, dim lighting and the telephone that gave people courage and allowed them to voice thoughts they wouldn't share otherwise? "No," he answered quietly. "Because of someone's brown eyes."

The silence at the other end of the line stretched out for several very long moments. Jake squeezed his eyes shut and mouthed a curse. He knew he shouldn't have said that, and now it was too late to take it back. What had possessed him?

"I'd better get some sleep," she said, and he could hear a touch of uneasiness in her voice. "Kylie's an early riser."

"Then I guess you'd better," he replied, at a loss for anything else to say. Obviously, he needed sleep, too, or he wouldn't have run off at the mouth the way he did.

Should he apologize? Tell her he hadn't meant his remark to sound like a cheap pickup line? "Sarah—"

"Good night, Jake."

Jake drew a long, deep breath as something inside him warmed. She'd finally called him Jake. Not Sheriff. Not Mr. Russell. *Jake.* "Good night, Sarah," he said softly. "Sleep tight."

"You, too."

On the other side of town, Sarah hung up the phone and pressed a hand to the fluttering behind her navel. How could he make her want him with only a phone call? Take her breath away just by lowering his voice? Had he been thinking about her all evening, too? Or was that call simply an amused man calling in the punchline to a shared joke?

Sarah blinked in shock as common sense brought her to a halt. She had to stop this! She wasn't looking for a relationship, and she wasn't into recreational sex. But if she didn't get a grip on herself, that's exactly what could happen.

Reaching across to her nightstand, she turned off the lamp and lay in the darkness. One thing was certain. She couldn't continue to keep quiet about his fatherhood. The more contact she had with him, the stronger her feelings were that he was a decent man and could be trusted not to topple Kylie's secure world.

At the same time, some people changed when faced with life-altering situations. Would Jake?

What would happen if they went head-to-head at a custody hearing? Betsy Chappell hadn't fared well against a doctor with connections. Could Sarah hope to do better against the law in this town?

Apparently, the café was Comfort's Saturday morning hotspot. Jake pulled off his black Stetson and walked inside to more noise and commotion than usual, the difference being the presence of kids. Kids in and out of the booths, babies tucked into high chairs, and frazzled parents trying to eat their breakfasts and oversee wound-up children at the same time.

It looked like heaven to Jake.

"Busy place today," he said, taking one of the vacant stools at the end of the lunch counter. He set his hat on the stool next to him.

Ruby brought him a cup of black coffee. Her waitresses were moving along at a fast clip, but the elderly proprietress proceeded at her regular pace—which, Jake decided, was whatever speed she felt like going at the time.

"School's startin' Monday. It's always like this the Saturday before. Stores'll be busy, too, what with last-minute shoppin' fer shoes and such." Her pale eyes twinkled behind her spectacles. "One a' these days it'll be you and some nice gal tryin' to keep yer kids in their seats."

"Probably not," Jake said, taking a sip of his coffee. "I'm not the marrying kind."

"Why not?"

Because marriage required a man and a woman to put each other first—above all others—and no woman had ever put him first. Not even his mother. With his track record, somehow he knew it would always be that way.

"Why not?" he repeated with a wink, "because I'm thinking of joining the priesthood."

With a delighted cackle, Ruby slapped her knee.

"Then you'll be breakin' a lot of hearts around here, young fella. Now, what kin I git you fer breakfast?"

"Just a couple of your cinnamon rolls to go, and an extra coffee. I have a few things to do this morning, and I need to get started." He'd already been to the building supply store, and his Mountaineer was loaded with plywood sheets, padlocks and tools.

"Guess yer boardin' up Babylon again," she said, then turned away to take two huge cinnamon rolls from a glass pie case. "You want these heated?"

"Sure, if it's not too much trouble." But Jake's attention was still on her first statement. "How did you know about Babylon? Got a crystal ball behind your counter, Miss Ruby?"

"Aunt Ruby," she corrected him. In a few seconds, she took the rolls from the microwave, wrapped them, then filled a foam cup with coffee. "And I don't need a crystal ball. Elvira Parsons was in this mornin' and said you brought it up at last night's town council meeting, along with the news that young Jimmy Ray Becker's gonna be yer new part-time deputy. Gave folks something to chew on this mornin' besides their bacon."

Jake drank from his coffee cup while she loaded his breakfast into a bag. No wonder the *Prairie Voice* only came out once a week. There was no need for a daily newspaper in Comfort.

A high red vinyl stool stood behind the counter. Ruby pulled it close and plunked herself down across from him. "Fact is, people chew about you pretty regular around here. Even me," she added, chuckling.

"Why is that?" He was amused by her candor, but he couldn't say he was surprised.

"Cause yer so tight-lipped about yerself." She pursed her own lips thoughtfully. "Fact is, you remind me of somebody. Maybe it's them blue eyes. Yer pa wouldn't be one of the Russells from over near Dillon, would he?"

Jake stood and finished his coffee, then grinned, pulled some bills from his jeans, and laid them on the counter. "Nope," he said, donning his hat.

Ruby handed him the bag containing his coffee and rolls. "Didn't think so. Big Timber?"

"Nope."

"That all yer gonna say on the subject?"

"Yep," he answered with a wink. But he was pleased that someone in his family had experienced at least a spark of recognition. "Thanks, Aunt Ruby. Have a good day."

"Same to you. And it's about time you called me by my proper name." He'd only taken two steps when he heard her mutter, "I suspect you have more right to use it than most."

Jake whirled in surprise, but Ruby had already grabbed a coffeepot and was making her way toward the other end of the counter to fill cups.

Had he heard her right? The noise level in the place hadn't eased up, and her voice *had* dropped at the last. He waited for several seconds to see if she'd look up from her pouring. But she was already involved in good-natured banter with a few men he didn't know, and Jake left, nerves buzzing and adrenaline high.

Chapter 6

The wind howled and raged, threatening to blow the burgundy Blazer off the road as Sarah drove through the pelting rain with her wipers going full force. She should have canceled her Monday night quilting meeting, but she hadn't expected the weather to get this bad. She glanced in the rearview mirror to check on Kylie. Safely snapped into her car seat, she was watching the downpour with typical two-year-old fascination.

"Will I get wet in the wain?" she asked.

Sarah smiled. "No, you won't get 'wet in the wain' because you're wearing your pretty yellow poncho, and we have a great big umbrella." But the last forecast from the car's radio had said temperatures were falling. If the rain changed to sleet or snow before they reached home, they'd have more to worry about than getting wet. Thankfully, they were nearly there. Area residents were fond of saying that Montana only had two seasons: winter and summer, sometimes in the same day. It wasn't far from the truth. Earlier, the skies had been sunny, and tomorrow, temperatures were supposed to climb again.

Minutes later, the row of pines fronting her property appeared in her headlights. Sarah pulled in and parked near the porch, doused the lights and grabbed her umbrella from the floor. Then she lifted Kylie from her car seat and carried her through the blowing rain. It was a relief to unlock the front door and hurry inside.

"Here we are, Miss Sweetie Pie," she said a little breathlessly as she set Kylie down and clicked on the light in the foyer. "Home safe and sound."

"I got wet," Kylie grumbled.

"I know, but not too wet, right?" Sarah set the umbrella in its corner stand to drain. Suddenly, she froze.

Something was wrong. She was sure she'd left the foyer light *on.*

Chills prickling her arms, Sarah turned around slowly, as the strong, unexpected smells of garlic and tomatoes assailed her nostrils.

Light from the entryway spilled straight ahead of her into the kitchen, and Sarah stifled a cry. Cupboards hung open and dishes were smashed on the floor. Food was everywhere. An ivy she'd had hanging in the window over her sink lay in the doorway, pot upended and soil everywhere.

Ignoring Kylie's shrieks that she wanted to stay, Sarah snatched her up and raced back into the rain, into the Blazer. Quickly, she adjusted her seat to make room for Kylie on her lap—tried to fit the key into the ignition with shaking fingers. She tried again. The engine roared to life.

"Mommy?" Kylie whimpered, obviously picking up on Sarah's fear as she backed out of the driveway.

"It's okay, sweetheart," she answered rapidly. "We're just going across the street to visit Uncle Pete for a minute.

Then—then would you like to sleep at Grandpa's tonight?''

"Okay," she answered in a small voice.

"Great," Sarah said, shivering as she sped the short
distance to Pete's clapboard home. "Great. Then that's
what we'll do. We'll go to Grandpa's."

Pete answered immediately when she hammered on his
door, and swiftly beckoned them inside. "What's wrong?"

The smell of bourbon was strong on his breath and he
looked a little worse for wear, but she couldn't concern
herself with that right now. "Pete, I need to call the sheriff.
My house was broken into."

"Again?" The big man hustled out of the way. "Sure,
sure. You know where the phone is, missy."

Still clutching Kylie, Sarah hurried through Pete's sad
little rooms to the dim kitchen. He followed, quickly finding the phone book beneath a pile of newspapers on a
counter.

"I'd get the number for you," he said, "but I don't see
so good in this light."

"It's okay, Pete, thank you." Sarah put Kylie down,
flipped through the pages and dialed. She was close to tears
when Jake answered the phone.

"Jake? Jake, someone broke into my home!"

"Sarah?"

"Yes! Yes, it's Sarah! We were at the Grange hall, and
when we got back the place was a mess. Plants were upended, food was dumped—"

"Sarah, get out of the house."

"I did. We're at Pete's. I was afraid to call from my
place. I don't think there's anyone inside now, but—"

"Good. Stay at Pete's. I'll see you in a few minutes."

Sarah waited nervously at Pete's front door, fidgeting
with the zipper on her jacket, mindless of the cold mist

coming through the screen. From the living room, she could hear Kylie and Pete making a game of throwing checkers into a box, and Sarah was thankful Pete had become their friend.

It seemed forever until she heard a siren split the air and saw red and blue lights flash in the downpour.

Sarah opened the door and watched the sheriff's Jeep fishtail into her driveway fifty yards up the straight stretch of road. Then she stepped back inside and continued to wait impatiently for news.

It was a full ten minutes before Jake pulled into Pete's driveway and parked behind Sarah's Blazer. She opened the door to him, noting that his tan Stetson and uniform jacket were both rain-splashed.

"Whoever wrecked your place is gone now," he said grimly. "But it might be best if you and Kylie spent the night at your dad's house."

Sarah nodded, shivering, her chills a combination of cold rain, fear and adrenaline. "I'll take Kylie to dad's right now, but I'm coming back."

Jake spoke in concern. "You should stay, too."

"No. I—I have to see."

"All right, but be careful traveling the roads. If it gets much colder, they could get slick."

"I will. Will you be at the house when I get back?"

"I'll be there." He squeezed her hand. Despite her fears, the simple gesture made her feel safe, gave her strength. "I have some men coming over to dust for prints and take pictures, so I'd better get back."

"Okay," she said through a shaky breath. "Okay, I won't be long. My dad's place isn't far."

"Just watch the roads," he repeated.

* * *

Sarah was wrong. She was detained at her father's home far longer than she'd anticipated. An hour after she and Kylie arrived, the phone rang. Sarah answered, holding the receiver close to her left ear and pressing a hand over her right one to muffle Kylie's high-pitched wails.

"Guess you decided to stay at your dad's after all," Jake said after he'd identified himself. He needn't have bothered; she would have recognized his voice anywhere.

"No," she said, relieved to hear from him considering the thoughts she'd been having for the past hour. "No, I'm still coming back. Kylie's a little out of sorts right now, and I don't want to leave until she's settled."

"I can hear her. What's wrong?"

"I think she's feeling a little insecure. Which is certainly understandable after being dragged into the rain three times in one night. She's probably picking up on my mood. Dad's trying to calm her down."

"All the more reason for you to stay," Jake returned. "I can leave the lights on and lock up as best I can. Anything you have to do over here can be done tomorrow."

But Sarah refused again, her voice starting to shake. "Jake, I have to come back. We need to talk. This—this isn't the first time this has happened."

"Your home's been broken into before?"

"Not broken into exactly, but entered. It was three years ago. Actually, it was…it was the night we met. I started locking my doors after that."

More surprise. "You didn't normally?"

"No. It's a small town, and I never dreamed I had to worry about that." She drew a deep breath. "I told you that I'd been away for two weeks. Since I came back, I've been losing things—rather, misplacing them. But my life's been crazy lately," she defended, "and I just assumed I'd been distracted when I put them away."

"You think someone was in your home while you were gone."

A new shudder moved through her. "Maybe even since I've been back."

"Okay," he said gravely. "We'll talk more later. Don't rush. Take all the time with Kylie that you need. I'll wait here for you."

"Thank you." For a second, she wondered how he'd found her. Then she remembered introducing him to her father last week. "And thanks for checking on us. I'll be there as soon as I can." Then she went back to the living room, where Kylie's sobs were finally abating.

Three full hours had elapsed by the time Sarah reentered her home, slipped off her wet sneakers and walked tiredly into her kitchen.

Jake was alone, with only the dim overhead light lit as he swept a mixture of flour, sugar, cereal and rice from her floor into a dustpan. She looked around, surprised that the place looked so good. Apparently, he'd already cleaned up the majority of the mess.

She watched him dump the dustpan into the wastebasket where its contents joined the broken sunflower canisters already in there. It was so quiet, Sarah could hear cereal and sugar granules falling into the basket's plastic liner.

"Thanks again for calling my dad's to make sure we were all right," she said over the lump in her throat. The canisters weren't expensive, but they were special, and losing them broke her heart.

"I was worried when you didn't come back right away. Is Kylie okay?"

"I think so. As it turned out, she didn't want to sleep upstairs in my old room, though she's always looked forward to it before. Dad talked her into a camp-out in the living room. When I left, he was dragging out pillows, flashlights and picnic food.''

''Sounds like he knows how to make her happy.''

Sarah nodded, then walked to the wastebasket and lifted out a ceramic shard. Sighing, she dropped it back in. ''These were my mother's. After Miss Lillian died…after she left me this place…I dropped the lid to her tea canister on the floor and it smashed.'' She tried to smile. ''Since my parents never drank tea, my mom said she'd trade me—said her sunflower canisters would look better in this yellow kitchen, anyway.''

Tears welled, and suddenly Sarah didn't have the energy to hold them back. ''Things are always breaking in this house.''

Setting the broom and dustpan aside, Jake came to her and gathered her close, and Sarah melted into his warmth. ''I'm sorry,'' she sobbed. ''I *hate* to cry. My eyes burn, my head aches, and my sinuses get all p-plugged up. It's such a weak, stupid thing to do!''

''Are you kidding me?'' he said, a smile in his voice. ''There's nothing weak or stupid about you. Someone ransacked your home. You have a right to be upset.''

She sobbed harder, grew angry. ''Homes can be replaced! Possessions can be replaced! But I live here with my daughter. What if Kylie and I had been home? What if we'd interrupted whoever did this while they were still in the house? She could have been hurt.''

''But that didn't happen, and we're going to find out who did this. For tonight, just leave everything as it is. Tomorrow, I want you to look around and see if anything's missing. Then we can talk about why anyone would want to do this, as well as a few other things.''

Shaking her head, Sarah released her hold on him to

wipe her eyes. "I'll do it right now. I won't be able to sleep, anyway."

"All right, but let's have a cup of coffee or tea or hot cocoa first."

"I don't need anything."

"Well, maybe I do," he said, his hands still linked at the back of her waist.

Sarah searched his caring eyes and reassuring smile. He didn't fool her for a moment. He wanted her to calm down, but he wouldn't say the words. The considerate gesture made her tears well again. "You're not going to believe this, but this is only the second time in my life that I've fallen apart this way. Twice in an entire lifetime. And you've been here both times."

"Just doing my job," he joked.

"I don't think so." He'd cleaned up a horrid mess, phoned to make sure she and Kylie were okay, and held her when the tears came. That was above and beyond anything he was required to do. Jake Russell was a decent, caring man...and somehow she'd always known that.

Brimming with warmth and gratitude, and something else she didn't want to name, Sarah eased up on tiptoe and kissed him softly. "Thank you," she whispered, feeling a new kind of trembling inside. "Really."

He nearly backed away. She could see the wariness in his eyes and expression, feel the impulse to bolt radiating from his body.

Then Jake shook his head as if to say that backing away was an impossibility. "You're welcome," he rasped. "Really." A second later, his hot, hard mouth was covering hers, and Sarah was returning the pressure.

It was pure heat, right from the get-go, the kiss of a man who'd hungered for this for a very long time.

Clutching the front of his shirt, she surrendered to its

power, inhaled his musky scent as the kiss deepened, then went deeper still. This was dangerous, and she didn't care—wrong, but she denied it. She tightened her arms around him, hating the jacket she wore because it kept their bodies from each other's. She loved the hot, slick stroking of his tongue against hers as the movement fired her senses and brought her to life.

Just a little longer, she thought, her mind spinning. *Just a little deeper. Dear God, it's been so long....*

Jake broke from the kiss and buried his face in her neck and hair, raining more kisses over her throat. His warm mouth and the shivery scrape of his beard were nearly her undoing.

Nearly. Because this pleasure she took so freely was tainted by lies. Suddenly she knew she couldn't withhold the truth from him any longer. She couldn't accept his strength and comfort without giving him the gift he so desperately wanted in return.

"Jake," she whispered shakily. "Jake, wait."

His hands stilled on her back, and she heard his breath catch. His low voice trembled near her ear. "I'm sorry, I shouldn't have—"

"No, it's all right. You didn't do anything I didn't want you to do. I just—we have to stop."

He didn't move for a moment. Then slowly, he eased away from her, his eyes troubled, his voice still passion-tinged. "Then I did misunderstand."

Sarah shook her head, wishing her heart would stop pounding so hard, wishing she didn't feel the need to speak so quickly. "No, I wanted you to kiss me. It's been a long time, and I was scared about the break-in, and we were alone, and—" And like déjà vu, the desire she'd felt for him that night three years ago came streaking back, begging for one more taste.

"But?"

"But I have to tell you something. And I'm afraid to do it."

His expression softened. "You don't have to be afraid to tell me anything. What is it?"

She was crying again, dammit, and she didn't want to! She wanted to be strong! Sarah blinked, cleared her throat and swallowed, all the while keeping her gaze averted. She'd waited too long to tell him, and she didn't want to see the loathing in his eyes when she said the words.

"She's yours," she whispered.

"I'm sorry?" he said.

She looked up at him. "Kylie. She's your child. Yours and mine."

It took several seconds for him to digest the news. It took only a moment for his rage to build. "Kylie's my child?"

Sarah nodded.

Jake cast around the kitchen, his eyes wild, thoughts sailing through those dark blue irises at a frenetic pace—and not a warm thought among them. His gaze stabbed hers, and his hands curled into fists. *"I asked you—point-blank—if she was mine, and you said no. I gave you endless opportunities to tell me! How could you lie to me about something so important?"*

"I didn't lie!" she insisted. "I never actually said she wasn't yours. I told you that an April birth date and black hair didn't automatically *make* her yours."

"A lie of omission is still a lie!" He turned away, turned back, didn't seem to know what to do with his anger. The air in the kitchen fairly crackled with electricity. "You knew how badly I wanted her to be mine—*you knew my past*. And you lied to me!"

"All right, I lied! But I was going to tell you."

"When? When she graduated from high school? When she celebrated her twenty-fifth wedding anniversary? When it was too late for me to know and love her as a child?"

"No! I was going to tell you soon—I swear. I didn't know what kind of man you were. I couldn't let a stranger into Kylie's life—she's too precious to me. I'd only known you for *one hour* when she was conceived."

"And when you found out you were pregnant, it never occurred to you to try to reach me? To *find out* what kind of man I was?"

"I didn't know your last name," Sarah shouted, embarrassed all over again.

"You knew I was a deputy up near Glacier. It would've taken only a few phone calls to find out which county."

Now Sarah got angry. "You're absolutely right," she snapped sarcastically. "That's exactly what I should have done. And of course, the second that I reached you, you would've rushed right back here, jumped into a tux and married me."

"Hardly," he drawled. "You know how I feel about marriage. It's a bad bet. But I would've supported you through the pregnancy, and made damn sure *my* name was on that birth certificate, not Vince Harper's." He frowned in disgust. "That was quite a legacy you gave my daughter."

This was too much. It was just too much. Drained, Sarah shed her jacket and hung it on the back of a maple chair. Then she walked to the sink where Jake had left dishes and refrigerator containers that were still intact yet needed to be washed. She started loading the dishwasher.

"Kylie had to be protected," she said wearily. "I couldn't very well tell them to write 'Jake Somebody' on that line."

Jake took several deep breaths, his joy at learning that Kylie was his damn near ruined because the woman he'd lain awake nights thinking about was a liar. But he had to get a grip on himself. He had to start thinking like a lawman, not a disenfranchised father.

He went to the sink where Sarah was still stiffly and methodically going about her task. "Okay, this isn't getting us anywhere. Let's shelve it for the time being and talk about the break-in."

"All right," she replied quietly. "Do you still want that hot cocoa? It's instant."

Jake started to refuse, then abruptly changed his mind. "I'll fix it while you finish loading the dishwasher. I doubt you'd be able to find it, anyway. I probably put everything back in the wrong cupboards."

They worked independently of each other, moving rigidly about. They didn't speak again until they were seated across the maple dinette from each other, their mugs of cocoa untouched, the autumn floral centerpiece in the middle of the table a tangible barrier between them.

"All right," he began brusquely. "First of all, I should tell you that the print guys came up empty. They said the place was so clean he wouldn't be surprised to find out you're an OCD case."

Sarah lifted her gaze from the study of her clasped hands, and despite her lies, Jake felt a little sorry for her. Her dark eyes were red and puffy, and the rain had her usually silky hair stuck together in damp clumps. "OCD?"

"Obsessive-compulsive disorder. There were very few prints on your canisters, plates, refrigerator or any of the other smooth surfaces they tested right away. Those they found obviously belonged to you and Kylie. Since we know the intruder touched these things, we have to assume he wore gloves." Jake took a deep breath. "Also, there was a faint flour trail leading out the back door, but the rain pretty much obliterated it as soon as he stepped off the porch. From the size of the footprints inside—and they weren't viable—we suspect the intruder was a man.''

"All right," she said, brushing her long bangs aside. "Where does that leave me? This was such...such an *angry* thing. What happens if this person tries again? How do I protect my daughter?"

"*Our* daughter," Jake said pointedly. "And I have that covered. But before we discuss Kylie's needs, let's think about what the intruder could have been looking for, because this was obviously a search. Do you have anything of value on the premises? Keep in mind what this person looked through: canisters, containers, ice cube trays. Plants were ripped out of their pots and the soil dumped." He let a little sarcasm enter his tone. "Think small and valuable."

"You know about the diamonds," she said wearily.

"Of course I know about the diamonds. Everyone in the state knows about the diamonds. I just didn't realize you were involved until—"

"I wasn't involved! I had nothing to do with any of that!"

"I'm sorry, poor choice of words. I should have said that, since I didn't know Harper was your ex-husband until last week, I didn't connect you to him."

"Well, let me save you some time, Sheriff. I don't have them. Although, there was a time when half the people in this town thought I did. I told you someone had gone through the house three years ago. I'm sure they were looking for the diamonds at that time. But now? Three years later? It has to be something else."

"If not for the type of search we saw here, I'd agree with you."

"Well, if someone's looking for them again, they're in for a disappointment. The FBI searched this place from top to bottom and side to side, and they found absolutely nothing—which is exactly what anyone else will find." She paused, drew a hand back through her hair. "Vince won't be giving you any answers, either. He was killed two months ago during an escape from a Florida prison. There was a...a car accident."

Jake eased closer, forearms on the table. "But he wasn't alone in the car, was he?"

"No." She sighed. "Apparently, someone from outside—the man who set up the escape—was driving, but he..." Sarah stopped and moistened her lips. "The driver got away. He hasn't been found yet, has he? You think Vince told the man about the gems, and he's behind this."

"When it appeared that this could've been a search for the diamonds, I made a few phone calls." Jake assessed her gravely. "The driver's name was Ike Paden. He's a skip from the Miami area."

"A 'skip'?"

"Someone who skipped bail—ran out before his court date and left a bail bondsman a lot poorer. Someone who fit Paden's description stole a car in St. Louis last month."

Sarah drew a trembling breath. "What was the charge?"

"Second-degree murder. He was out, pending an appeal." Jake watched her pale. "I'm not saying it was Paden who stole the car, and I'm not saying he was the man who broke in here tonight. It could be anyone. But considering the time frame, we can put him on a suspect list. If he was dodging police, it could have taken him this long to get here. Do you know him?"

"No. Vince took off for Florida almost a year before we divorced. And I wasn't in the habit of visiting my ex-husband in prison, much less meeting his new friends."

"What about strangers? Have you noticed any unfamiliar faces in the area recently?"

"Jake, I see strangers all the time. Vacationers, hunters, fishermen. Some of them—the ones who brought their wives along—have even boarded here."

"I'll have a photo faxed to me in the morning." He paused to meet Sarah's troubled gaze. "Didn't your ex-sheriff warn you that Paden could come calling?"

Sarah shook her head. "Cy Farrell was up to his ears in graft and corruption. He didn't have time to do his job. What am I supposed to do now? What about Kylie's safety?"

"I told you before. I have that covered." Jake took a long swallow of his cocoa, put the cup down and stared at her candidly. "The idea of Kylie staying in a home where she's at risk is unacceptable to me. We'll be making some changes, Sarah."

Instantly, her eyes widened in horror. Then her fear was replaced by a cold determination Jake knew he shouldn't test.

"If you're trying to tell me you're taking Kylie out of this house, you're sadly mistaken."

"Not at all," he said solemnly. "I'm trying to tell you to get my room ready. I'm moving in."

Chapter 7

"You're joking."

"Not even a little bit." His cool blue gaze held hers. "I'll pay you, of course, whatever your former tenants paid, and I don't need any extras. I'm perfectly happy taking my meals at the café."

Sarah stared, incredulous. "And what do you think your living here will accomplish? You can't protect us twenty-four hours a day. You have to work."

"But I'll be here at night, and that's when the break-ins occurred. I can stagger my work hours with my deputies, leave my car parked in the driveway occasionally when I'm gone, and avoid the life patterns that criminals are quick to spot."

Suddenly anxious again, Sarah left her chair and flipped on the rest of the lights in the kitchen. The maple chandelier over her dinette, the light on the range hood, the spotlight over the sink. "No way. The gossips in this town would have a field day, and that wouldn't be good for either of us. You don't want to risk the November election, and I don't want to be the reason everyone stops talking when I walk into a room.''

"That won't happen. My presence here is easily justified. You run a bed-and-breakfast.''

"Which has been closed for nearly a week.''

"Because of me.''

"*Yes,* because of you.''

Jake went to the sink where she stood with her arms crossed over her red sweater. "Then reopen it,'' he said, irritation flaring in his eyes again. "I know about Kylie now.''

"*Reopen?* Has it occurred to you that if I reopen, I could end up giving a room to the very man we're trying to keep out?''

"Yes, it has. And again—that's not going to happen.''

Sarah snatched up a damp sponge, squirted dish soap on it and scrubbed it over her smeared countertops. "You can't know that.''

"Yes, I can, because I'll be your only boarder. After I move in, the No Vacancy sign goes back up.''

Sarah blew out a sarcastic breath and kept working. "Oh, yes, that's a wonderful idea. No one will bat an eye if I reopen just to accommodate you.''

Jake turned her around to face him, his agitated gaze piercing hers. "It's common knowledge that I've been looking for a temporary place in town while I hunt for an apartment. People will assume you're doing a favor for the sheriff—nothing more.''

Sarah jerked away.

"If anyone asks,'' he continued, "you can feed them the same line of crap you fed me. Your catering business is taking up a lot of your time, and you'd rather spend it with Kylie. You can tell people that you're not even giving me breakfast.''

Sarah almost laughed as she moved to the range to gather up spilled rice and dump it into the wastebasket. Didn't the man have a mirror? With his looks, people would think he was getting a whole lot more than breakfast. From his thick black hair to the tips of his boots, he was the most exciting, most rawly attractive man to hit this town in years. People would absolutely think the worst.

And there was a fear in Sarah that their gossip would eventually be justified. Though he was furious with her now, they'd been locked in each other's arms only minutes ago. She could still feel the imprint of his mouth on hers, still feel that crackle of awareness in the air. Eyes met, blood stirred and memories ran rampant whenever she got within ten feet of him. How could they possibly live under the same roof without giving in to the heat?

"And before you object again," he said firmly, "you might as well know that, gossip or no gossip, I'll do whatever it takes to protect my daughter."

Sarah stood motionless at the range. Did he mean that he'd publicly claim Kylie to end the speculation and explain his presence here? Slowly, she turned to face him. "Was that a threat?"

"It was a statement of fact. Nothing more."

But the set of his jaw and the determination in his eyes told her that she couldn't completely discount Jake's announcing his paternity.

Sarah began to tremble inside, half fear, half anger. She couldn't allow that to happen. Her dad didn't even know yet. How would he react when he learned that Kylie's father hadn't just suddenly materialized, but was living in her home? Until now, Bill Malloy had been Kylie's only solid male influence, and he cherished that role—he desperately needed it to make up for the role of husband that had been taken from him.

Kylie needed to be prepared for the news, too. She wasn't just two and a half, she was two and a half, going on five. She knew what a daddy was, and she knew she didn't have one. Sarah didn't want her to be hurt and confused if Jake suddenly bailed out because the idea of being a father was more attractive than the reality of it. And again…she, Jake and their libidos would all be living under the same roof.

Sarah stared coldly into his eyes. It didn't appear that she had much choice. If she wanted his silence, she had to let him stay. "All right," she said, flipping the sponge into the sink. "You can have the room across the hall from mine. But you have to promise me something."

"What?"

"You can't breathe a word about being Kylie's father to anyone. Not until we both agree that it's time."

Jake's face turned to stone. "Forget it."

"Jake—"

"I said, forget it. Considering the length of time you kept it from me, you might want to keep it a secret forever."

"I won't. I give you my word."

"Your word?" He expelled a mirthless laugh. "Sorry. The word of a liar isn't worth much to me. I intend to claim her. But I won't do that until I'm sure it won't hurt her in any way. Now, will you be all right here alone tonight? I have to get back to the office before Jimmy Ray comes in. It's his first night."

Fighting tears, Sarah spun around to the sink again and rinsed out the sponge. "I'll be fine. No one will bother me if I leave all the lights on."

Showing him her back didn't seem to faze him.

"A couple more things," he continued. "Some of the other rooms appeared to have been searched, too, but nothing was destroyed. Seems like he didn't get really pissed off until he got to the kitchen. And the intruder came through the back door. I fixed the broken door frame as best I could, but you'll be needing a carpenter.

"When I put the memo board back on your refrigerator, I noticed the name of a building and remodeling place on it. Do they do your carpentry work?"

"Yes."

"Then you'd better give them a call first thing in the morning."

Sarah spun angrily to face him again. "All right, that's enough! I've made mistakes—I'll admit that. But don't give me orders. I'd already planned to phone Clyde."

"Good."

"No, good *night*," she said curtly.

Jake nodded. "I'll have Jimmy Ray drive by a few times during his shift. If something comes up, call me at the office. I'll sleep there tonight. See you tomorrow."

Sarah didn't move a muscle until she heard his Jeep leave in a spin of tires. Then, emotionally drained, she walked to the table and sank into a chair. She stayed like that for a long while, listening to the silence, just being still, too tired to cry. Jake Russell wanted to claim his daughter.

Kylie would never be hers alone anymore.

The morning brought warm sunshine—and a series of disruptions. While Sarah was trying to scrub away the residue of the break-in, she received three phone calls from neighbors, asking what last night's commotion was all about. Apparently, while she was getting Kylie settled at her father's, Jake had knocked on a few doors and asked if residents had seen anyone coming or going from Sarah's home that evening. But that wall of trees had kept any criminal activity secret.

She'd just said goodbye to neighbor number three when Clyde Hoskins showed up to fix the splintered door frame out back and haul away the spouting beside her shed.

"That was quick," she said, grateful to see him. "I didn't expect you until this afternoon."

"I didn't plan on being here until then," he returned, smiling. "But the sheriff phoned and said you'd need this door fixed before the security people got here, so I came right over."

Sarah went numb all over. "Before the security people get here?"

Clyde eyed her strangely. "Yeah. You knew about that, right?"

Sarah excused herself and went to the phone. It took only a moment for Maggie to patch her through to Jake, who was en route to the Wilson ranch again. "Who gave you permission to take over my life?" she demanded the instant he said hello.

"I'm not taking over anything," he replied evenly, obviously understanding the reason for her call. "I'm doing what needs to be done to keep my daughter safe. The locks on your windows and doors are fifty years old. Some of the windows don't even *have* locks."

"So you called a *security firm?*"

"No, I called a man who has a locksmith business over in Livingston. He's not planning to put in a mine field and surround the place with razor wire. He's just going to upgrade your locks, put in some spotlights with motion detectors and install an alarm."

"This is *my* home," she said belligerently, "not yours. It's not up to you to make these decisions."

"Would you like me to cancel?"

"No, if the locks are bad, they should be replaced. But the next time you decide to do something that affects my life, I'd like to be informed about it first."

For a long, drawn-out moment, an accusing silence hung in the air, broken only by the crackle of static on the radio. Then Jake answered politely, "Yes, that *is* the only fair thing to do, isn't it?" The underlying message was clear; sharing information was a two-way street, and Sarah had failed badly on her side of it.

"The truth is," Jake continued, "I tried to reach you several times, but your phone was busy. Now, I need to get back to work." And without saying goodbye, he broke the connection.

Sarah slammed down the phone, her cheeks burning. All right, she'd had that remark coming. But he'd still overstepped his bounds, and they *would* talk about it when he moved in. Then she picked up the phone again and called her father. Quickly, she brought him up to date and asked him to keep Kylie for another hour.

"The sheriff will be boarding at your place?" Bill asked.

"Do you...have a problem with that?"

"No. In fact, I'm relieved. I just thought you'd decided to close."

Wearily, Sarah combed her fingers back through her hair. "Yeah, Dad, I did. Technically, I'm still closed. But with the break-in, and having Kylie...I'll feel safer if the sheriff's here for a while. Actually, this will help us both out. He's been looking for a place closer to his office while he hunts for an apartment."

Everything she said was true, yet it felt like a lie because Jake had practically spoon-fed her the words.

"He thinks someone's looking for those damn diamonds again, doesn't he?"

"He's not sure. He's not ruling out anything, even though it's been three years since the first break-in." A hard knot formed in Sarah's throat, and she paused. She felt like the biggest liar in the world again. "Dad, I...I have something to tell you. But I want to wait a bit, okay? In a few days, we'll get together and have a long heart-to-heart over coffee. I'll make us some cinnamon rolls." Of all the pastries she baked, warm, frosted cinnamon rolls were her dad's favorite.

He didn't reply for a moment. Then he said quietly, "Want to give your old man a hint as to what it is?"

"Not just yet." When she'd told her parents that Kylie's father had been a stranger, her mother had understood— or rather, she'd understood as well as anyone could. But Sarah had seen a disappointment in her father's eyes that she never wanted to see again. She wasn't eager to turn back the clock. "I really have to go now, Dad."

"Okay, honey. If it helps, I can keep Kylie for the day. Roy'll understand."

That wouldn't help, it would hurt. "Thanks, but winter's coming. You and Judge Quinn won't have many more days to go fishing. Besides, I miss her to pieces already."

She needed time to cuddle her daughter close and smell her hair. She needed time to push her on the swing out back, and hear high-pitched baby giggles echo off the tree-tops.

She needed time alone with Kylie that, in essence, she would never have again.

Sarah was grateful for those tall pines out front at three-fifteen that afternoon when Jake pulled his Mountaineer up close to the house and lugged his things inside. With the trees shielding most of the activity, at least she didn't have to worry about judgmental neighbors for a while yet. Not until someone saw his car leaving in the morning and realized it had been there all night.

When he'd finished, he came back downstairs and took a half step into the kitchen where Sarah was peeling carrots for stew. He'd changed from his uniform to a chambray shirt and snug jeans, and despite her leftover anger, her pulse raced as she imagined him shedding his clothes across the hall from her. His black Stetson dangled from the fingertips of his right hand—the strong, familiar hand wearing that police academy ring.

"I guess Kylie's still asleep?" he said soberly.

Sarah nodded. "You probably saw the single bed in the toy room last night. Most afternoons, she naps in there." But she didn't want to discuss Kylie right now. Sharing her was still too new. "Is your room all right?"

"Yes, it's fine—very nice, actually." He sent her a faint, wry smile. "I'm not used to having the drapes match the bedspread."

"Oh. I'm glad you approve."

"I do."

"Good."

His steady gaze rested on hers while they waited through another uneasy moment, and Sarah wondered how she could want him here and resent his presence at the same time.

Then he spoke quietly. "I'm sorry about this morning. I shouldn't have phoned the locksmith without your consent. It was impulsive, and I apologize."

Sarah set her peeler aside. "That's not all that's going on here."

Jake nodded. "I imagine you're feeling threatened where Kylie's concerned, especially after my behavior last night."

"Not threatened, exactly. But, Jake...she's my life."

"She's a lucky little girl. Not every kid gets to be his mother's life."

No, not every kid did, she remembered. Jake hadn't.

"I won't push anything," he said. "I'll do my best to let her come to me." He studied the tips of his brown boots for a moment; when he faced her again, his tone was almost gentle, a man trying to make peace.

"I've waited a long time for this, Sarah. Some days, I thought it would never happen. I'm not going to screw it up by pushing too hard."

Despite all the harsh words between them, Sarah felt a tug of sympathy. She'd been loved and cherished by her parents her whole life. She'd never experienced the kind of loneliness she heard in his voice. "Thank you."

"Sure." He nodded toward the door. "Think I'll go over to Brokenstraw for a while—groom Blackjack. We have a few hours of daylight left."

"If you get back after dark, the door will be locked, but you have your key."

A small, faintly teasing smile touched his lips. "There aren't any more spare keys outside in flowerpots or taped to the back of porch lights, are there?"

Sarah had to smile, too, and it felt good to break the tension for a moment. "The locksmith told you." When he said "Yep," she shook her head. "No. No more spare keys in obvious places."

"Good. I'll be back before dark." But as he headed for the door, he seemed to remember something and turned back. "I received that fax from Florida today, but it's too dark. They're overnighting a clear photo of Paden. I'll have it tomorrow."

He pulled on his Stetson. "You'll be okay?"

She nodded.

Then he walked toward the door, paused for a fraction of a second beside the toy room to his right, and left.

Sarah rinsed the carrots and added them to the bubbling beef stock on the stove. She would try to make this new arrangement as easy a transition as possible—as she suspected Jake was doing by giving her some space on his first day here. She'd already explained to Kylie that the sheriff would be staying with them for a while—just as other people had before Mommy, Kylie and Grandpa had traveled to Helena to help Aunt Vera. Now they just had to live through it.

It would work out a lot better, though, if he didn't smile at her. When he smiled and his voice dropped low, she got rattled and old memories came rushing back.

On the other hand, she thought, whisking the carrot peelings into the colander for disposal, his not smiling would probably bother her even more.

Jake returned shortly before sundown. But after a quick hello to Sarah and Kylie, who were straightening the toy room, he said good night and went to his own quarters.

Sarah's conflicting feelings about him kicked in again. There was a television set in the room she'd given him, so it wasn't as though he didn't have some sort of entertainment if he wanted. But signing on to watch over Kylie had undoubtedly changed his life.

Did he usually go to Dusty's when his shift was through? she wondered. Was he a have-a-beer-with-the-guys sort of man?

Did he date?

That thought gave her an unpleasant jolt, and she worked faster at picking up the stuffed animals and building blocks strewn around the room. Well, she thought in annoyance, if he was missing the nightlife around here—such as it was—he'd brought it on himself by demanding to stay. This hadn't been her idea. No, sir, it certainly hadn't.

"Okay, sweetie," she said with a smile when the last toy was in the box. "Let's go find a bedtime treat and a storybook. Which one should we read tonight?"

Kylie came running and jumped into her arms. "Fwee Little Pigs!"

"I like that one, too," she laughed, and dropped a kiss to her daughter's freshly shampooed hair.

At eight o'clock Sarah removed the gate at the bottom of the staircase, swallowed her apprehension, then carried Kylie and her storybook up the steps. The closer they got to Jake's closed door, the more Sarah's stomach shook.

Get used to it, she told herself. He could be here for weeks, possibly longer if he didn't find an apartment. *Longer still if he didn't look for one.*

It was a relief to settle into the rocker in Kylie's room and surround herself with ruffles and pink-and-white gingham checks.

Sarah opened the book, snuggled Kylie close and began to read softly. "'Once upon a time, there were three little pigs who lived with their mother in a cozy cottage.'"

"Then they maked their *own* houses."

"Yes, they did because it was time for them to grow up." *But don't you grow up too fast, sweetheart,* Sarah thought, her gaze drawn to the closed door and the man beyond it. Grown-up life was too stressful. But it was also stimulating, and exciting and daring. And sometimes...sometimes it positively took your breath away.

Kylie was asleep before the Big Bad Wolf blew down the house of sticks.

Sarah carried her to the youth bed and tucked her in, then kissed her softly and turned out the light. Then she left the room, leaving the door ajar, and went to the staircase to secure the top gate.

It was already in place.

Sarah shot a quick glance at Jake's door. But the door was closed, and the room, silent. Still, he had to have hooked the gate, and she couldn't help wondering if he'd listened while she'd read to their daughter.

A new rash of nerves struck, and Sarah hurried to her room. But once there, she was faced with yet another problem. It was rare for Kylie to wake in the middle of the night and want to crawl into bed with her. But Sarah always left her bedroom door open, just in case. Could she still do that with Jake here?

A shiver moved through her. No. No, she couldn't. She'd feel too vulnerable. Moving quickly to her nightstand, she turned up the volume on the baby monitor, then sank to her bed and shook.

He'd been right when he'd said there'd be some changes made around here. And not all of them were welcome.

Jake didn't give her "space" for too long. The next afternoon, he appeared at the top of the stairs just as Sarah carried the monitor out of Kylie's room. She froze as he came toward her, his broad-shouldered presence filling up the narrow hallway and making her pulse race. Somehow, she hid her awareness of him and whispered a sober "Hi."

"Hi," he whispered back, equally sober. "She went down for her nap already?"

Sarah nodded, wishing the sun hadn't moved to the back of the house already. Only diffused light came through the window at the top of the stairs, and it seemed to add intimacy to the moment. "She was up early," Sarah murmured. "You can look in on her if you want."

He did, just for a moment. But that look was filled with pride and tenderness—and totally different from the look he gave Sarah when he closed the door and turned to her again. It didn't seem to matter that he still held a grudge against her. He still saw her as a woman.

Sarah swallowed as his somber gaze grew heavy-lidded...slid over her hair and face, and dropped to her plaid shirt and jeans. Then he seemed to catch himself and nodded for her to walk with him toward the stairs.

He's feeling it, too, she realized, nervy chills drizzling down her backbone. And he's playing the same game I am. The change in temperature, the weak-kneed feeling, the wanting to touch...*to clutch*...he feels it, too.

"I have the photo of Paden downstairs," he said gravely. "I think you should take a look. And...there's something else you should know."

"About the break-in?"

"Possibly."

Sarah stepped over the gate and led the way downstairs, then turned up the monitor so she could hear Kylie if she stirred. When they'd taken seats at the table, Jake slid a photo from a manila envelope.

A shudder went through her. The man's face was chilling—cold stare, straight black hair that hung in his eyes, gaunt, pockmarked features, uneven teeth.

"Familiar?" Jake asked.

"No, thank heaven."

Jake slid the photo back into the envelope. His forehead creased as he moved on to the next subject. "When I went down to Babylon the other day, I surprised someone," he began. He filled in the details, ending by describing the travel mug he'd slipped into an evidence bag.

The story made Sarah uneasy. Somehow this affected her, or he wouldn't have brought it up.

"I didn't follow through on the mug at first, because it would've only led to a trespassing charge. But the other night, when officers were here dusting for prints, I gave it to them. It was an easy match. The driver of that truck's been printed before."

Uneasiness became fear, and Sarah's heart thundered in her chest. "Ike Paden?"

"No. The prints belonged to an Idaho bounty hunter named Blanchard."

She blinked in confusion. "A bounty hunter? What would a bounty hunter be doing—" Then she knew. "He's after Paden."

"I won't know that until I talk to him."

"But if he is, that means that Paden's *here*," Sarah said, vaulting nervously to her feet.

Jake stood, too, cupping her upper arms to calm her. The automatic gesture sparked something between them again, and he withdrew his hands. He was still stinging from her lies.

"I don't want to jump to conclusions," he said gruffly. "Blanchard could be looking for someone else, or simply be on vacation."

"People don't take vacations at Babylon, and they don't race off to avoid detection without a reason. Vince was caught there, Paden was Vince's friend, and federal agents searched for the diamonds there. You think there's a connection." When Jake didn't speak, Sarah glanced at the manila envelope. "Do you have another photo in there?"

Jake shook his head. "I only have a description of Blanchard, and it fits half the men in the state. He's white,

medium height, medium weight and in his early forties.
Brown hair and mustache. Ring some bells?''

"At least two dozen."

"We'll watch for him, but I doubt he'll stop at the office
to get his mug back." Frowning, all business, Jake picked
up the envelope. "In the meantime—with your permission—I'd like to conduct my own search of your home. If
I find nothing, no surprise. But if the gems turn up, you
won't have to worry about any more break-ins."

"*If* whoever broke in was looking for the diamonds."

He nodded. "But I think it's worth the time."

"So do I," Sarah agreed. "When and where do we begin?"

Jake raised a brow. "We?"

"Yes. I'd rather feel like I was doing something to help
the situation instead of obsessing about who might or
might not be thinking about ransacking my home again."

He considered her for a moment, then said, "All right.
I'd like to start now. Beginning with the attic and working
our way down. I'll need some duct tape if you have it, and
about twenty feet of rope—clothesline will do. I also want
to know everything you can remember about the night
your ex-husband showed up here."

Sarah nodded, thinking that that night would be easy to
recall. She just wasn't looking forward to sharing it with
Jake.

The chain clinked against the attic's bare bulb as Jake
brushed against it, on his way to marking off another section of the open room. It was hot in the attic, and he wore
only a sleeveless white undershirt with his jeans. A fine
sheen of sweat glistened on muscles that were accustomed
to hard work. He moved aside a dressmaker's dummy.

"Go on," he said, and Sarah pulled her gaze back to the box of clothing in front of her.

They were searching systematically, dividing the attic into small sections with the clothesline, taping it down, then examining each section inch by inch—something the feds hadn't done.

She'd already told him it was late when Vince showed up that night, and that despite their divorce being final, he'd insisted that he wanted to reconcile.

"He was sweet as honey that night," she continued, working to keep the derision from her voice. "Which was strange because he'd been cruel and bitter since he learned his grandmother had cut him out of her will and left everything to me. It was a considerable gift. That's why closing the bed-and-breakfast wouldn't have hurt me financially."

She sealed the box, then stepped over the new rope and into the next section, and the next corrugated box. Dropping to her knees, she removed the lid.

Sarah glanced at Jake again, watched him shine the flashlight over rough beams, feel along dusty rafters. Then she returned to work.

"Vince made the usual empty promises," she said, taking an old dress from the box and checking the pockets. "But every time I looked at him all I could see was ugliness and deceit. He never hit me, but he used his fists on other people. And he liked women. He even slept with two of my friends. Excuse me…former friends."

"And you let him *stay* that night?" Jake asked in disbelief.

"I felt that I had to. This had been his grandmother's place, and for a while, our home." She set the dress aside. "We had an apartment at first, but then we had money problems and Miss Lillian insisted we move in with her.

I suspect she did it mostly to give me a home. She loved Vince because he was a part of the son she'd lost, but she couldn't accept his lies and his cruelty.''

Reaching into the box again, Sarah withdrew a pair of old dress pumps with rhinestone clips, then examined them and set them aside. ''Anyway, I told Vince he could sleep on the downstairs sofa, and made him promise to leave the next day.''

''Did he?''

She didn't answer right away as the memory came back, every bit as distasteful as the original event. ''No,'' she said. ''No, he left an hour after he arrived.''

Slowly, Jake wandered back to her, clicking off the flashlight as he crouched down nearby. ''What happened?''

''He came upstairs and tried to sweet-talk me into unlocking my bedroom door. When I told him to get out, he broke in.''

The rage that widened Jake's eyes was so powerful and immediate, Sarah hurried to correct his thoughts. ''It's okay. Nothing happened. I had a gun. He knew I'd use it before I'd let him touch me that way again.''

Jake bit back a curse, thinking that even though Sarah wasn't emotional, it was a damn good thing Vince Harper wasn't here now. He didn't know what he'd do to the creep, but it wouldn't be pretty.

After a few moments of trying to come up with something comforting to say, he gave up and sat next to her on the floor. He would have liked to take her in his arms. He would have liked to tuck her head under his chin and hold her close. But that wasn't a good idea. Despite the fact that she'd lied to him, whenever he touched her...he wanted to *touch* her.

''What in hell made you fall for a jerk like that?''

She grinned wryly. "I was young and stupid. He was the charming, good-looking town rebel, and every girl in the county thought he hung the moon. When he picked me... Oh, my. I thought I'd died and gone to heaven."

Her blond hair shimmered in the faint sunlight coming through the attic window, and Jake caught the flowery scent of it, remembered the feel of it in his hands.

"I didn't see the crazy side of him until we were married for almost a year and a half—or maybe I didn't want to see it. Then he beat up his boss at the garage where he worked and lost his job. Poof. No money, no security. I had a job waitressing at the café, but that didn't pay the rent."

Jake blew out a disgusted breath. "Is that when you moved in here?"

She nodded. "I couldn't ask my parents for help after they'd tried everything to stop me from marrying Vince. I had too much pride to admit that I'd made a mistake. That probably sounds ridiculous to someone as sensible as you are."

He blew out a derisive breath. "Oh, I'm sensible, all right. I told you once that there was a woman in my life...."

"Heather. She was unfaithful."

Jake glanced at her, surprised that she'd remembered. "I looked the other way, too, even though I suspected something wasn't quite right." He shrugged. "It wouldn't have worked out, anyway. She didn't want kids. One night, we were talking about rings and wedding dates, and I added a crib to the equation. She said to get that thought right out of my head. She wasn't interested in stretch marks and two o'clock feedings, and she had no intention of giving up her shape, her job or her freedom." He paused. "I suggested adoption, but that was out of the question, too."

"Having kids meant that much to you?"

"Having a family did. Looking back, the signs were there all the while. But I was like you. I didn't want to see them."

"Looks like we're both destined to pick losers."

"Not anymore. My 'picking' days are over. Besides, I don't have to pick anymore. I have a daughter."

Sarah's smile faltered, and something uneasy registered in her eyes. "But a daughter isn't a family," she reminded him.

"It's close enough. Besides, where is it written that every man on the planet should be married? You name me one happy couple and I'll name you three who won't make it to their fifth anniversary. Life's a lot less complicated when you're alone."

"I used to think that way, too," she said, rising to brush off the seat of her jeans.

Jake stilled. Was that a tremble in her voice?

"After Vince, I really didn't think I had the heart to try again. But lately...well, I think I've changed my mind. I don't want to be alone forever."

Startled, Jake pushed to his feet. "Are you leaving?"

"Yes, I should check on Kylie. It makes me uneasy leaving her this long without looking in on her. Plus," she said, turning away, "the heat's beginning to get to me. I should get out of it for a while."

Jake followed. He knew it was hot, he just hadn't thought it was *that* hot. She wasn't even flushed. "I'm sorry. Go ahead, I can finish." He watched her pick up the monitor. "You aren't dizzy, are you?"

"I'm fine. I'll see you later."

Bothered by her sudden departure, Jake watched her

stride across the linoleum runner in the center of the attic floor, then disappear down the steps. *Was* she all right? Or had he said something that made her want to run off?

And what—or who—had changed her mind about remaining single?

Chapter 8

Sarah peeked in on Kylie, then closed her door and hurried downstairs. What was wrong with her? Why was she reacting so emotionally to things she already knew about him? She'd known he wasn't interested in an involvement. He couldn't have been any clearer in the kitchen two nights ago.

She wasn't looking for involvement either—especially from Jake. Even if she changed her mind about being alone for the rest of her life, she'd never make the mistake of falling for someone who'd refuse to let himself fall back.

But that wasn't all that disturbed her about his statement upstairs. His growing affection for Kylie bothered her as much as it pleased her. He'd practically said that she was all the family he needed. And that made Sarah think of shared custody again.

What if he wasn't elected in November? He could take a job elsewhere—possibly a distant job—and take Kylie with him for six months out of the year! It wouldn't be the abomination that Betsy Chappell was facing, but aside from her father, Kylie was her life. How could she handle even one day without her?

Trying to tamp down her fears, Sarah set the baby monitor on the kitchen table and went to the refrigerator for the chicken breasts she'd thawed earlier. She was gathering the remaining ingredients for chicken cacciatore when a long, sleepy sigh and a mumble came from the monitor, and she smiled. Kylie was waking. Sarah hurried to wash and dry her hands.

She'd just started into the hall when she heard her daughter's wispy, sleep-fogged voice and stopped dead in her tracks.

"I waked up, Jake."

Chills prickled her arms as Sarah slowly returned to the kitchen to stand over the monitor and listen to Jake's deep, low reply. She could hear a smile in his voice. "I can see that. Did you have a nice nap?"

"I dweamed."

A yawn and a rustle of bedclothes issued from the monitor, then Sarah heard a soft "Up you go" and knew he'd lifted Kylie into his arms. Suddenly, she didn't know what to do. Did she want this? Could she stop it if she tried?

"What did you dream about, pretty girl?" he asked.

"I swinged with Mommy."

Sarah hurried to the staircase, then stopped at the bottom when Jake appeared at the top, removed the gate and carried Kylie down the steps.

"She dreamed about swinging with Mommy," he said, grinning.

"So I heard on the monitor," Sarah murmured.

"Feel better?"

"Better?" she asked, not understanding.

"The heat?"

"Oh. Yes, I'm better." Hiding a guilty twinge, Sarah smiled and took Kylie from Jake's arms. "Maybe we can swing a little later, sweetheart. Mommy's just starting supper."

Jake's deep voice gentled. "Then maybe *we* could swing until Mommy's finished."

Sarah stiffened. "She always has juice and a cookie after her nap." The sharp reply was out of her mouth before she could soften it. Embarrassed by her outburst, she had to turn away.

To her surprise, Jake cupped her chin and brought her face back to him. "Is there any reason I can't push her on the swing after her snack?"

"No," Sarah returned, feeling a thrill at his touch. "I just thought you wanted to search the attic. I—I can take her out as soon as—"

"Why don't we both take her? You do what you need to do, and I'll sit with her while she has her juice. Then we can all go outside together. Okay?"

There was nothing she could say but yes. Telling him the truth had set a chain of events in motion that couldn't be stopped anymore. There was no turning back.

Fifteen minutes later, with the sun shining and a light breeze blowing, Kylie raced across the grass to the swing set, Jake striding along behind her.

Sarah took a seat at the small white table at the rear of the wraparound porch. After much deliberating, she'd decided to give him his own time with Kylie while she prepared her shopping list for the church dinner she was catering in Livingston on Sunday.

But it was difficult to keep her mind on her task, and she glanced up often at the tall man and small child who were getting to know each other in Kylie's private park.

Constructed of thick wooden beams, the swing set boasted a tiny attached clubhouse with a slide, a horse, a seesaw and two sturdy swings. To the right of it, beneath the broad branches of a huge cottonwood tree, sat the covered turtle sandbox Grandpa Malloy had bought for Kylie's second birthday.

It didn't take Kylie long to leave the swing for the sandbox, chattering nonstop to Jake as she dragged aside the turtle shell lid.

But a few minutes later, when they hurried to the outside spigot, filled a pail with water and carried it back, Sarah frowned. She nearly called out that they had a rule about mud-making in the sandbox. Then she heard Kylie's shriek of delight and was glad she hadn't.

Father and daughter sat head to head, Jake sprawled in the grass, Kylie in the sandbox, laughing and whispering together. Then Jake dunked a fistful of sand into the water and let the wet sand escape his hand in a drizzle of fine, curling "fairy castles." He added moats, added turrets...added happy giggles to the afternoon air as he guided Kylie's tiny hand, and she made a castle, too.

Sarah was feeling terribly left out when Jake turned around and called, "Come on, Mommy. You should try this, too." She didn't have to be asked a second time.

"Okay, give me your hand," he said when she'd settled in the grass beside him. His hand was warm and strong in hers. Jake turned to Kylie. "Tell Mommy—what's the first thing we do before we pick up the sand?"

Kylie's pixie smile stretched wide. "Count! One, two, free, four, five fingers!"

"Very good," he said, chuckling, while Sarah's skin tingled beneath his grasp. "Does Mommy have five fingers?"

Kylie nodded excitedly.

"Then she can make castles." He glanced at Sarah in amazement. "She really *can* count to five."

"No, she can count to twenty-five," Sarah corrected, and they shared a proud grin.

The castle building was fun. But soon Kylie's attention waned, and she ran to the swings again, leaving them alone to move closer to the tree and rest their backs against rough bark.

Sarah hid a shaky breath when Jake took her hand again, then lightly brushed away the sand clinging between her fingers. She studied the high slope of his cheekbones, slid her eyes over his perfectly carved mouth and the faint beard shadow that had begun to appear around it. Only a few days ago, she'd kissed that mouth, stroked that face. *So why was she constantly thinking these things if she only wanted his friendship?*

"She's a wonderful little girl," he said quietly, looking up at her again. "You've done a great job."

"Thanks. I try. She'll drive you crazy now, you know. She'll want to make fairy castles every day."

"Then I guess I'll have to quit my job and go into castle construction."

"Probably doesn't pay much," she laughed softly.

"Maybe not in money," he said warmly. "But I hear the benefits are awesome."

They fell silent then, and watched Kylie swing back and forth on her horse, silky hair flying out behind her. After several minutes, Sarah gathered her courage and spoke again. "You're still holding my hand."

Jake nodded, unconcerned, his eyes still on Kylie. "Do you need it for anything right now?"

"No," she said, barely breathing. "Not right now."

"Then let's just sit here and watch her for another few minutes. Okay?"

Nodding, Sarah eased back against the tree trunk, her hormones suddenly quieting as understanding dawned. He needed this. The little boy in him who had never known the love of family needed this moment. Maybe he didn't really need *her,* but he did need to share this time with someone. So with their fingers linked loosely and the solid warmth of his arm against her shoulder, Sarah gave him what he couldn't quite ask for.

When Jake left for the office a little later, Sarah's feelings about him were so mystifying, she didn't know whether to stand, sit or pace the floors. She wanted him here...and she didn't. There was no disputing the fact that he'd been wonderful with Kylie; she already looked at him in that adoring way little girls looked up to their daddies. But sitting under the tree with him hadn't done her heart or her hormones any good. Her physical attraction to him was still there, as strong and unsettling as ever. But now caring had moved in, and that was dangerous. Because caring could turn to love in a heartbeat, and Jake Russell wanted no part of it.

She was even more convinced that she was in trouble that night as she stood over the ironing board in the utility room off the kitchen, listening to his restless movements in the room overhead. She slid the blouse she'd pressed on a hanger and hung it on the caddy nearby. Once again, her nerves were raw.

He'd been in and out of that cherry four-poster at least three times since he'd turned off the TV. What was he doing up there? What was he thinking?

Swallowing, Sarah took Kylie's wrinkled white pinafore from the laundry basket and slipped it over the ironing board. Was he looking out his window? she wondered. Staring at the crescent moon? She pictured his smooth

back and broad shoulders—that thick shag of black hair—
and ironed faster.

Steam whooshed and spit over crisp white cotton.
Maybe he was wondering why it was nearly midnight and
she hadn't come upstairs to bed yet.

That was easy. Holding hands under the cottonwood this
afternoon had brought back the memory of another time
when they'd held hands, and for the past few hours, she'd
been reliving every second of their lovemaking three years
ago. The hint of vulnerability she'd glimpsed this afternoon had only made him more attractive to her. Now she
was so wound up, she just couldn't—

"Enough, Sarah," she muttered as her nipples hardened
and that airy feeling swept through her abdomen again.
She had to stop fantasizing about a man who wasn't interested in anything more than a casual fling. Besides, she
reminded herself, he wasn't here because of her. Kylie was
his prime—

Something banged loudly and clattered against the side
of the house. In a flash of adrenaline, Sarah dropped the
iron onto its stand and ran for Jake.

He was already rushing down the stairs, bare-chested
and zipping his jeans, his gun and holster slung over his
shoulder.

"Somebody's out there! Something hit the house!"

"I know." Barefoot, Jake bolted for the door and hurried onto the porch, drawing his gun. He kept going until
the motion-detecting spotlights on the side of the house
flared and shone on the grass, low shrubs...and a section
of spouting, dangling from the roof. Another long piece
lay on the ground.

Sighing, shaking his head, Jake retraced his steps and
went back inside. He found Sarah a minute later, sitting
protectively at the side of Kylie's bed, the room illumi-

nated by two angel night-lights. Her gaze flew to him, nervously questioning.

"A section of spouting came down," he said quietly from the doorway. "There's a length of it dangling, too, so if the wind kicks up, don't be too alarmed if you hear some thumping against the siding." He nearly suggested that she read Clyde Hopkins the riot act in the morning, but remembering their fight over the locksmith, he thought better of it.

"Spouting?" she murmured, leaving the room and closing the door behind her. "My heart almost stopped because of spouting?" She shook her head and mustered a weak grin. "Clyde's going to hear about this. I can't be jumping at shadows."

"Well, it was a pretty noisy shadow," Jake attested with a smile. "I think you were entitled."

Her eyes softened. "Thank you."

"You're welcome."

A few seconds ticked by, while the realization that they were alone in the semidarkness seemed to settle over them. Jake knew she didn't mean for him to see it, but Sarah's gaze passed over him for just the briefest of moments, from his bare chest and midsection to his unbuttoned jeans.

It spiked an arousal he'd been fighting all night long. But as the air began to thicken between them, he remembered her lies. He didn't need to get hung up on another woman who colored the truth to suit her own purposes, even if she felt it was justified. He wasn't just through with commitment, he was through with deceit and all its cousins.

Still, he couldn't continue to be angry with her. "Well," he said, drawing away. "I guess I'd better get some sleep. Early day tomorrow."

She blinked but kept her poise. Had she wanted him to

kiss her? "And I'd better get back to my ironing. Thanks again for checking outside."

"Sure. Good night."

"'Night."

Jake went into his room and closed the door, then flopped on his bed and stared at the ceiling. It had taken him a long time to get over Heather, but he'd done it. Mostly by reminding himself that trust and love had to go hand in hand. If he couldn't trust her, he couldn't love her—and if he didn't love her, he could get past the hurt. But it had been a long transition from pain to apathy...and he sensed that if he let his guard down again, he could easily begin to care for another liar.

Sarah was relieved to see Jake's door ajar and his room empty at seven-thirty the next morning when she answered Kylie's call. After the night she'd had, her mind didn't need any more stimulation. Every thought she'd had before falling asleep had been X-rated. Her relief was short-lived. Just before noon, as she was preparing lunch for herself and Kylie, she heard Jake's Mountaineer pull in, and blew out a long, defeated sigh.

"Hi," he said, taking off his hat as he came into the kitchen.

"Hi." Sarah set the bread and chicken salad aside and put the knife down. Tiny nerve endings bounced and vibrated beneath her skin. "Did you forget something this morning?"

"No. I was just wondering if you'd mind my spending a few minutes with Kylie before she took her nap. It looks like I'll have to work later than I planned tonight. She'll be in bed by the time I get ho—back."

He frowned, seemingly at his slip of the tongue, then went on in a faintly embarrassed tone. "When I came out of the café this morning, I saw this little girl, and she sort of reminded me..." He cleared his throat. "Well, I was just hoping for a quick visit while Kylie ate her lunch."

Sarah's heart softened, much the way it had yesterday as they sat together watching their daughter swing. But beneath Jake's amiable exterior, she sensed an urgency, a need to make up for lost time. Time, she thought guiltily, that he'd lost because of her silence.

She moistened her lips. "You've probably noticed that it's really warm inside. I've been cooking and baking all morning. Would you like to join us for a picnic lunch out back? Nothing fancy—sandwiches and fruited gelatin on paper plates, and a brownie for dessert."

"I'd like that," he said gratefully. "How can I help?"

You can help by staying out of my dreams, she thought. *By not making my nerves dance and my stomach dive whenever you look my way.* "If you want, you can carry the drinks to the table on the back porch. Kylie and I are having milk—she likes the Mickey Mouse cup in the cupboard to the right of me—and you can help yourself to whatever you want."

The last few words hung in the air between them for a long moment. Then Jake said, "Water's fine," and went to the cupboard.

Once they were outside watching Kylie mangle her sandwich and pick the fruit cocktail out of her red Jell-O, things relaxed somewhat, though currents still passed between them.

"This is nice. Thanks." Jake nodded at his empty plate. "Guess you'll be raising my rent now."

Grinning back, Sarah wiped Kylie's hands and face with the wet washcloth she'd brought out. "Why don't you just do the dishes and we'll call it even?"

"Paper plates? I can handle that."

Sarah imagined he could handle anything he tried. Lifting Kylie out of her booster chair, she kissed her nose, then set her down. "Want to swing a bit before we read a story and take a nap?"

She did. Sarah walked to the end of the porch with her. Then she watched as Kylie held the railing and descended the four wide steps, one at a time. She flew across the yard so quickly her sneakers seemed to have wings. When Sarah returned to the table again, Jake's face was tense.

"She's careful," she assured him. "It's a big world out there. She needs to learn how to navigate it."

"But she's still so small."

"And getting bigger every day. I still use gates over the stairs."

With a sigh that told Sarah she was the boss, Jake gathered their plates and napkins and pushed them aside. After taking a swallow of his water and glancing at his watch, he grew serious. "As long as I have a few minutes, I should bring you up to date on a few things."

Instantly, Sarah's heart kicked into high gear. "Paden?"

"No, nothing on him yet. No news on the bounty hunter who left his prints at Babylon, either, but we're looking closely at strangers and talking to area merchants. The more I learn about this guy, the less I like him."

"Why?"

"He's unscrupulous."

"Unscrupulous enough to break into my home, thinking that diamonds are a better reward than what he'd get for bringing Ike Paden in?"

Jake smiled, a compliment in his eyes. "Ever think of going into law enforcement?"

"You haven't answered my question."

"Gut feeling? It's possible, but I don't think so. He's done some shady things, and he'd know enough to wear gloves. But *shady*'s the key word with Blanchard. He wouldn't alert us by making a mess. He'd be neat and sneaky about it so he could come back in and try again.''

''Unless he found what he was looking for,'' Sarah said.

Jake nodded. ''Unless. And that brings me to your attic and the search we started yesterday. I'd like to get back to it.''

''It's hot up there again today.''

''It's hot everywhere. But the heat's due to move out soon. Do you have any objection to my searching while you're not there?'' His voice dropped teasingly. ''Any skeletons in your closets you'd rather I didn't know about?''

Smiling, she shook her head. ''I've already trotted out all of my skeletons, remember? I was an incorrigible teenager who married a jewel thief. My other sins are minor compared to that. Well, most of them, at any rate.'' The look in his eyes said he knew what she meant.

''That wasn't a sin,'' he said softly. ''That was a miracle.'' Jake took her hand, and Sarah's heart rocketed as he kissed her palm. ''Thank you.'' Then he stood, kept her hand and bent to cover her mouth with his own. It was a simple kiss, a mere brushing of lips, a soft exchange of breath. The contact nearly fused her to her chair.

''See you later,'' he said huskily. Then he was gone, leaving Sarah tingling, breathless and wanting more.

Dear God, she was in trouble.

Late that evening, Jake broke the connection with Dusty Barrows, the owner of Dusty's Roadhouse, then dialed Sarah's number. While the phone rang, he grabbed his hat and keys. To his annoyance, an adolescent quivering began in his gut.

''It's Jake,'' he said when she answered. ''I know I said

I'd be back before dark, but all hell's breaking loose over at the roadhouse. Will you and Kylie be all right alone for a while?''

"We'll be fine," she said. "I doubt anyone's going to bother us with the sheriff's car parked in the driveway."

"That was the plan." Just hearing her voice made him relive that unintentional kiss on her porch. He had to be losing his mind. Why was he playing games with her? Why was he using the chemistry that zipped so freely between them to indulge his needs? "Joe's already on his way, so I'd better get moving. Please—leave a bunch of lights on. If I'm going to be later than ten, I'll call again."

"Okay, but I think you're overreacting."

He probably was. But Kylie—and her mother—were beginning to mean a great deal to him. "Talk to you later."

"You, too."

Hanging up, Jake grabbed his keys, locked the office and headed for Dusty's, forcing Sarah out of his mind for the moment to concentrate on the problem at hand.

What possessed testosterone-charged cowboys to thump their chests and flex their muscles every damn Saturday night? Maybe the unusually warm September weather was to blame. But this was the third complaint since he'd hit this town, and the brawling and chair-smashing was going to stop.

It was nearly ten when he left Joe in charge of the three cowboys he'd put in the lockup, and pulled into Sarah's driveway. He forgot how tired he was when he saw her sitting on the swing.

"You're up late," he said, climbing the steps to the porch. The ringing of crickets filled the night, along with the muted sound of a retreating vehicle and the musical chink of ice cubes.

Sarah cradled a glass in her hand. "Just waiting for the

house to cool down. It's really muggy inside, especially upstairs in the bedrooms. I put a fan in your window.''

"Thanks." He studied her for a moment, taking in her light tank top and chinos while a sultry breeze carried the tantalizing scent of wildflowers to him. It was the same heady fragrance he inhaled every night as she showered in the family bath across the hall—the same scent that was responsible for his now-chronic bouts of insomnia.

Against his better judgment, Jake removed his hat and wandered a little closer to sit on the sturdy porch railing. She was beautiful in the light spilling through the parlor's lace-covered windows. "Kylie doesn't mind the heat?"

"She's not here. Dad called a while ago, and when I told him how stuffy it was upstairs, he offered to take her overnight. He'd planned to keep her while I do the church dinner, anyway, so it was a big help."

The news of Kylie's absence registered and slid away. The disturbing thought it provoked didn't.

They'd be alone all night.

Suddenly, Jake got jittery as he detected something powerfully familiar in the air. Its name was knowledge, and it was more potent than wildflowers and silky hair, more dangerous than the gun still holstered at his hip. Tonight, there would be no two-and-a-half-year-old chaperone in the room next to Sarah's. They were on their own.

Ice cubes chinked again in Sarah's glass, and she cleared her throat. "There's lemonade in the fridge if you'd like some. Although…you're probably tired."

"No, not at all," Jake replied, suddenly teeming with energy. "If it's okay with you, I'll grab a glass when I go inside to change."

"Sure. Help your—" She stopped before she repeated her invitation of this afternoon, but she might as well have finished.

He'd love to help himself, Jake thought upstairs a minute later as he stripped quickly and pulled on a pair of jeans and a chambray shirt. It had been a long five days, listening to that brass bed clank across the hall. He should probably offer to tighten the head- and footboards to the frame for her, but then she'd know he was aware of the sound and probably feel even more uneasy around him. And she *was* uneasy. It seemed as though the only time they weren't cautious around each other was when they were arguing.

A minute later, he was carrying a glass of lemonade out on the porch. His high energy fizzled as he took in her position on the wooden swing. She was tucked into a corner, with her knees drawn up, and her sneakers planted midway on the seat. Out of nowhere, a webbed lawn chair had sprouted up beside the windows.

Jake dragged the chair away from the light and the moths fluttering nearby, then settled it in front of the swing and sat. After taking a long swallow of lemonade, he rested his glass on the arm of the chair. "This is good. Maybe you should think about becoming a caterer," he teased.

"Maybe I should," she joked back. "So…how did the big bust go over at Dusty's?"

He nearly said that the only big bust at Dusty's belonged to a redhead named Brenda who worked for a local insurance agency, and who'd been way too interested in giving him the details of the fight. After the first few minutes with her, it was obvious that she was looking for male company.

"No big deal. I locked up a couple of cowboys for their own safety. They'd all arrived in one pickup, and no one was sober enough to drive. When I took the keys, they got belligerent, and Joe and I had to haul them in."

Sarah blew out a tentative breath. "That's a first. I can't recall anyone ever being jailed for blowing off steam at

Dusty's. It's almost expected that a few guys will drink too much, act like jerks for a while, then find a quiet place to sleep it off.''

Jake grinned. "So how is that different from what actually happened?"

"Oh, it's different. And you'll probably hear about it. Your constituency loves living in a time warp, Sheriff. They don't like people messing with their 'Wild West' way of life. I assume you've taken a good look at Frontier Street."

"Yes, and I like it. It's nice to keep a little of the past around. But if I start seeing vigilantes and people wearing breakaway holsters—"

"Oh, heavens, they don't go that far. They draw the line at rowdy cattle drives and public lynchings."

Jake chuckled, then sipped from his glass, aware of the chemistry ebbing and flowing between them—chemistry they were trying to bury in conversation.

After several long moments, Sarah said in a softer voice, "You know, you were quite a hit with Kylie yesterday. She chattered about you all day. She started all over again when Dad picked her up tonight. Now *he* wants to know how to make fairy castles."

"I'm glad she had fun." He paused, feeling a little more of the snap and sizzle they were ignoring. "Did her mommy have fun, too?"

"We both had a good time." A much better time than she'd deserved. From the beginning, she hadn't played fair with him. Slowly, she slid her feet to the floor and eased forward on the swing. "I'm sorry for not being truthful with you right away. About Kylie, I mean."

He shrugged. "As you said, you didn't know what kind of man I was. The longer I know her, the more protective I feel toward her, too."

Sarah felt a tingle as his shadowed gaze met hers, then dipped to her mouth. "I'm beginning to feel the same way about you," he continued. "It bothered me that you were alone tonight."

"I was okay."

"But I wasn't. I was worried."

"About Kylie," she said.

"And about you."

Sarah drew a soft breath. His voice, once merely soft, had dropped to a sexy rumble. She knew what was coming. Maybe she'd even invited it, sitting out here, waiting for him tonight…but this was a bad idea.

Jake set his glass on the floor. Freed his hands.

"I should go in," Sarah said, not wanting to.

They stood at the same time, and their legs filled the narrow space between the swing and chair. They were so close the tips of her breasts brushed his chest.

The warm, male smell of him took her uneasiness to a new level. Suddenly, the sounds of crickets and night birds were lost in the rush of blood to Sarah's ears.

He said something. But she didn't know what. She muttered something in return, *We can't do this?* But he couldn't have heard her because his heavy-lidded gaze and perfect mouth kept drawing nearer.

At the first brush of his lips, Sarah closed her eyes and floated on the sweet sensation of it. Then he took them with total command, and she was lost.

Back came the memory of soft grass and hips that throbbed to be joined. Back came the need to touch and be touched, the need to feel shoulders and spines and hips. The need to fumble with buttons and feel springy chest hair beneath her fingertips.

Sarah's mind swam as the kiss deepened and became

more demanding—she felt herself sail away as his tongue thrust into her mouth again and again.

Jake slid an arm under her legs and lifted her, bringing her down with him on the swing. Chains creaked and wood careened beneath them as he arranged her on his lap and she felt the hard ridge of his arousal against her bottom.

Sarah claimed his mouth again. He was heat and heaven, and she wanted him desperately. All those nights of hearing him across the hall from her, of missing his talented hands and body could be over if she just…let him. Because there was no one around to shake a finger or say that what they were doing was wrong.

Jake worked a hand under her tank top, deftly disposed of the front closure on her bra. And Sarah shuddered as her nipple hardened against his palm.

Some faraway sound tried to penetrate the muzzy wave she rode, but she refused to listen. She knew it wasn't the phone—wasn't a call about Kylie. She wanted his hands, his mouth; she wanted all of him. Everything inside her pulsed and buzzed. Pulsed and…

And buzzed?

With difficulty, Sarah made herself think, stopped breathing for a second. The buzzing was coming from the inside of her right thigh. She broke from the kiss.

"Jake," she whispered raggedly as his mouth moved down over her neck again. "Jake, your pants are buzzing."

He lifted his head and stared at her, passion-fogged and unknowing. Then he blinked, swore softly and eased her off his lap, just enough to retrieve the pager in his pocket. He checked the illuminated number, then spoke through gritted teeth. "I'm sorry. I have to call the mayor."

"Now?"

He released a shuddering breath. "Good point." Threading his fingers through her hair, he ravaged her lips again. Sarah was warm, melted butter when he finally rested his forehead against hers. "Okay," he gasped. "Now I'll call her."

He found a wry smile somewhere as he lifted her off of him and stood them both up, and they moved in a shuffling walk to the screen door. "Guess I should thank her when we speak."

Sarah groaned. "Why?"

"Because if she hadn't called, we might've finished this out here." He chuckled wickedly. "I would've had to arrest both of us for indecent exposure."

Sarah stopped playing with the hair at his nape, stopped moving her feet as reality came rushing back. Her face heated in embarrassment.

Only dim light came through the windows, but there was certainly enough to give someone an eyeful if they were to pass her house. The driveway between the trees made a perfect keyhole…and they'd been anything but discreet.

Pushing away from him, she went inside.

"Sarah?" Jake came up behind her. He nearly cupped her shoulders, then seemed to think better of it. "What's wrong? What happened?"

"We happened," she said quietly as gooseflesh ran the length of her. "Or we almost did. God," she breathed. "I'm so stupid."

"Don't say that."

"I'm your landlady. You're my boarder. This can't happen between us." She started up the steps.

He came after her. "Wait. Let me call Eve, then we can talk about this."

"Not now. Please…just go make your call."

"This isn't all your fault. There were two of us on the porch, Sarah."

She turned wearily on the stairs to face him. "Look, I

appreciate what you're trying to do, but it's not helping. I really need to be by myself right now. Please."

He didn't speak for a moment, then he finally seemed to realize she was serious. "All right. But I can't say I'm sorry. That would be a lie. I *liked* kissing you. I liked the way you kissed me back." He drew a shaky breath. "You're the most exciting woman I've ever known…and I *liked* it."

"That didn't help, either," Sarah murmured.

She was still sitting in her darkened bedroom a few minutes later when Jake paused outside her room. She heard a sigh, then the soft pat of his hand on the door.

"Sarah?" He waited, then continued when she didn't speak. "Sarah, do you want me to leave? I can go back to the motel. Just say the word."

That would have simplified things. But they had other considerations.

Sarah opened her door, and her face heated again when she saw that his shirt was opened to his waist and his hair fell over his forehead. Had she done that? Probably. "No, I don't want you to leave. Kylie still needs your protection."

"*Kylie* needs me?" he repeated grimly.

"Yes," she said. Because that was all she *could* say.

Neither of them moved for a moment. Then Jake nodded and walked inside his room. The next sound Sarah heard was the shower spray running full force.

Chapter 9

The next two days were difficult. On Sunday, Sarah managed to make herself scarce because of the church dinner in Livingston. On Monday, an extended shift kept Jake away from the house until nearly six o'clock. But a half hour after he arrived, as Sarah prepared to leave for her quilting meeting at the Grange hall, trouble erupted again.

Jake was pushing Kylie on the swing out back when Sarah came to the porch steps and called that it was time to go. Suddenly Kylie burst into tears. Sarah was so startled, she could scarcely believe her eyes. While she watched in utter bewilderment, Kylie hopped off the swing—which Jake quickly caught—then scurried to Jake and latched on to his leg.

"Sweetheart," Sarah said, feeling a sharp twinge as she crossed the lawn to the two of them. "What's wrong? You like visiting with the ladies, remember? You help them pass out the cookies when we have our lunch."

"No," Kylie shrieked, hugging Jake tighter. "I want to pway with Jake!"

"You can play with him tomorrow," Sarah said patiently as she crouched beside her. "And the day after that, and the day after that. Jake lives with us now. Tonight you have to go to the meeting with Mommy."

Kylie simply cried louder, her high-pitched wails echoing off the treetops.

"I'll watch her, Sarah," Jake said, smoothing a hand over his daughter's dark hair.

Sarah glanced up at him, fighting her own hurt feelings. She knew he wasn't trying to steal Kylie's affection from her. He wasn't that kind of man, and, after all, what little girl *wouldn't* choose a sandbox and swings over spending two hours in a room full of chattering women? But as Kylie continued to cling to him, Sarah felt threatened nevertheless. "You're not helping."

"So you've said," he replied, making her remember their conversation on the stairs. "She doesn't want to go. When she's there, you obviously have to divide your attention between her and the women, and that has to be distracting."

"My daughter is *not* a distraction."

A nerve leapt in Jake's jaw. "I didn't say that *our daughter* was. I merely said—"

Sarah unhooked Kylie's arms from around Jake's thigh, then lifting her, rocked her until her sobs ceased. But as moments ticked by, the sensitivity and common sense that jealousy had blocked out came back to her. All Kylie wanted was to be allowed to be a child. She was so mature for her age, and usually so well-behaved, Sarah sometimes forgot that she wasn't quite two and a half yet. Another thought finally reached her. If Grandpa Malloy had offered to baby-sit tonight, there wouldn't have been a problem.

Sighing and feeling small, Sarah brushed away Kylie's tears and kissed her cheek. "Okay, honey, you and Jake can play. If Jake really doesn't mind watching you."

"He don't mind," Kylie said, her lower lip still trembling.

"Then I guess I don't mind, either," Sarah said, hugging her again, then setting her down. "Have fun, and I'll see you soon." Instantly, Kylie's smile was back, and she was racing to the sandbox for her pail and shovel.

How quickly children let go of anger and sadness, Sarah thought. Adults had a much harder time getting over the rough spots. She turned to Jake. "You're sure about this?"

"I'm sure. Joe's on tonight, and I have no plans."

Briefly, Sarah studied her keys. "All right. I'll be home early enough to get her dressed for bed. If you run into a problem, phone me at the hall. The number's on the memo board beside the kitchen phone, along with all the emergency numbers."

"We'll be fine. Drive carefully." He paused. "Be aware."

His subtle warning sparked a reminder. "Nothing on Paden or the bounty hunter yet?"

"Not yet. Keep looking closely at the people you pass."

"I will," she said soberly. "I'll be back by nine."

The meeting flew by in a blur. Sarah set up the quilting frames, then set out refreshments and assisted the dozen or so women who showed up.

But mostly Sarah worried—though not about Kylie's welfare. She'd finally admitted to herself that her daughter couldn't be in better hands. What worried her was Elvira Parsons and her band of merry gossips.

As she drove home with their conversation still ringing in her ears, Sarah's nerves were still on edge.

"Where's our little Kylie tonight, Sarah?" Elvira had called across the tables. And before the group had their needles threaded and their thimbles on, the whispers and supposedly good-natured teasing had begun. The *sheriff* was baby-sitting? Well, yes, they'd heard that he was renting a room from her. And wasn't that nice? Then they'd gotten personal.

"Don't pay any attention to them," Maggie Dalton had said. "Every woman in this town wants Jake's attention, the nosy old biddies at that table included. A day doesn't go by that he doesn't get two or three call-outs for the silliest things." She'd laughed softly. "Boy, do I get an earful when I send Jimmy Ray out to answer their calls."

"I just don't want them speculating about Jake and me," Sarah had replied. "I told them that I feel safer with him in the house after the break-in. Why can't they just let it go at that?"

Sarah pulled into her driveway and shut off the car, hearing Maggie's answer again. *"Because that's who they are."*

Jake and Kylie were huddled in one of the parlor's mauve wing chairs looking through a photo album when Sarah stepped inside a moment later. A shiver ran through her as her gaze settled on Jake. She'd never seen anyone look so out of place in her life. Broad shoulders and five o'clock shadow didn't belong in a room full of Victorian lace, pretty pinks and glass tables topped with silk flowers. His tall frame and raw good looks were better suited to mountains and open prairie.

With a happy squeal, Kylie jumped down and ran to Sarah for a hug and a kiss. It bothered Sarah that—for just a moment—she wished her daughter were already settled for the night.

"Kylie's idea," he said, raising the album then placing

it on the end table. "She said she was allowed to look at it."

"With supervision." Sarah sent him a smile she hoped he'd realize was an apology for her earlier behavior. "She likes checking out pictures of herself when she was 'little.'"

"That's what she told me." His tone softened as he walked to them. "We saw pictures of her before she was born, too. When she was in Mommy's tummy. You didn't get very big."

Sarah felt her face warm. "Big enough. Clumsy enough."

"Never," he said quietly. Then he shifted his gaze to Kylie. "Does it ever amaze you?"

"What?"

"Just…the way things worked out."

Sarah nodded, knowing what he meant. Fate had brought them together to create this child. Now, if it would just see their situation to a decent conclusion, she'd be deeply indebted. "I'd better get her into her pajamas. She's had a big day."

Thirty minutes later, Sarah knelt beside her daughter's bed, smiling while Kylie God-blessed everyone she knew and every stuffed animal lined up on the toy chest across the room. She was about to crawl into bed when Sarah stopped her. "Did you forget someone? Someone who makes fairy castles and looks at 'Kylie pictures' with you? Someone who loves you very much?"

Then, gleefully, his daughter God-blessed Jake.

When Sarah left Kylie's room a minute later, she wasn't surprised to see Jake lounging against the wall at the top of the stairs. There was a faint sheen in his blue eyes, but neither of them acknowledged it.

"Thanks for that."

"It's time." She shrugged, crossing her arms over her plaid shirt and walking toward him. "You're her daddy."

"And I do love her, Sarah. I didn't think I'd ever say those words again, but watching her play...seeing how excited she is to learn new things..." He broke off. "I do love her."

"I know." But there was little risk in loving a child. For the most part, children returned love unconditionally. Adult relationships demanded so much more. Like trust and forgiveness. Like friendship and acceptance. Maybe it was time she took those words to heart.

"How would you like to join me downstairs for *Monday Night Football* and hot buttered popcorn?" she asked suddenly.

Jake's grateful smile said it all.

They talked about unimportant things while she rattled the kettle on the range top, and the wonderful smells of popcorn and melted butter filled the kitchen. Then, with the volume turned low on the game, they sat on the sofa drinking iced tea and eating from the same bowl, and for a change, arguing about plays and the referee's calls instead of Kylie. Every so often they'd share a glance that said something was going on—a liking, a growing friendship. But it was fragile, and like the sentiment in Jake's eyes after hearing his daughter bless him, neither of them mentioned it. Just as they didn't mention what happened on the porch swing...or the attraction still pulsing between them. Though they could ignore it for a while, it just kept bouncing back.

At halftime, when they returned to the kitchen, Sarah finally brought up the meeting.

"The ladies had a good time gossiping about a local man tonight," she said, and set their bowl in the sink.

Jake tossed their napkins in the wastebasket. "Oh? Who'd they go after?"

"You."

He froze for a second. Then he set their glasses on the countertop, took the iced tea from the refrigerator and poured. "Good or bad?"

"Good *and* bad. They're fascinated by our living arrangements."

His expression darkened as he put the pitcher back in the fridge. "What did you tell them?"

"The same thing I tell everyone—that I'm relieved to have you here because of the break-in. I thought bringing up the diamonds would give them something else to talk about."

"But it didn't?"

"No." Her tummy fluttered, remembering. "They were still more interested in how you like your eggs, and where you sleep at night."

Though he scowled, Jake didn't appear to be surprised. That made Sarah wonder. "You've heard this before."

"Yes, but don't worry about it. I'm not."

Even though she'd been expecting his answer, hearing him say it floored her. What was *wrong* with the people in this town?

"All right, I'm *not* worried anymore. Now I'm mad. In fact, I'm so irritated, I feel like telling them all off." She paused, but just briefly. "You know, maybe you should start accepting the perks around here. If they think you're getting the whole package, you might as well *take* the whole package."

He raised a brow, and she pointed a finger at him. "Don't start. I was talking about eggs. When your schedule permits, maybe you should have lunch with us. It would be good for Kylie to—"

Without warning, Jake cupped her neck and kissed her soundly. Then he put her iced tea glass in her hand. "Thank you. I will." If he noticed that she nearly fell over, he didn't mention it. "Halftime's probably over," he said with a nod toward the living room. "Let's go see who's winning."

Later, as Sarah showered before bed, her lips were still tingling from that kiss. She was more confused than ever. The stressful mood in her home had finally been put to rest, and that was a happy relief. The only problem was, with apprehension and mistrust making their exit, there was nothing to balance out attraction and appeal. And those two things could get her in real trouble if she let them.

Jake was in a foul mood late the next morning as he used his key to enter the quiet house, then climbed the stairs. He shouldn't have kissed her last night. His stomach had been in knots ever since, and his mind... Well, forget his mind. That wasn't working worth a damn. He walked up to his door, saw that it was ajar and pushed it open.

He froze.

Sarah stood at the far side of his bed, still as a deer caught in headlights, her arms full of his sheets, her hair falling around her face like a halo in the sunlight streaming through the window.

"Hi," she said, color staining her cheeks. "I didn't expect to see you until lunchtime. I was just stripping your bed, but I can come back later if that's better for you."

"No, no, it's okay," he returned, coming inside. "I'm not staying. I forgot my wallet this morning when I left for work, and just came by to pick it up."

Except he didn't go to his dresser to get it. Instead, he

came to the bed to remove the mattress pad, and stuffed it into the half-filled laundry basket.

"Thanks."

"No problem. Toss me those pillows and I'll take off the cases."

The pillows came at him, one, two, and he shook them out of their cases. There was a smell in the air that grabbed him and wouldn't let go—the combination of her perfume and his musky sheets. The knotted feeling in his stomach intensified.

"How's your morning going?" he asked.

"Fine. Busy." She walked around the bed and added his sheets to the basket. "Yours? Aside from forgetting your wallet, I mean."

"I've had better." And he wasn't just referring to his libidinous urges. "Our chronically needy mayor's been buzzing me since I opened my eyes, and I just met with a half-dozen men who want to nail my hide to a wall."

"Why?"

Jake retrieved his wallet, then sank to the edge of the mattress. "Remember the cowboys I locked up the other night?" She nodded. "Well, their friends think I'm too heavy-handed in defending the law."

Frowning, Sarah sat beside him. "I warned you that people get upset about things like that."

"Yes, you did. And they can have all the 'Wild West' way of life they want as long as it doesn't break the law, or cost someone their property. Drunks don't drive in this town, and if it happens again, they can expect the same treatment. Maybe your former sheriff subscribed to the boys-will-be-boys philosophy, but I don't."

Sarah moistened her lips, and Jake had a hard time tearing his gaze away. "I agree with everything you've done," she said. "But it's a bad time to be making enemies. In two months you'll be asking these same people to vote you in for a full term. What happens if they decide they want someone else?''

"According to Eve, the November election's a formality. Mine will be the only name on the ballot.''

"That doesn't mean the town council couldn't look elsewhere at the last minute. They didn't have a problem finding you to replace Farrell, did they? And even if the mayor and town fathers back you, you could still lose to a write-in vote.''

"Then I guess I'll have to find some supporters.''

"Jake—''

It was getting harder and harder to sit here on the mattress beside her. The room seemed to be shrinking around him. He gave her hair a playful tug. "Do you always obsess about things you have no control over? You're taking this whole thing too seriously.''

"And you're not taking it seriously enough.''

Jake's heart skipped. Was that a tremor in her voice?

"I grew up here. There's so much machismo in this town, if enough men get riled up, they'll talk to their friends, and their friends will talk to their acquaintances, and before you know it, you'll be looking for a job in another county.'' She ran out of breath and drew in air.

Their eyes met—wary, knowing eyes. She wasn't out of breath because of her lengthy reply. The pulse at the base of her neck was pounding. She was wound as tightly as he was.

Blood pumped hard in Jake's veins, making him bold. "Would you miss me if I had to leave, Sarah?''

Sarah's heartbeat accelerated. It was too early in the day for this much tension.

She stood up.

Jake tugged her back down on the mattress.

"I—I should check on—"

"Kylie's not here," he cut in. "There were no gates across the stairs when I came up. Not at the top, and not at the bottom. She's with your dad, isn't she?"

"Yes," she whispered. The room with its masculine woods, navies and burgundies seemed to fade away until all that was left was the subtle smell of Jake's aftershave and the lingering scent of musk on his sheets.

Would she miss him? Oh, yes, she'd miss him. Except for the time they'd spent together the night Kylie was conceived, she'd been walking through life a mere spectator, enjoying the sights and sounds, but never really feeling. Now, as she lost herself in his eyes, she knew she never wanted to go back to that. She wanted to experience everything, wanted to feel this shiver of excitement running through her forever. They were only inches apart, and he eased forward, waiting for her. Sarah eased forward, too.

And seconds after his mouth covered hers, they were lying on the mattress and kissing deeply.

Everything in her shuddered as Jake rolled on top of her, and they drank from each other again and again, hands searching and seeking, roving at will over slopes and swells that had been denied them for three long years. She'd known only one other man in her life, and compared to Jake, that man had been fumbling and inexperienced. As his tongue stroked and glided along hers, everything in Sarah opened to him. Loving him on the porch had been dizzying…being here on his bed was a whirlpool of sensation. His hands smoothed, and coaxed and persuaded, pressed her to his body so that hard met soft and their movements and breathing took on a slow, deep rhythm.

His eyes were fevered as Jake broke from the kiss to make short work of the buttons on her shirt and the closure on her bra. Then with a ragged sigh, he lowered his face to her breasts. Chills drizzled through her as he kissed each swell. He took a nipple into his mouth and she fought for air.

Then his hand was at her waistband, popping the snap, tugging down her zipper. She'd just lifted her hips to let him hook his fingers into her jeans when the enormity of what she was about to do stopped her. Grabbing his hand, she stopped him.

She wanted him. Nerves were twitching in places she never knew they resided, and her belly quivered with need. But making love meant making a commitment to her. And even if Jake were a committing kind of man, memories of her life with Vince had left Sarah too afraid to think about taking that risk again without some soul searching.

Jake unhooked his fingers from her jeans and rolled onto his back to stare up at the ceiling. Everything above his belt buckle needed air, everything below throbbed for fulfillment.

They lay there in silence for several long moments, waiting for nerve endings to stop snapping and arousal to fade to a tolerable level. Then, seconds apart, they came to seated positions.

Sarah spoke in a raw murmur. "I'm sorry I put you through that. But I just…can't."

"It's okay."

"No, it's not," she returned, sighing. "I wanted you. I still want you. But making love is more than just satisfying a need to me—and that's all this would have been."

Jake couldn't deny it.

"Are you all right?" she asked.

"I'm fine." Trying to ignore the clawing feeling in his gut, he looked at her. Her lips and chin were red from his kisses, and though he'd shaved only a few hours ago, her breasts were rosy, too. His marking her up like that took a little more wind out of his sails.

"Where do we go from here?" he asked quietly.

Tentatively, she met his eyes, then slowly turned away to fasten her bra, button her shirt and zip her jeans. "I'm not sure." Swallowing, she left the bed and picked up the laundry basket. "Maybe I'll know later. But right now...I just don't."

Jake nodded. That was better than he'd hoped for. Then, standing, he took the basket from her and carried it down the stairs.

Where did they go from here? As he drove toward town, he came up with the only possible answer. He hadn't gotten much advice from adults growing up, but there was one thing his mother had always told him. If you fall off your bike and get banged up, you need to get right back on. You just have to be more careful when you ride the next time.

Jake gunned the Jeep down Prairie Street, then swung into the parking space beside Maggie's truck and cut the engine. He kept his composure when he walked inside the office and Maggie's eyes widened in surprise. Okay, so he should have combed his hair, and his uniform was wrinkled. At least his fly was up.

"The mayor's been trying to reach you all—"

"I know," he said, heading for his private office. "I'll call her back in a few minutes. I have another call to make first."

Jake closed the door behind him, strode to his desk and flopped into the swivel chair. Then he tapped in the number from memory, and hoped she'd answer. She did, on the second ring.

"Can your dad keep Kylie for a little longer?" he asked,

trusting that she'd recognize his voice. "I should be able to get out of here by three."

"I—I don't know. Why do you want—"

"Because we need to get past this right now. I don't want to move out, and you need to feel comfortable in your home. We have to get back on solid footing."

"And you know how to do that?"

"I think so. I want to take you somewhere. Will you go?"

Chapter 10

A brisk wind tossed Sarah's hair as she rode beside Jake, her dark green parka unzipped over her white sweater, her knees hugging the chestnut mare's ribs. She breathed in deeply and caught the not-too-distant promise of snow. Jake had been right. This was exactly what they'd needed to relieve the coiled tension between them.

She'd been right about something, too. She glanced at him as they loped through the north pasture's tall, pale grass, en route to his secret destination. This was where he belonged. All around them, aspens and poplars studded rich green hemlocks and pines with gold, while high above, snow-capped granite peaks rose out of the timbers to scrape the blue sky. He looked so right here...so easy in the saddle with the collar on his denim jacket turned up, and his black Stetson tugged low to shade his eyes. He seemed... Sarah searched for the right word. He seemed complete here.

"How much farther?" she called to him over the rhythmic thud of their horses' hooves.

"Not far," he called back. "Are you getting tired?"

Sarah felt her smile stretch wide. Tired? With the wind in her face, and wilderness all around them? "No!" she yelled, urging her horse into a gallop. "This is glorious!"

Laughing, Jake kicked Blackjack into a gallop, too.

Twenty minutes later, as they followed a slightly worn path up a steep hill, a small, shabby building came into view, nestled among the firs and poplars. Blond prairie grass rolled out before them, a mile long and stretching from the sagging gray-stick porch straight into the face of the mountain. Tugging back on the reins, Jake halted his horse a short distance from the shack, and Sarah did the same.

There were no fences here, no signs of habitation. Not a sound except for the faint rushing of water somewhere, and the blowing of their horses. Light steam fogged the air as Sarah exhaled. They were high.

When they'd dismounted and left their horses to graze, Jake took Sarah's gloved hand in his. Her pulse skittered in remembrance, but she didn't pull away.

"What is this place?" she asked as they walked up to the ramshackle dwelling.

"An old line camp. Probably built around the late 1930s when Jess and Ross's granddad was just handing Brokenstraw over to their father."

"You know this for sure?"

He grinned. "Nope, just aimless chatter for the folks I take on the tour."

Sarah grinned back, knowing he was kidding.

"I almost asked Jess about it once. Then I decided that…well, maybe they wouldn't want me coming up here anymore if they knew I'd found this place."

"Why not? I thought you were free to roam since you board your horse here."

"I am. But every time I come up here, it feels sort of off-limits. Unless you're family."

If she hadn't been staring up at him, she would have missed the flicker of disappointment in his eyes. Sarah's chest tightened. Suddenly she understood Jake's fascination with this corner of the ranch. From border to fence line, Brokenstraw had a raw, wild beauty. But this old line shack obviously pulled at his heartstrings. It was run-down to the point of being condemned, windows smashed out and tar-papered roof sagging. But it was also filled with memories of another era, memories of a close-knit family's past. Something Jake had never known.

"Have you looked inside?"

"Yep, the first time I came up here." He hadn't been able to stop himself. But there'd been nothing to see. Years ago, someone had taken everything of value and burned the rest out back where a makeshift privy stood. He'd never looked again.

Shaking off the sentimental mood before it could get a grip on him, he grinned and tugged at her hand. "Not much in there but broken glass and a few friendly mice. Come on. Time for the second leg of the tour."

They walked past dormant huckleberry bushes and scrub pine, a stand of larch, willows and cottonwoods, then visited a small, rocky creek where cutthroat trout flashed in water his father had probably fished. But after a few minutes, Jake realized that, from Sarah's standpoint, there wasn't much to see, even though felled logs and a scattered fire ring whispered memories every time he walked the area. When they'd finally returned to their horses, he was surprised to see her smile.

"Thank you."

"For what?" he asked.

"For bringing me here. It's beautiful."

His heart swelled with something akin to pride, but he hid it. "It's also high and cold, and probably lousy with ticks in the spring."

"But you like it."

"Yeah. I like it." Jake snared their reins, then put Sarah's in her hands. She considered them for a few seconds, then glanced up.

"So...how many people have had this tour?"

"Oh, seventy or eighty," he joked, unable to stop himself from threading the zipper on her parka. He tugged it up against the falling temperatures until only her sweater's white turtleneck showed.

She looked fresh-faced and wholesome standing there, with her cheeks pink with color, and the light from the setting sun streaking her hair...stealing his breath.

That wanting began again in his belly, and everything in Jake began to stir.

This trip to the mountains had been designed to clear the air and forge a new trust and confidence between them. But he wanted desperately to touch her.

Don't do it. Wasn't messing with her zipper enough?

No. It wasn't.

Jake flipped up her collar, then let his wrists rest on her shoulders. When she didn't move them away, he searched her eyes and sent her a silent question. Should he go ahead? Or should he back away? Here in this special place with no one to see, how terrible could a simple kiss be?

He spoke soberly. "Can we do this just once before we get back on those horses? It doesn't have to mean anything. I don't know if this mountain's ever seen a kiss before, and I've been thinking that...maybe it should."

Jake felt a shiver move through her as her wary eyes

searched his. "I need an answer first. How many? How many women have taken your tour?"

Didn't she know? Couldn't she tell? Jake exhaled raggedly, feeling the rush of blood to his temples as he drew her into his arms. "One," he whispered. "Only one." Then he turned her face up to his, parted his lips and sealed her welcoming mouth with his own.

Several moments later, Jake helped her mount her horse and they rode back to the barn in silence—partly because sunset had streaked the painted sky, and commenting might have diminished the moment. But mostly because he didn't know what to say.

Something was happening—something complicated— and Jake didn't like the uneasy feeling it gave him. Having a daughter had enriched his life. Wanting anything more was just asking for another kick in the teeth.

Reality shattered their mood the instant they entered Sarah's driveway and saw the sheriff's white Jeep sitting there, red and blue lights flashing. Her pink Victorian was drenched in light. Motion-detecting spotlights flared from the corners of the roof, and every light on the first floor burned.

"Jake?" Sarah cried. *"Jake, what's going on?"*

Jake's heart pumped. Quickly, he stopped the Mountaineer behind the Jeep and leapt out to speak to his deputy, who was just rounding the house. Sarah flew to the porch to take Kylie from her father's arms.

"What's going on, Joe?"

Joe nodded toward the back of the house. "Mr. Malloy called in. He said he heard a noise out back, and the rear spotlights came on. He got concerned because of the break-in. Said he'd have checked on his own, but he was alone with the little girl."

"Did anything turn up?"

"Nothing. Doors and windows don't appear to have been tampered with—no trail to follow being it's so dark. Might've been kids. There's a bunch of them down the road on bikes, but they claim they don't know a thing about it. Could've been a deer or the wind, too. You know how finicky those motion lights are sometimes."

Jake nodded, then glanced at the tense threesome on the porch again. It could easily have been deer. But the image of Ike Paden's face soured his stomach. "Did you talk to anyone else?"

"Not yet. I'll see some neighbors."

"That's okay, Joe," he murmured gravely. "I'll take it from here."

Jake waited until the Jeep left the drive, then walked up the stairs to the porch. Sarah and her father both met his eyes expectantly. "Joe didn't find anything," Jake told them. "He said it could've been kids who tripped the sensors—even an animal." The look on Sarah's face told him she thought that explanation was too easy.

"It's okay," Jake said. "I'll still knock on a few doors and see if anyone's seen anything out of the ordinary tonight." He smiled at the child in Sarah's arms. *His* child. "Why don't you two take Kylie inside, and I'll go talk to some people?"

"Now that I think about it," Malloy said a little sheepishly, "it *could've* been deer. Kylie and I saw two does grazing at the edge of the property earlier this evening."

"That's probably all it was," Jake said, "but I'll take a look around, anyway."

Jake wanted to slam the door when he walked back inside forty minutes later, just to relieve some of his tension. It was just as well that he didn't. Bill Malloy was still there, and Kylie was in bed.

Apparently, he wore his mood on his face, because all Sarah had to do was meet his eyes to know he was angry and churning inside. Her face paled. "Someone saw something."

"No. No one saw anything. But your sweet, lovable neighbor down the road went off like a box of blasting caps as soon as I knocked on his door."

"Pete?" She stared as though that was hard to believe.

"Who else? He was all rummed up and ticked off at the world. What was I accusing him of? He hadn't been outside all evening. I was determined to pin something on him, wasn't I? If I'd do my job instead of—" He stopped as Pete's insults echoed in his mind. *Instead of sniffing around Sarah like a buck in the rut.*

"Don't take offense, he was just under the weather. He's usually not like that."

"Sarah, he *is* usually like that. Why are you defending him? Every time I speak to the man, he gives me attitude."

Her tone inched its way toward testy. "Then you probably didn't approach him in the right way."

"I said good evening. How was I supposed to approach him?"

Bill Malloy glanced from his daughter's face to Jake's, then back again. "I think I'll head for home. I need to pack a few things yet." He hugged Sarah and kissed her cheek. "Honey, I don't have to look in on Vera if you think you need me here. The visiting nurse still comes by every day, and her back is healing...."

Sarah hugged and kissed him back. "We'll be fine. Give Aunt Vera our love, and I'll see you in a few days. And thanks for staying with Kylie tonight."

The second her father was out the door, she picked up

the argument exactly where it had stopped. "The simple truth, Sheriff, is that *you* don't like *Pete,* and he feels that animosity every time you look at him. He told me so himself."

Furious that she'd take the word of a nasty drunk over his, Jake put an end to the conversation. "I'm going out back to look around. Maybe Joe missed something. And if I may say so, what a thoroughly *crappy* ending to a wonderful evening."

"I'm going to bed," Sarah said coldly. "Please lock up when you come inside."

Nothing on the grounds was amiss, but that scare convinced Jake that they needed to finish searching the house for the diamonds.

On Sunday afternoon while Kylie napped, Sarah and Jake donned sweatshirts and climbed the stairs to Miss Lillian's dusty repository. They left the hall door open in the hope that a little heat would follow them up. The first snowstorm of the season had blown in overnight, fluffy and fierce, blanketing the entire town. Temperatures outside had dropped into the thirties, and it was barely fifty in the attic.

Sarah's mood wasn't much warmer.

They were nearly finished upstairs when the bickering started again. Jake dragged the box they'd just searched back under the eaves, then sighed and walked slowly to where she sat on the floor. "Can we call a truce? It's not getting any warmer up here, and I'd really like to finish today."

"Fine," Sarah answered crisply, and nodded toward the brass-trimmed steamer trunk that was next in line. "Is that the last one?"

Jake nodded. Then he sighed again and crouched down

to kiss her cool cheek. He stared into her dark eyes. "Okay," he murmured. "I'll ease up on Pete. He's the best. If I were running for governor instead of sheriff, I'd ask him to be my running mate."

"Thank you. He'd do a good job." Then she showed him her first faint but genuine smile in two days. "And I'm sorry I've been such a pain."

He was wrong, Jake thought, feeling an annoying little tickle of arousal in his gut. It *was* getting warmer in here.

Leaving her, he dragged the trunk over to the small window overlooking the front yard, then opened the latches and crouched beside her. "Last chance to find anything up here."

"But I doubt that we will." Sarah lifted out a pair of purple throw pillows—both fringed in gold and factory-embroidered with a tacky likeness of Niagara Falls. "I just don't believe Vince was up here that night." Her voice cooled again as she laid the pillows aside and withdrew a yellowed party dress. "I never heard him climb the stairs until he broke into my room."

Jake bit down on his molars and reminded himself that the man was dead and couldn't hurt or bother her anymore. But there was a nasty urge in him to dig Harper up and kick his behind to Texas, anyway. "Still have that gun?"

"No, once Kylie started walking, I got rid of it."

"Good. Guns make me nervous. Even in the hands of people who know how to use them." He withdrew an afghan, then a patchwork quilt. It had a few rips in it, but a quick check proved it wasn't hiding anything. "What did you do after Harper left?"

"Went through this house in a rage. I threw out everything of his that remained from when we lived here together. Clothes, pictures, an old boom box, even the beer he brought with him that night. I put anything that even *remotely* reminded me of him out for the trash collectors the next morning. I was glad when he was extradited back to Florida the next day. Then I didn't have to think about *him* anymore, either.''

Jake stared blankly. ''You threw out *everything?*''

''You bet.''

''Did the feds search the trash before it was hauled away?''

''No, it was gone by the time they got here. But I think I would have noticed if I'd thrown out a bag of diamonds.''

''What about the boom box?'' Jake persisted. ''Did you look inside the battery compartment?''

''Of course not. I didn't have any reason to. But Vince wouldn't have put something that valuable inside the boom box, then left it here in the house. It's too portable.'' She paused, met his eyes again. ''Jake, I really don't think the stones are up here.''

''I don't, either.'' He sighed. ''But we've come this far, so let's finish.'' He reached inside the trunk again, unloading more linens and a silky, yellowed white turban. At the very bottom, he spied a smallish book hanging out of its tissue-paper wrapping, and lifted it out. The worn tapestry cover was old, and like the rest of the trunk's contents, smelled strongly of mothballs.

Jake untied the ribbon around it and flipped through to see if the center had been hollowed out. But the only thing he saw was faded, fluid handwriting and a few words he probably shouldn't have read. The author of the diary— Miss Lillian?—had been well loved in her time.

Suddenly, the wrongness of his disturbing the woman's memories got to Jake, and slowly, carefully, he rewrapped the journal and returned it to the trunk. An emotional hole opened in his heart as he buried it beneath the turban and party dress Miss Lillian might have worn for her lover. The dress and the journal and that faded, hand-stitched quilt were just more reminders that he was short on memories.

"Kylie's a lucky little girl," he said, meeting Sarah's waiting expression. His gaze swept the attic. "To have all this, I mean."

She seemed to know what he meant. "You don't have any mementos from your mother?"

He shook his head. "Other than knowing she was an ex-California flower child, it's as though one day I was born, and there's no record of anything before me."

He couldn't believe he was telling her this. Especially since he'd been embarrassed for days after spilling his guts to her three years ago. The only thing that had saved his pride was the fact that she'd been a stranger he never expected to see again. But now, sitting beside her with Kylie's soft snores coming from the baby monitor, it was easy to share his thoughts. Maybe because she already knew so much. Or maybe because she was no longer a stranger.

"You told me once that your late father and brothers were from this area," she reminded him quietly. "That's why you applied for the sheriff's position, isn't it? So you could know them."

"Yep."

"Are your brothers still here?"

"Within tripping distance, actually."

"Tell them," she said earnestly. "Tell them who you are."

"Nah. It's not time yet."

"How will you know when it's time? Jake, you're a good man. They won't turn you away. Don't you want to see *their* trunks? *Their* letters? I'll bet they have wonderful memories in their attics. Don't turn your back on that."

"I'm not turning my back. I'm just indulging in a little cowardice until I get a handle on some things."

"Stop it, you're the bravest man I know."

"Yeah, right," he scoffed, then looked at her face, her hair. There were no dark roots there...no artifice. Just one-hundred-percent honesty from the top of her head to the tips of her sneakers. How could he have called her a liar? It simply didn't apply to her, because she'd done what she felt she needed to do out of love for their daughter. "Tell me something," he said.

"If I can."

"Why is it that I can tell you things I'd never discuss with anyone else?"

"Probably because men don't tell other men the things that really matter. They're too afraid of seeming weak."

"I didn't ask why I don't discuss things with men, I asked why I *can* discuss them with you."

"Don't you know?"

He shook his head.

Sarah smiled softly. She knew. He knew it, too. He was just too afraid to accept it yet. He could feel the trust and caring that was steadily building between them...day by day, hour by hour, minute by minute.

That ride into the hills with him had told her a lot more about him than he'd wanted to betray. And not just about their growing affection.

She strongly suspected that Jess and Ross Dalton were his brothers. The night they'd met, he'd confided that his brothers had both been at the Founder's Day celebration; Jess and Ross were there. He'd also worried that his brothers might think he wanted a chunk of their ranch; the Daltons owned Brokenstraw, and there were no other ranchers close by who'd had only two sons, and no daughters.

Then there was Jake's resemblance to Jess. If she hadn't

been looking for it, she might not have seen it, but it was there. Coupled with the emotion she'd seen in his eyes when he looked at that old line shack, she was almost positive that Jake was Ross Dalton Senior's illegitimate son. But she wouldn't guess. She'd let him confirm or deny it in his own time.

Right now, with hard bits of ice and snow pelting the window and their daughter sleeping soundly on the floor below, she would be content with whatever Jake felt comfortable sharing with her.

Because she loved him. Two days ago, she couldn't have said that. Today the specter of Vince Harper was gone, and she knew. She loved his tenderness, and she loved his strength, and she loved the way he made her feel when he held her in his arms. Kylie wouldn't be here now if Sarah hadn't intuitively recognized his decency and goodness three years ago.

The moments stretched silently between them, during which decisions were made and justified, and easing closer was both contemplated and feared. Coming to his knees, Jake was the first to bridge the gap between them.

He touched her hair, and Sarah turned her cheek into his caress. She traced his full, lower lip with her thumb, and he drew it into his warm mouth to suck softly. Sarah's breath caught.

They came together in a clash of fiery emotion, chest to breasts, navel to navel, two people who'd wanted this since they set eyes on each other again.

They kissed deeply, drank freely, giving themselves over to the rush of passion raging through their bloodstreams. With a low growl, Jake plunged his tongue deeply into Sarah's mouth and she welcomed it, took it all and gave hers back.

This was the dance, she thought in the part of her mind

that was still functioning. She loved him and this was the dance she'd wanted forever. She savored his taste, gloried in the commanding pressure of his hands as they moved over her, opened wider as their tongues coupled in that shivery prelude to mating. This was the dance, and their hammering heartbeats and rapid pulses would supply the music. Neither of them would be left with that raw, helpless ache in their bellies today.

Gasping, Jake broke away to kiss her forehead and her eyelids, then reached behind him to grab the puffy quilt and those purple pillows. Then he yanked off his sweatshirt. Heart pounding, Sarah shed hers, too.

"You're sure?" he rasped.

Hands shaking, she unhooked her bra and bared her breasts to him. Her nipples hardened in the cool air. "Do I look like I'm having second thoughts?" she asked in a trembling whisper.

Jake took her breasts in his hands, then he moved his lips over them, taking each nipple into his warm, wet mouth.

Sarah clutched his head and urged him deeper into her softness, thankful that his strong hands steadied her. She gripped the smooth, taut muscles of his shoulders, slid her palms down his spine. She felt the hard knot below her navel tighten to a dull ache.

With a tremulous breath, Jake drew her to her feet to unsnap and unzip her jeans. Then dropping to his knees again, he hooked his fingers into her waistband and drew both rough denim and silky panties down over her hips. He kissed her breasts, kissed her rib cage and belly, tugged the jeans lower and kissed her thighs. Sarah's legs nearly buckled, and she gripped his shoulders as he pulled off her sneakers and finished removing her jeans.

Then he stood and it was her turn.

Sarah's heart raced. She wanted to touch all of him at once. Shaky hands unbuckled his belt and popped the button on his worn Levi's—shook harder as she lowered his zipper and her hands brushed his manhood. Her touch went through him, and Jake kicked off his boots, finished stripping off his jeans and briefs.

Sarah ran her trembling hands over his broad, smooth shoulders again, then slid them down to the mat of hair that all but covered his tanned chest and flat nipples. Her fingers went lower, over his lean rib cage and taut belly, following that narrowing strip of hair that arrowed downward. She brought her fevered gaze back to his as she paused just below his tan line. Just below his navel. Just above his hard arousal. She took him in her hands.

Jake covered her lips in a crushing kiss, then eased them down onto the quilt and pillows. He felt for the afghan behind him and drew it over them.

There was no waiting. The electrifying anticipation wouldn't allow it. Not after a three-year absence. Hard, corded legs twined with long, smooth ones as Jake sought her beneath the colorful yarn and Sarah opened to him. Then, with a sure, swift thrust, Jake buried himself in her heat.

Sarah tightened around him, and they fought for space as they rained kisses over anything their lips could reach. Shoulders, necks, chins, cheeks and hair.

Jake plunged his tongue into her mouth again, making her yearn all the more for shivery release. This man cared about a woman's needs, not just his own satisfaction. In the part of her mind that wasn't floating on pure sensation, Sarah remembered that. Even that first night, he'd been more concerned with her pleasure than his own. Which is why she would give him everything she was.

Sarah arched to him as Jake began the slow, sleek ritual,

making her his, making her strain to meet him stroke for stroke. Her breath deserted her, and a tingling began in her limbs. And suddenly, though she knew he wanted to take things slowly, she couldn't wait. Her hands found his hips and pulled him to her.

Jake groaned a warning, but the rush of blood to her ears was deafening and Sarah couldn't make it out. All she knew was that his patient lovemaking had found a new pace, a new vigor, and that blissful feeling of release was seconds away.

He found her mouth again and kissed her deeply, deeper still, stealing her air. Then points of light exploded behind Sarah's closed eyelids, shudders racked them both, and holding on tightly, they carried each other to fulfillment.

Lying there with her eyes closed and those sweet, lovely aftershocks pulsing through her, Sarah smiled. She stroked his powerful back with a boneless hand, ran her fingers over his long, straight spine…pressed soft kisses to the top of one shoulder.

It took her a long time to find her voice. "That was delicious," she whispered.

"No," he chuckled groggily. "That was fast."

"And delicious," Sarah repeated.

"And delicious," he agreed. He nuzzled her ear, and his warm breath spilled over Sarah's neck, raising a brand new crop of gooseflesh.

Eventually, he rolled onto his side and propped himself on an elbow to smile down at her. His hair was mussed and sexy, and his eyes held the look of a contented man.

"Tired?" she asked.

"Mmm-hmm." He brushed a few blond strands out of her eyes. "But it's a nice kind of tired. Will you hear Kylie if we cuddle up and doze for a while?"

Sarah nodded, pleased that he wanted to linger here, too.

She wasn't ready to give up this special closeness yet—if ever. "I'll hear her," she whispered, smiling. "I'll hear her if she turns over in her bed. She's my life."

A stark look rose in his eyes, but it appeared and vanished so swiftly, she barely had time to give it a name. Which was just as well, because she didn't want anything spoiling this moment.

She'd never known joy like this. To love someone, truly love someone, was a gift no one could best. Unless it was to have that love returned.

"What are you thinking?" she murmured, smoothing a hand down his tanned throat to his chest.

"That I was right before. Kylie really is very lucky."

But the light in his eyes seemed to have dimmed a little. "That's a good thing, right?" she asked uncertainly.

"You bet."

Then, to Sarah's bewilderment, he rolled to a seated position, stared through the window, then looked toward the stairwell. Drawing a long breath, he let it out slowly. "You know, the snow doesn't show any sign of letting up. Maybe I should check in with Joe to see if he needs a hand."

Shock jolted her nerve endings. "You're leaving?"

"I think I should." He bent to kiss her briefly, then moved away to dress. "If the snow keeps up, there could be more call-outs than Joe can handle. I should get to him before he phones here and wakes Kylie."

Mind spinning, Sarah sat up. This didn't make any sense. This was his day off. Suddenly embarrassed by her nakedness, she pulled the afghan around her and stood. "Isn't that why you hired a part-time deputy? Can't Jimmy Ray Becker help Joe if he needs it?"

"Probably, but I should be there, too."

"Then...you'll be gone for a while," she said, feeling an uneasy distance grow between them.

He nodded. "I can always find paperwork to do while I wait to see how the storm shakes out."

Sarah watched him finish dressing, then pull on his boots. With shocking clarity, she realized that looking for love from Jake Russell was a pie-in-the-sky dream. The only way he could love a woman was physically. Emotional love was impossible for him, and he'd told her that several times. She'd been a complete fool not to believe him.

Scooping up her clothes, Sarah walked toward the steps, unable to look at him anymore. She didn't want to see her own pathetic reflection in his eyes.

"Hey," he said softly—almost apologetically, "aren't you going to dress first?"

"I'll do it downstairs. It's warmer." Although to be honest, she hadn't felt the cold until just now. "Since you're going to get some work done, I should probably do the same while Kylie sleeps." She started down the steps, too upset to cry, pulling the afghan high to avoid tripping. "But thank you, really. That was lovely."

As she approached the door to the hall, her words grew colder with every syllable. "Let's do it again sometime. How about when hell freezes over?"

Chapter 11

Jake strode to the top of the stairs, then winced as the attic door closed behind Sarah—loud enough to make her point, but soft enough to keep from waking Kylie. Another door shut seconds afterward. He let out a long, rattled breath as he stared down into the stairwell, fear gripping him as it had at no other time in his life.

Maybe he should be thankful for her anger. It had saved him from having to make an explanation that was as pathetic as his willpower. And God knew she deserved an explanation. But how could he tell her that the reason he'd pulled away was jealousy—a jealousy that sickened him.

For a moment—for one selfish, loathsome moment—he'd been jealous of his own daughter. Jake scowled in disgust. How could he have felt that vile emotion for even a second? He *wanted* Kylie to be first in Sarah's life. He wanted his daughter to grow up secure and happy and knowing that she was loved above all others. But a life of never coming first with any woman, had all converged to make him insist on that number-one position if he ever got involved again. Just for that millisecond, he'd seen himself relegated to second or third place, as he had been so many times with his mother, and the old hurt had splintered unexpectedly through him. On the heels of that jealousy came the fear that he faced that again. But it was patently ridiculous, because he was *not* falling for Sarah Harper. And he absolutely wanted Kylie to know the love of a mother who put her first.

With a self-damning oath, Jake pushed it all out of his mind and crossed the attic floor to the baby monitor. It was all irrelevant, anyway. He carried it down the stairs and tapped softly at her door. "Sarah? Sarah, do you want the monitor?"

Nothing. Not one forgiving sound.

"I'll put it beside the door." Still nothing. Jake waited another few seconds, then sighing in frustration and knowing he was to blame, he strode to his room to shower and change. Fifteen minutes later, he was on his way to town.

Amazingly there were no call-outs. For some reason, people either stayed off the roads or used caution. But Jake couldn't make himself go back to Sarah's, not even when Joe left and Jimmy Ray Becker came in to take his place. Finally around four-thirty, tired of trying to find money in the budget for a new computer, Jake bounced his pen off the thick blotter on his desk and stood. The idea of food wasn't all that appealing, but he did need to eat something before he returned to Sarah's. He seriously doubted that she was keeping anything warm for him. Literally or figuratively.

With a wave to Jimmy Ray and a promise to be back in an hour, Jake hunched into the fur collar of his black leather uniform jacket, tugged his Stetson low and sprinted through swirling flurries to the café. But as he stepped up onto the boardwalk and approached the warm glow and delicious smells emanating from Aunt Ruby's, he wondered if he'd made a mistake coming here.

He'd given the blunt little woman a wide berth since she'd hinted that she knew about his roots. He wasn't sure he was ready for another trip down memory lane.

He opened the door, anyway.

The top of Ruby's gray hairnet bobbed behind the lunch counter as Jake walked inside and stamped the snow from his boots. He stared curiously. She couldn't be stocking shelves. She wasn't moving around enough for that.

Suddenly, Ruby's head came up, and she peeked through her spectacles at him. Then she cackled happily and all but the hairnet disappeared again.

Grinning, pushing his apprehension aside, Jake left the thick mat by the door and went to the counter to peer down at her. He chuckled softly. She was stretched out on one of those summer chaise longues, her red high-top sneakers stuck out in front of her, her knobby fingers finishing the Sunday paper's crossword puzzle.

He set his tan Stetson on a vacant red stool, then slid onto the one next to it. As he'd crossed the floor he'd noticed only a half-dozen patrons sipping coffee in the back booths. Apparently, the storm had discouraged the usual supper crowd.

"Well if it ain't my favorite sheriff," she finally said, tucking her pencil in her apron pocket and sliding the newspaper under her chair. "Leastwise, you *look* like the sheriff. Ain't seen you fer a while." She folded her bony arms across the red sweater she wore over her white dress. "You quit eatin'?"

"Nope, I've just been taking my meals at Sarah's since I moved in."

"That's what I been hearin'."

"Oh?" Obviously the gossip hadn't stopped at the Grange hall. "If you already knew, why did you ask?"

Ruby cackled softly. "Didn't seem right to tell you I know *all* yer business. Thought I'd leave some fer you to tell me."

"Gee, thanks."

"Yer welcome." The old woman held his gaze for a long moment, then when he didn't say anything, she sighed. "Well? Anything you want to get off yer chest?"

"Like what?"

"You know what. We gonna talk about it, or are you gonna keep it to yerself fer another thirty years?"

Resigned, Jake smiled. Maybe it was time. The restaurant was nearly empty, so their conversation would be private. And he somehow knew Ruby wasn't one to carry tales. "I guess we're going to talk about it."

"Good. But let's git us some coffee first, and order you a supper. Might as well find us a comfortable booth, too."

When all three of Ruby's requirements had been met, she hunched over the table toward Jake and spoke in a conspiratorial undertone. "Shame on you. Why didn't you tell me straight out who you were?"

"Didn't think anyone would believe me, I guess. And, I didn't want you thinking I expected anything because of who my father was. How did you know?"

"Guess you never seen a picture of yer daddy." When Jake shook his head, she went on. "You look so much like him, I knew you had to be kin."

"Then why did you ask if I was related to the Russells in Livingston?"

Ruby stirred sugar into her coffee. "Playin' detective. I'da been shocked silly if you'd said yes. I knew yer ma wasn't from these parts. Somewheres around San Francisco, I think I heard her say once."

"Then you know more about her than I ever did."

"Well, that might be," Ruby admitted with a kind smile. "But, my, she was a pretty little thing. All them ribbons dangling from hair the color of sunshine. Fact is, I think if yer pa hadn't met Emily Russell, he'd still be mourning Jess's mama. That was a hard year fer him," she continued. "I never saw a man so broke up and hurtin' in my whole life."

"What happened to his first wife?"

"Heart trouble. Back in them days, there was no such thing as transplants and such. Then a year or so after Laura went to live with the Lord, Ross was in here, just goin' through the motions of livin'. Eatin' cause it was expected of him, breathin' cause he couldn't figure out how to stop."

She grinned. "Then, all of a sudden, in comes yer pretty ma, wearin' a long dress that looked like an embroidered feed sack, and a smile that lit up the whole town."

Jake nodded, remembering she'd liked to dress that way.

"Yer pa needed someone like her then," Ruby explained gently. "Someone who laughed just cause it felt good. I still don't understand why any woman would want to paint flowers on her face, but that's how it was back then." She paused, met his eyes again. "She still around?"

"No, she's gone now, too. When I was fifteen."

"But she told you about yer pa."

"No," he said, sighing. "I only found out a few years ago when I ran into a friend of hers."

With a sad frown and a shake of her gray head, Ruby murmured, "That was cruel."

"Maybe. But not intentionally." For some reason, he wanted to defend her. "She never cared about her own past, so she probably didn't think it mattered to me, either.

I did ask her once who my father was. All she said was 'a good man.' She said my eyes were like his.''

"Eyes, chin, hair. You might even have the same ears if I could see more of 'em. You look a lot like Jess, too, except he got his ma's brown eyes.''

Jake looked up from his coffee. "So why haven't Jess and Ross seen the resemblance?''

"Probably would have if the boys had known about their daddy's time with Emily Russell.''

"No one knew but you?''

"Oh, others knew. Can't keep things like that a secret in this town. Yer ma and her friends turned heads around here for a while. But she didn't hang around long, and some memories fade after a time. Ross wanted her to stay, of course, but you can't rope the wind. She wouldn't have been happy here.''

"You're right. She wouldn't have.''

"Yer daddy knew it, too. He was a rancher and pledged to the land, and she was…well, she needed her freedom. The next summer, Ross's mama caught his eye, and that was that.''

Ruby squeezed Jake's hand. "But I know in my soul that wouldn't have happened if he hadn't met Emily first. It was *yer* ma who helped him heal. I always wished I'd told her that.''

With a nod, Jake wondered if Emily would have cared. Then he decided that she probably would have. She'd always been drawn to wounded people. Maybe if he'd let her see his own pain, things would've been different. But he'd always had too much pride to let anyone know.

Until Sarah.

Jake pushed that thought away as quickly as it came to him. "Can I ask you a tough question, Aunt Ruby?''

"If you can handle a tough answer.''

"Did my father know about me?"

Ruby pursed her lips thoughtfully for a time, then said, "No. No, I don't believe he did. He loved his boys. If he'd had an idea Emily'd given him another son, nothin' could've stopped him from knowin' you." She smiled. "Now what—"

Ruby paused until Jeannie had served Jake's food, accepted his thanks and left. Then she went on. "Now, what else can I tell you about yer daddy?"

"Everything," Jake replied, ignoring the turkey dinner in front of him. "I want to know everything you remember." He smiled and checked his watch. "Or whatever you can remember in the next half hour. I told Jimmy Ray I'd be back by then."

When Jake left the café thirty minutes later, it was with conflicted feelings. Talking with his great-aunt hadn't just soothed his soul, it had filled one of the many empty spots inside him. Now he wanted to tell someone who cared that his dad had liked chicken gravy on his waffles, and that he'd treated his animals better than most people treated their relatives.

But if Sarah wouldn't talk to him, it was a sure bet she wouldn't listen to him, either.

Days went by, and while Sarah was civil to him and encouraged his bonding with Kylie, she kept any personal feelings she might've felt for him under wraps, which was probably for the best. It made it easier for Jake to concentrate on systematically searching a few more of her rooms in the evenings. He'd decided it was best not to take his meals at Sarah's anymore, but he still visited Kylie at lunchtime, and along with Sarah, heard Kylie's prayers each night.

Strangely, on the evening of the day he and Sarah made

love—when feelings between them were most strained—a new tradition was born in Kylie's bedroom. Kylie started kissing Jake good-night. It was almost as though she sensed the friction between her parents and was trying to comfort them both. The outpouring of love he felt for his daughter made Jake realize something. Maybe it wasn't as important to be number one as it was to be part of a family. Because now that he'd had a taste of it, he never wanted to give it up.

On Thursday night, instead of going to his room to read after Kylie turned in, he followed Sarah downstairs to the foyer. When she turned to him with a question in her eyes, he said, "I want to tell her I'm her father, Sarah. I love her, and it kills me every time she calls me Jake."

"No. And you *told* her to call you Jake." Her expression was cool, but the flickering in her dark eyes said she still felt the electricity between them. That compelling need to touch had never gone away.

"That's your answer? Without even discussing it?"

"We have discussed it. I don't want her told until she won't be hurt by it. Telling her now is a bad idea."

"What makes it a good idea two months or two years from now? She's not even three yet. By the time she's old enough to care, she will have accepted me, and the gossips will have moved on to someone else. I want her to know."

"You want her to know?" Sarah repeated. "Well this isn't about what you want."

"No, it's about what you want. You get to be Mommy. I get to be Jake. Not even *Uncle* Jake. Sarah, she's my little girl."

Sarah sent a glance upstairs, then nodded for him to follow her into the parlor, presumably so they wouldn't wake Kylie.

"My dad doesn't know yet. I don't want Kylie to call you daddy until he's been prepared."

"Then prepare him. When's he due back from Helena?"

Sarah sent him a trapped look, and Jake felt a tug of sympathy. He didn't want to be stubborn about this, but dammit, he was entitled to *some* perks. He might be an accidental father, but he was still the only father Kylie would ever have. "Sarah?"

"Aunt Vera's nearly well. He'll be back tomorrow."

"All right, I have to work. But you and I both know that he'll want to see Kylie, first thing. When he arrives, call me at the office. We'll tell him together."

To Jake's shock, Sarah's eyes filled with tears, and she fled through the French doors into the dining room.

Confused, and wondering what he'd said to set her off, he followed her to the long windows and cupped her shoulders. "Hey," he murmured. "If you don't want me here when you tell him, that's fine. I just thought it'd be easier that way."

"It won't be easy any way I do it," she said in an emotional voice. Outside, Kylie's sandbox was a snow-covered lump beneath the huge cottonwood, and beyond, thick pines rose high and black against the star-spattered sky.

"I don't understand. Your dad already knows you had Kylie out of wedlock. How much more difficult will it be to explain that her father is here and wants to be part of her life?"

"That's not why I'm upset," she answered, sniffing. "Not the whole reason, anyway."

"Then what is?"

"I don't want to tell him that the man who got me pregnant is living in my home. He'll think we're sleeping together again." She swallowed and cleared her throat.

"When I told him I was pregnant, he was *so* disappointed that I'd been with a man I didn't know. I don't want to see that look in his eyes again."

"Okay…I can understand that." He wasn't eager to see Malloy's disapproval, either. "You said that was only part of it. What else bothers you?"

He gave her some time. Just when he thought she wouldn't answer, she murmured, "Dad's had some problems. He was extremely fragile after my mom died. They had a wonderful marriage, and he missed her so much he slipped into a serious depression. Kylie was his salvation. If he thinks someone else is trying to take his place, he could be hurt again."

Gently, Jake turned her around to face him. The light from the parlor was faint, but enough of it spilled into the dining room to illuminate her sad features.

He stroked her hair, looked deeply into her eyes. "I would never do that. I want to be Kylie's father in every way. But she needs her grandfather, too. And her aunts and her uncles and her cousins. Some cultures believe that it takes a whole village to raise a child. I promise you that your dad will be included in anything we do as a family."

Sarah stopped breathing. *Anything they did as a family?* "I'm…I'm not sure what you mean."

"I mean that, in a way, we're already a family. But we could be a lot more conventional if you'll agree to something I've been considering for a few days."

"That depends on what it is."

"I want Kylie to have my name. I could never use my father's. I want her to have mine."

"You…want to adopt her?"

He nodded. "I shouldn't have to, but if that's the only way we can do it legally, then yes. I want to adopt her."

Disappointed without really knowing why, Sarah stepped out of his arms. "That makes no sense."

Jake coaxed her back to him. "It does if her mother's last name is Russell, too."

Sarah's heart stopped, and she stared numbly into his eyes.

He smiled. "Marry me. I've given this serious thought, and it's the best solution for everyone concerned."

"For everyone concerned?"

He stroked her cheek, kissed her softly. "Marrying me will put out a lot of fires. First, it'll quiet the gossips in this town. They can't accuse us of living in sin if there are wedding bands on our fingers. That goes for your dad, too. Second, Kylie will have a daddy and I'll have a daughter I can claim. Third, whoever broke in here may give up searching for whatever he was looking for, because I wouldn't just be rooming here. This would be my permanent residence. And fourth…"

Jake's low baritone was almost hypnotic now. "And fourth, we'll be able to funnel all the energy we've been using to stay away from each other into giving each other pleasure."

His hands slid down Sarah's spine to her hips, and her breath caught as he nudged her closer. "Every day, every night…no more closed doors between us. No more wondering if you missed me in your bed as badly as I miss you in mine. Sarah, the attraction's there. You said it yourself."

Sarah's eyes closed as Jake's warm breath fanned her hair and he kissed her forehead, then bent to her temple and ear. Then he kissed her with the passion she remembered, and throwing her arms around his neck, Sarah returned the tantalizing pressure without reservation. Her heart broke into song. He wanted to marry her.

"Is that a yes?" he gasped, breaking from the kiss and burying his face in her hair. "If we go into this with our eyes open, there won't be any disappointments. We can give Kylie the family she needs, and we can enjoy this chemistry between us forever."

But chemistry tended to blur reasonable thought.

Sarah paused to sift through Jake's entire speech, trying to recall something close to the words a woman needed to hear from the man she loved. But, regrettably, all she could remember were his logical statements about how their marriage would benefit Kylie and their strained-to-the-limit libidos.

Yes, he loved their daughter; he'd told Sarah so—many times. But Jake didn't love *her,* and the last thing she needed was another sham of a marriage. Now that she'd faced her fears and decided that she wanted to risk loving again, it had to *be* love before she said I do. She wouldn't settle for being part of a package.

"No," Sarah said quietly. "Unlimited sex and a shot at Elvira Parsons's brand of respectability aren't good enough reasons to get married. If I ever marry again, it will be for love."

Jake didn't move for a long moment. Then, slowly, he backed away from her, taking his warmth and strength with him.

"All right," he said. He wasn't quick enough to hide the hurt in his eyes, and Sarah felt her heart sink. "I still intend to adopt her. Kylie's not Vince Harper's child. She's mine. Now, if it's okay with you, I'd like to finish searching upstairs. I'll be quiet."

Sarah nodded, then stood there while he retraced his steps and climbed the stairs, wishing she could have said yes. No one had ever made her heart race and her blood thunder in her ears the way Jake did. Even if he didn't love her, life would be good with him. He was hardworking and respectable, kind and generous, and he had the power to buckle her knees with one look, one kiss. But she wanted more. After her marriage to a selfish, callous womanizer, she wanted a man who had eyes only for her. Not someone who saw her as the means to having the family he'd always longed for.

The next day, Jake walked through the empty reception area of the mayor's office, not surprised that Eve Markham's secretary was nowhere to be seen. Delores was never at her desk when he responded to a direct summons. Grimacing, he tapped at the door to Eve's private office, then at her "Come in, Sheriff," stepped inside.

There were no surprises inside, either. Comfort's beautiful redheaded mayor sat behind a massive walnut desk, dressed in a feminine version of a power suit. But there was no blouse under her fitted green jacket. Just a white lace panel that covered half of her ample cleavage and left her long, smooth throat and the top of her chest open to admiring glances. Jake would have been lying to himself if he didn't admit that it was a turn-on—especially in light of the cold showers he'd been taking lately.

Eve Markham was a good decade older than his thirty-four years, but she had smooth, flawless skin, and could have passed for younger. The only thing that betrayed her age was the experience in her shrewd green eyes. Or maybe that was hunger he saw.

"Have a seat," she said, waving him into a chair before her desk. "I won't take much of your time. You're busy and so am I."

Jake sat, startled by her brusqueness. Maybe she'd tired of his ignoring her advances and was ready to give up the chase. Or maybe she was ticked off because he'd stopped answering his pager.

"Thanks. What can I do for you today?"

She stared at him for a long moment while his words hung between them, then folded her hands in front of her chin and said, "You're making a lot of enemies for a man who wants to be reelected. How badly do you want this job?"

"Who's complaining?"

"Who isn't? The men in this town don't like power-drunk officials locking up their friends because they've had one too many beers. And the women don't like the idea of two unmarried people of the opposite sex living under the same roof. Especially when those two people are young and attractive."

That raised his hackles, but Jake didn't react, and she went on.

"Personally, I suspect most of the animosity that's coming from the women is rooted in jealousy. Of course, that'll be small comfort to you when someone else is sitting at your desk come January."

Jake sent her a level stare. "What do you expect me to do? Let men drive drunk? Move back to the Twirling Spur? Everyone in this town knows that Miss Lillian's was broken into, and they know that's a good part of the reason I'm there."

Eve sent him an insincere smile. "I see. Then it would naturally follow that if someone else's home were ransacked—mine, for instance—you'd offer me the same personal protection."

"What's the bottom line, Eve? Are you planning to withdraw your support? Thinking about backing someone else in November?"

Her smile stretched and she sent him an innocent look.

"Of course not. I believe you and I can do great things together...for the town. I just thought you should be aware that people are talking, and if you want to keep this job, you might have to smooth some ruffled feathers—or take other steps to regain some support."

"What steps might those be?" he asked coldly. "I'm not political. I'm not big on kissing babies and pressing the flesh."

"No?"

"No."

Eve stood, indicating that their meeting was over. "In that case, I think I should remind you—once again—that the people in this town just got rid of Cy Farrell. They're not eager to vote in another sheriff with dubious morals."

"I'll keep that in mind," Jake drawled. Then he rose, pulled on his Stetson and walked to the door.

"And pressing the *right* flesh isn't always a bad idea," Eve added indifferently as he grabbed the doorknob.

Jake turned around, hearing the veiled threat in her words. Obviously, the right flesh was hers, but he wouldn't bed Eve Markham to keep his job. Not in this lifetime. "Say hello to your husband for me," Jake said grimly. Then he walked out and shut the door behind him.

He was so angry when he tore out of the courthouse's parking lot that he spun snow and cinders for half a block.

"Damn women," he muttered. He checked his watch, saw that it was lunchtime, then yanked the steering wheel toward the bed-and-breakfast. "Damn them all." Except Kylie. The rest of Eve Markham's gender were free to go their merry way, making life hell for some other poor sap. Sarah included.

He should have his head examined for asking her to marry him. Love? Where in hell did she think she was going to find true love? That was a fantasy for romance novels and silly movies of the week.

But what happens if she does fall for someone? a voice in his mind asked. *Where would that leave you? And how would it affect your relationship with Kylie?*

In that instant, Jake knew how Bill Malloy might feel when Sarah told him the truth.

Chapter 12

Bill Malloy's dark sedan was sitting in Sarah's driveway when Jake pulled in several minutes later. Faintly uneasy, he parked and climbed the steps. What was the old expression? If you want to dance, you have to pay the piper? Well, he'd danced up a storm. And today, Sarah's dad was holding the pipe.

Some of his apprehension turned to joy when he stepped inside and saw Kylie in front of the TV, totally transfixed by a Disney video. As he pulled off his snowy boots and set them on the mat, he considered tiptoeing up behind her for a silly, growly hug. Then Sarah's voice—and Jake's name—filtered in from the dining room's partially opened French doors.

"Then you knew?" she said in surprise.

"I suspected," Malloy answered. "There had to be a reason for your being so troubled. Considering his frequent visits long before the break-in, and his coloring... By the

time you told me that we needed to talk, I had a fair idea.''
Malloy paused. ''What happens now?''

''For now, he wants to be part of her life,'' Sarah said.
''When the time's right, he wants to adopt her.''

''What does this mean for the two of you? Are you
planning to get married? I can't see him adopting Kylie
and living here without a commitment.''

''No. There won't be a wedding. The only commitment
will be between Jake and Kylie. He's a good man, Dad.
But I want more out of marriage than he's able to give
me.''

That stung, even though Sarah's reply came as no surprise.

''Has he asked you?'' Bill Malloy pressed.

Unable to stand his ground any longer, Jake walked
through the parlor and opened one of the French doors.
Sarah and her father both gave a start. ''Yes, I've asked
her,'' Jake said, staring at Sarah. ''She said no. Even
though it's the best thing for Kylie.''

Sarah's gaze never left his. ''A marriage without love
isn't the best thing for Kylie.'' She turned to her father.
''I grew up with two parents who adored each other. That's
the kind of marriage I want. Mutual respect and
chem...compatibility aren't enough.''

Malloy slid a look into the parlor where Kylie was still
entranced in her video, then slowly faced his daughter
again. ''Honey, I have to be honest. This bothers me.''

''I know, Dad. And after you've had a chance to really
think it through, I want to hear all of your reservations.''
She released a long sigh. ''Right now, I think we should
eat.''

''Oh, that'll solve everything,'' Malloy remarked
sternly.

''No, it won't. But it'll give us a chance to get some

perspective." Sarah glanced between them. "Would one of you put Kylie in her booster seat? Lunch is on the table."

Jake stepped back, recalling Sarah's fear that he might try to usurp her father's position. "Go ahead, sir," he said. "I'm sure Kylie missed you while you were away."

Malloy didn't reply immediately. Then his demeanor seemed to soften a little and he said, "Be right back."

Mouthing her thanks when her father stepped into the parlor, Sarah motioned Jake into the kitchen, where she took a pitcher of milk from the table and filled four glasses. "How much did you hear?" she asked quietly.

He faced her stonily. "Enough to know we aren't getting married." Jake nodded at the table with its bright floral arrangement and country place settings. "I don't need to eat anything. I just came by to see Kylie before her nap."

"I know." Sarah put the pitcher down. "But I wish you'd stay. Last night, you offered to be with me, and I said no. Today, I'm asking. Dad's taking this really well, but I think it's important that he spends time with you. I want him to see what kind of man you are, and know he can trust you."

"The way you do?"

She didn't answer for a moment while they continued to study each other. Then she said, "Yes, the way I do."

That touched him. Was he forgiven, then, for his deplorable behavior after they'd made love? "We haven't been on the best of terms lately," he reminded her.

"But that has nothing to do with what we're discussing now. I do trust you."

It touched him just as deeply the second time she said it. By the time Jake left to drive back to work, things seemed more relaxed all around. Malloy had been guardedly friendly, the goodbye hug and kiss Kylie had given Jake hadn't appeared to bother her granddad, and Sarah's offering her trust had buoyed him. It was as close to a feeling of belonging as he'd had in a long time.

Still, the closer he got to town—the more distance he put between himself and Sarah's warm country kitchen— the more he realized that he could lose it.

His conversation with Eve Markham played again in his mind. He didn't believe for a moment that jailing a few cowboys would cost him the election. Even if a small group voted him out, enough people in this county cared that their streets were safe. The moral issue was something else. If someone decided to make a big deal of his living at Sarah's, in light of Comfort's just getting rid of a cheat and a liar, that could hurt him.

Jake halted at the stop sign, then drove through the slushy intersection and headed for his office. What if he *wasn't* elected in November and he was forced to look for another job? He'd been a wrangler and worked on a few construction crews during his college days, but his lone, marketable skill was being a lawman. He was good at it, and he enjoyed the work. If he wasn't elected, he would have to leave.

Sarah had already said there would be no wedding.

Maggie was looking paler than usual when he walked in at one o'clock. "Ready for some lunch?"

"Please," she groaned. "Don't talk about food."

"Sick again?"

She nodded. "Jess's wife and I were talking about reviving Brokenstraw's annual barn dance this year. The second Casey mentioned pumpkin pies, I got heartburn." She bent to retrieve her purse from a desk drawer, then took her jacket from a peg on the wall and slipped it on. "Oh—Joe said to tell you he's still trying to get a current photo of Blanchard."

"Good." But Jake wasn't hopeful. Bounty hunters didn't want their photos passed around; that tended to hamper their effectiveness. Still, showing a likeness to area merchants might ring a few bells and give them a place to start looking. "Did the bail bondsman return my call?"

"Not yet. Sorry."

Jake paused while she zipped her jacket and turned up the fur collar. "You said you're planning some sort of barn dance?"

"Uh-huh. Ross's mom and dad used to host one every September, but when they passed on, the tradition passed with them. Now that the family's growing, Casey and I thought it would be fun to start having them again."

Jake hid a twinge of envy. "Sounds nice."

"You're invited, of course. Joe and Jimmy Ray, too, though I suspect someone will have to stay behind and mind the store." Her eyes twinkled then, as if she knew a secret. "Sarah and Kylie are invited, too."

"You're grinning again."

"Am I? Imagine that." Then she waved and left the office.

Jake blew out a lung-clearing blast of air. His life was chaos. He had brothers, sisters-in-law, and a niece he couldn't claim. He had a pseudo-family that could be snatched away in a heartbeat if Sarah fell in love with another man. And his job was probably in jeopardy if anyone learned that Kylie was his child and that he and Sarah had slept together again. If that happened, Comfort's oversexed mayor would undoubtedly find another candidate for sheriff, and back him all the way to the cot in Jake's private office.

There was also a skip and a bounty hunter out there somewhere who didn't want to be found, and someone who'd ransacked Sarah's home, possibly looking for Harper's diamonds.

Jake walked to the phone in his office. Dropping into his swivel chair, he checked a number in his Rolodex and dialed the Miami bail bond outfit that employed Blanchard. This time he got a person instead of a machine. It didn't help. Blanchard hadn't called in for days. They had no idea where he was.

Hanging up, Jake massaged the tension over his eyes, discouraged that he couldn't clear at least one problem from the nagging inventory in his head. He needed to speak to Blanchard. If he found Blanchard, Paden—who was a potential threat to Sarah—couldn't be too far away.

But after a few minutes of shuffling papers around on his desk, it suddenly occurred to him that he *could* look into one of the issues. Jake lifted the receiver again. He needed to talk to an attorney.

At three-thirty that afternoon, Sarah was exiting Hoffer's Dry Goods when she glanced across Frontier Street and saw Jake leave Mark Walker's law office. A feeling of dread settled over her. What was he doing there? Why would he need a lawyer?

With difficulty, she pushed her doubts aside. Jake was a lawman. There were any number of reasons why he might seek legal advice. He could even be holding someone at the jail. Except...if a suspect needed legal representation, it was a simple matter for Jake to pick up the phone.

Before the decision had fully formed in her mind, Sarah found herself crossing the street to Jake, and falling into step beside him on the covered boardwalk. Light snow swirled in the wind, sticking to his uniform jacket and Stetson, and her green parka.

"Hi," he said, smiling and glancing at the package she carried. "On your way to your car?" Parking was forbidden on restored Frontier Street, so shoppers left their vehicles in a nearby lot.

"Yes. You, too?"

"Yep." Taking her hand, he smoothly guided her in front of him so that she was now walking on the inside. He nodded at her package. "Early Christmas shopping?"

"No. I've been meaning to pick up a gift for someone for a while, and today seemed like a good time to do it. Dad's with Kylie. Their reunion ran a little long, so she went down for her nap only a half hour ago."

Jake chewed the inside of his cheek, then spoke. "Did you and your dad get things settled after I left?"

"Sort of. He doesn't like our arrangement, but he knows I make my own decisions and he has to abide by them. I think I told you that I've been pretty headstrong all my life."

"Maybe that's why we get along," he said, chuckling. They walked a few more feet, passing the café. "Kylie'll sleep for at least an hour yet, won't she?"

"Probably closer to an hour and a half. Why?"

"Just thinking that I'm through for the day, and I could go for a cup of coffee. Want to join me?"

"People will talk."

"Let them. After the day I've had, I need to look at a pretty face for a while. How about it?"

Teasing? Flirting? Sarah warmed at the compliment and a bubbly nervousness filled her chest. There was no way his visit to Mark Walker's office could have been threatening. Not if he could smile so innocently and ask her out. "Make it a French vanilla cappuccino and you're on."

"The café serves cappuccino?"

"No, but Hadley's convenience store outside of town just got one of those new dispensers. I hear it's not too bad, even out of a foam cup."

"Great. One car or two?"

"Two. Then we won't have to come back to town for the other one."

Ten minutes later, they were sitting in Jake's idling Mountaineer, sipping hot, frothy cappuccino and watching snowflakes melt on his windshield. It was cozy and warm inside with the heater on low, their easy intimacy heightened by sixties music from an oldies station on the radio. But even though she was snug and comfortable, her body still remembered him, and the vague seclusion of the car was exciting.

"You know," she said, "when I saw you coming out of Mark Walker's office a while ago I got a little uneasy." He'd removed his hat when they climbed into the car, and his hair was slightly mussed. A faint stubble shaded his jaw, and beneath his open jacket, his tie was gone and the top button of his shirt was undone. Memories flashed in Sarah's mind.

"Why were you uneasy?"

She took a sip of her cappuccino. "Because I thought— just for a second—that you might have gone to see him about Kylie."

"I did."

Sarah couldn't move, couldn't breathe. Then she released a long, shaky breath. "How nice. Right after I told you that I trusted you." She cleared her throat and hoped. "Adoption?"

"No. Shared custody."

Blood rushed to her head, pounded in her ears. How could he do this to her only hours after she'd let down her guard, given him her trust? Casting about, she sloshed her cappuccino into a cup holder and groped for the door handle—threw the door open.

Jake grabbed her jacket to keep her from leaving. "Sarah, wait."

"Let go of me!"

"I will. Just shut the door and let me explain. I didn't even see Walker."

She slashed him a look. "Because he was out?"

"No. Because I changed my mind. Now, will you please close the door? I'll tell you all about it, I swear. I was going to, anyway."

Sarah studied his face. He looked genuinely apologetic. After a moment, she pulled the door shut and waited.

"What I did was a stupid reaction to something that was said to me today," he began. "When I got to Mark's office, I realized that exploring my options was wrong without talking to you first. And that's all I planned to do— explore my options. I want everything about Kylie to be totally up-front with us."

"Why do you think you need a legal document to have time with Kylie? Is trust a one-way street with us?"

"No, I trust you, too. Seating me on one side of her and your dad on the other at lunch today told me that you want to be fair. I was just concerned because..." He sighed, then shook his head and waved the subject away.

"Don't do that. Tell me what's going on."

"All right. I had a meeting with Madam Mayor today. She had some of the same reservations that you did about my being elected. At first, I dismissed everything she said. Then I started wondering what I'd do if I had to move on, and it hit me that moving away would mean leaving Kylie behind."

But you weren't worried about leaving me, were you?

A new lump rose in Sarah's throat. "Didn't you realize that if that happened, we'd work something out?"

"Yes, I did. But only after the fact. That's why I canceled the appointment." He sent her a weak smile, handed back her cappuccino and raised his own cup in front of him. "Can we drink a toast to two caring single parents? Even if one of them isn't the brightest bulb in the box sometimes?"

Sarah nodded and they bumped cups.

"No more secrets between us," Jake murmured.

"No more secrets," Sarah repeated, and they raised their cups to their lips. *No more secrets except for the big one. I'm hopelessly in love with you, Jake Russell. But I can't say those words knowing that you aren't able to say them back.*

"I had a reason for asking you to have coffee with me," he said after a moment. At her questioning look, he asked, "How would you and Kylie like to go to a barn dance with me?"

"A *barn* dance? Where? When?"

"I'm not sure about the when, but it'll be sometime soon—this weekend or next if Maggie and her sister-in-law can get things together. They want to revive the shindigs Jess and Ross's dad used to throw years ago. Maggie said it used to be the ranching families' last big social event before the heavy snows came."

Hearing Jake refer to Ross Dalton Senior as "Jess and Ross's dad" tugged at Sarah's heart. "I remember. My parents took me to one when I was pretty young."

"Well?" he asked, smiling. "Would you like to do it again? The Daltons put up a big barn a few years ago, and they only use it to store hay and farm machinery. Maggie said it's perfect for the dance."

Though his expression revealed little, Sarah could guess

what he was thinking. Going to the dance was another chance to interact with his brothers and walk his father's land. A chance to pretend at belonging. But Sarah knew that it was also a chance for him to see happily married couples laughing and talking with their families and children—and maybe instill a little trust in Jake that sometimes, love did last. Maybe then he could put his fears behind him. Because that's the only reason anyone refused to love—the fear that trust would be betrayed. All this man needed was a little faith.

"Do you think the house will be all right unattended?" she asked uneasily. "Pete *did* see someone..."

"You have new locks, motion detectors and a good security system. But if someone does get in and doesn't know enough to disarm the system within thirty seconds, that alarm will blast him right out of the house."

"It's that loud?"

"It'll sound like a civil defense siren. If that's not enough, I'll ask Jimmy Ray to cruise the neighborhood a few more times than usual. We won't be gone that long."

Sarah smiled. "Then we'd love to go. In fact, since I don't have anything coming up for the next two weekends, I'll phone Maggie and offer to help with the food."

"She'd probably like that," Jake returned. Then he added with an impulsive grin, "Let's buy Kylie something special to wear. Something fancy. I want to show her off."

Sarah laughed. "You want to *shop?*"

"Yeah," he said. "Yeah, I want to shop. How about tomorrow?"

"All right. But right now I'd better get back and start supper. I told dad he could eat with us tonight." She paused, then added warily, "You *are* having supper with us, aren't you?"

His eyes gentled on hers. "I'd like that."

"About six? I'll put a few baked potatoes in the oven, make a salad, and you and Dad can brush the snow off the grill and do steaks on the porch. If you want."

"I want." Jake put his cup down, then raised the hood on her parka and took a moment to rearrange her bangs. For a breathless moment, Sarah thought he would kiss her.

"I wouldn't want you catching cold," he murmured. "I'd hate to miss out on a steak dinner."

"Looking out for your own interests, Sheriff?"

"Have to. No one else wants the job."

But someone did want the job. Perhaps one day she could tell him that. "See you at home."

"See you at home," he repeated.

Kylie was still asleep when Sarah returned. After thanking her dad, she went to the parlor, opened the bag containing her "gift," and removed the five-by-seven-inch gold picture frame. Then, smiling, she slipped a photo of Kylie behind the glass and carried it to Jake's room.

Chapter 13

Preparations for the dance at Brokenstraw took longer than anticipated because heaters had to be placed inside the barn, and decorating and menu ideas kept getting more elaborate. But when Jake and Sarah crossed the snowy threshold and entered the noisy barn on the first Saturday night in October, they had to agree that the wait was worth it.

The cavernous interior had been transformed. Cornstalks and hay bales abounded, set off by colorful spills of Indian corn, pumpkins and gourds. Thousands of miniature lights twinkled from rafters, support posts and a tall pine lavishly festooned in ribbons, gingham and crafts. At the back of the barn, a spotlit three-piece band performed on a raised platform, while neighbors and friends sat at the long tables covered with yellow-and-white checked tablecloths that were positioned around the room. More energetic guests two-stepped to an old Willie Nelson song.

Jake tossed their jackets on the row of hay bales that

served as coat racks, then lifted Kylie into his arms. Maggie hurried over to greet them as they moved farther into the room.

"Hi!" she called over the music and chatter. "Glad you could make it."

"Thanks, we wouldn't have missed it," Jake said, meaning it. He'd been looking forward to this for more than a week.

"The place looks spectacular!" Sarah exclaimed.

"Thanks, but all I did was supervise. Ross wouldn't let me bend, stretch or lift anything heavier than a spoon."

Sarah smiled. "Exactly as it should be."

While Maggie thanked Sarah again for helping with the food, Jake slid an appreciative eye over Sarah. She looked beautiful. Her blond hair was pulled up in a kind of soft bun laced with black ribbons, but deep bangs and a few soft strands curved around her face and neck. She wore a long-sleeved, lacy white blouse over her black skirt, and that was long, too—patterned with tiny pink roses. With a cameo at her throat, she looked like a pretty prairie schoolmarm.

All he'd thought about on the drive here was finding a baby-sitter and introducing Kylie's mommy to the delights of a secluded hayloft.

Maybe it was her smile, or her forgiving nature. Or maybe it was her thoughtfulness in putting that photograph of Kylie on his dresser...but Sarah Harper was growing more important to him every day.

"Looks like half the county's here," Sarah said, breaking Jake's musings.

"Not that many," Maggie answered. "But at last count, we had well over a hundred guests. Most of the ranching families came, and a few friends from town." Her smile warmed as she took in Kylie's white-fringed cowgirl dress, white hat and boots. "And *you* look precious," Maggie gushed.

"I'n a cowgirl!"

"You sure are." She laughed, then nodded toward the door as more guests arrived. "Sorry, gotta go. I'm the designated greeter. Help yourselves to the food and snacks on the tables. There's cider, juice, punch, soft drinks and coffee over there, too." She started away, then turned back to call "Oh—and Casey has an area partitioned off where the little ones can play."

"Thanks, we'll find what we need," Jake replied. Then his gaze moved between his two pretty dates. Pride, and an incredible warmth, filled him. "Now, what would you ladies like to do first? Eat? Have something to drink?"

Kylie bounced in his arms, her eyes shining. "No! No, I want to dance!"

Laughing, Jake set Kylie down on the floor, keeping one of her small hands while Sarah took the other. "Well, then," he said over the music as they walked her to the center of the crowded floor. "I guess we should dance." His smile softened, and his gaze found Sarah's, though he pretended he was still speaking to Kylie. "And maybe a little later, your mommy and I can dance all by ourselves."

Sarah's smile made him think about haylofts again.

For the better part of an hour, all they did was watch over Kylie and exchange proud smiles as she twirled and spun in her cowgirl dress. Then Jess and Casey moved in with their little girl, and Kylie had a partner her own size.

Lexi Dalton's resemblance to Kylie nearly struck Jake speechless. Or maybe he only noticed it because he knew Kylie and Lexi had the same granddad. Still, suddenly, Jake was so uneasy he had to get out of there. He inched close to Sarah so she could hear him over the fiddle music, then smelled her perfume and nearly changed his mind about leaving. "Want some punch or a cola?"

"Not right now, thanks." Her bright smile went straight to his heart. "Maybe later."

"Be back soon."

But just as he turned away, he intercepted a startled look from Maggie that swiftly turned curious. He knew what she'd seen. He and Jess were practically mirror images standing there with their black hats, dark-haired little girls and blond women.

With a quick wave, he hurried to the refreshment table. Aunt Ruby was there, wearing a red-and-white-checked dress, and ladling out cider. After a cautious look around, she moved closer and said in a stage whisper, "Y'got a fine lookin' family over there. What're you gonna do about it?"

Jake shook his head. "I don't know. I guess I need to tell them soon. I'm starting to feel damn uncomfortable accepting their hospitality and keeping them in the dark about this. Maybe when this shindig's over, we can talk."

"Good idea," Ruby agreed. "Only I wasn't talkin' about Jess and Ross."

Jake stilled. She wasn't? Did she know about Kylie, too?

Suddenly, he didn't care about any of it anymore. He'd keep his job or he wouldn't. People would gossip or let things be. "Aunt Ruby, how'd you like to dance with me?"

"I'd like it right fine, nephew," she said with a gleeful cackle. She put down her ladle and slipped her arm in his. "Only, I need to ask you an important question first."

Jake waited, ready to tell her whatever she wanted to know. She was family.

Ruby's eyes twinkled. "Are ya any good at this, or do I hafta lead?"

* * *

The night went by in a blur. Jake spoke to Ross, Jess, Casey, and was introduced to Maggie's aunt Lila and uncle Moe. He also spoke to her ladyship the mayor more times than he cared to count. Several times, when the band played a slow song, he tried to find Sarah to collect that dance. Once, he even caught her eye, mouthed an invitation and received her eager nod.

But halfway to her, two members of the town council waylaid him with complaints that Jimmy Ray Becker was too young and inexperienced to be a deputy sheriff. By the time he'd assured the men that Jimmy Ray just needed time to mature in the job, the song was nearly over and Sarah was in someone else's arms. When he apologized later, she smiled and shrugged, but she looked disappointed.

Their luck didn't improve after Casey took Lexi and Kylie up to the homestead to unwind. On the rare times the band played a ballad, Jake was busy with people who wanted his views on everything from taxes to higher penalties for cattle thieves. He was pleased that there were no complaints and no accusations, veiled or otherwise. In fact, despite all the backbiting and gossip, he got the feeling that no one even minded his being there with Sarah. Well, no one except Eve Markham. Which made him suspect that her warnings the other day were pure drivel.

Jake suppressed a frown of annoyance as Eve sidled up to him again. "Your husband couldn't make it tonight, Mayor?" He craned his neck over Eve's head to look for Sarah. He hadn't seen her for a while, and she hadn't looked happy when they'd last spoken.

"Donald's not much for barn dances," the mayor said with a coy smile. "Unfortunately, he lost his joie de vivre years ago."

She slid her arm through Jake's and pressed her ample breast against his bicep. "You know, I've been thinking about the new computer you mentioned a while ago, and I believe you're right. Maybe it *is* time to discuss it." With her green eyes locked on his, she felt for Jake's hand, brushed his thigh, then laced her fingers through his. "Let's talk about it while we dance."

Irritated, Jake took back his hand. "Sorry, it'll have to wait. It's getting late, and it's time that I—"

He'd been about to say it was time that he took Sarah and Kylie home. But just then he saw Sarah hurrying out the side door, looking upset.

Eve ran a fingernail down the pearl snaps on his shirt. "All right, we'll talk at your office."

Suddenly, her constant pawing was more than he could take. Jake grabbed her hands and stuffed them one by one into the pockets of her skirt. "Eve," he said, holding her shocked gaze. "Get some help."

Then he half ran to the hay bales, grabbed his denim jacket and burst into the clear, crisp night.

Pulling on his jacket, he scanned the ranch yard. All he saw was snow, sparkling on the roads and clinging to trees and corral posts. The outbuildings were on low ground, the house much higher. Jake hurried up a rise, heading for the long, plowed path to the Dalton homestead.

He spotted her thirty or forty yards ahead of him. Quickening his strides, he called to her, but she couldn't have heard because she kept walking. Jake broke into a loping run. "Sarah, wait!"

When he reached her, one glimpse of her face in the light of the hunter's moon told him she was well beyond upset.

"Tears? Sarah, what's wrong?"

"Nothing."

"People don't cry for nothing."

"Women do."

"Not this woman," he said, snaring her hand when she tried to bolt. "You hate to cry. Your eyes burn and your sinuses get all clogged up. You told me that yourself. Now, what's going on?"

He knew it was serious when she pressed her forehead to his shoulder and sobbed into his jacket. God, he didn't want her to be sad. Not ever. Jake stroked her hair and back, kissed her temple—and wondered if he'd heard right when she whispered two names.

"What do Maggie and Ross have to do with this?"

"*And* Casey. *And* Jess."

Concern turned to anger. If his brothers or their wives had said anything to hurt her—

"I've been watching them all night," Sarah said, pushing away and fumbling for the tissues in her coat pocket. "They're just so—so damn *happy!* The tender touches, the longing looks!"

Now he *really* didn't understand.

She wiped her eyes, blew her nose. "Just as I was leaving, I saw M-Maggie and Ross s-standing in a corner away from everyone. They were smiling and kissing and he was rubbing his hand over her stomach—over their baby."

"Sarah, I'm sorry..." Jake said, at a loss. "I just don't see why that should upset you."

"*I* want a life like that," she sobbed in frustration. "A *love* like that! Is it too much to ask for a little happiness?"

That was it? Jake's heart took off. *He could fix this.*

"No—no, it's not too much to ask. Sarah, *we* could be a family. You and me and Kylie. We could have more babies. I want the same things you do." He turned her face up to him, kissed her mouth and tasted salty tears.

"All you have to do is say the word and we're on our way to the altar. Sarah, I do care for you. So much."

"I know you do," she returned in a tear-clogged voice. "But I'm talking about love. Gut-level, can't-live-without-you love. I *want* that. I *need* it, and I won't settle for anything less."

"Sarah, don't say no—say you'll think about it. It makes so much sense for us to be together."

"Sense? Caring and sense? Well, I'll admit it's better than what I had with Vince." She wiped her eyes and looked up at him. "But it isn't enough. Now, let's get Kylie and go home. I'm tired."

Jake watched her walk toward the lit porch, frozen in a rush of thoughts and emotions. He needed to *do* something, *say* something before his future slipped away. His heart was pounding so loudly that he scarcely heard his own reply.

"Okay," he called. "Okay, I love you."

Sarah stopped, then turned around to face him from several yards away. Her breath clouded the cold night air as heartbeat after heartbeat thudded in Jake's chest and he waited for her to react. It wasn't what he expected.

With a shake of her head, she continued up the porch steps to the door. Jake was beside her before she could open it.

"Did you hear me?"

"Yes, I heard you," she returned quietly. Then she tapped softly at the door, opened it a crack and called to Casey.

Casey's welcoming smile wavered a little when she clicked on the light in the foyer and saw Sarah's face. Then she caught herself, and with a new smile and a finger to her lips, led them into the living room.

Kylie and Lexi were both asleep in a swaddling pile of

afghans, pillows and toys. Again, Jake was struck by the cousins' startling resemblance, more so because their eyes were closed. He had to resolve this soon. But there would be no heart-to-heart talk with family tonight. Right now, he had to convince Sarah that marrying him was the best thing for all of them.

They were silent on the way home. When they got there, Kylie was out of sorts at being awakened again, and it took a long time to settle her down. Eventually, though, they left her room and faced each other in the hallway.

"Can we talk now?" he asked, keeping his voice low.

"It's nearly eleven o'clock," she said, folding her coat over her arm. Jake held his jacket, too. "We should sleep."

"How can I sleep with you feeling this way?"

Sarah looked at him, resignation in her eyes. "What do you want me to say? That I believe you?" She shook her head. "That had to be the most terrified profession of love in the history of the world. Not to mention convenient. You don't love me, Jake. You're tired of being alone, and you want a family. You want a daughter you'll never have to be afraid of losing."

"You're right. I want all of those things."

"Then please, be honest with yourself. That 'I love you' wasn't something you'd intended to say, you felt pressured to say it."

Jake stared guiltily at her, then sighed. "Sarah, I do have feelings for you. I've never known a woman with your capacity for—"

The phone rang.

He fought hard to keep the frustration out of his voice. "Let it ring. Let the machine get it."

"I can't. If Kylie wakes up again, I'll never get her back

to sleep." She walked into her room. "Besides, it's late. It could be important."

Jake heard her say hello. In a moment, she stepped into the hall again. "It's for you. Your office."

Gritting his teeth, he strode into her room and snatched the receiver from her nightstand. "Yeah, Jimmy Ray."

"Sorry to call so late, Sheriff, but there's somebody over here who wants to talk to you."

He squeezed the receiver in a death grip as Eve Markham's face bloomed in his mind. *"Now?"*

"Yes, sir. I said you were off-duty, but—"

"Tell him who I am," a gravelly voice said in the background.

"Sheriff, he says his name's Paden, and that you'd know what it was about." His voice lowered. "He doesn't look much like that mug shot, though."

Jake's momentary shock vanished, and he drew an annoyed breath. "Jimmy Ray?"

"Yes, sir?"

"Is there a gun on your hip, Jimmy Ray?"

"Uh…yes, sir."

"Good. Take it out of your holster, point it at the joker in front of you and escort him to one of our cells. Make sure you Mirandize him, and make sure you check him for weapons. Then come back to the phone and tell me it's been done."

Jake listened intently for almost a full minute, straining to hear Jimmy Ray's shaky tenor and the deeper, amused voice of the man he was detaining. Presently, his new deputy reported back.

"Sheriff? He's locked up."

"Fine," Jake replied dryly. "I'll be right there."

Sarah's face was lined with concern when he rejoined her in the hall.

"I have to go into the office, and I'm not sure how long I'll be. Set the alarm and leave some lights on. I might be there all night."

"Jake, what's going on? I couldn't help overhearing your end of the conversation."

"I'm not sure," he said, planting a quick kiss on her lips, then shrugging into his jacket and starting down the stairs. "But I'm damn well going to find out."

Sarah hurried to the head of the steps. "Watch the roads."

"I will, thanks. Set the alarm."

"Jake?" He turned around. "Remember, the code is Kylie's birthdate, 0-4-1-8. Come home when you're through."

He was so overwhelmed he couldn't think of anything to say. Then he grabbed his hat from the table in the foyer, murmured, "I'll see you when I can," and left with one thought in mind. No one who'd eluded a fugitive warrant for months would be fool enough to waltz into a sheriff's office at eleven o'clock on a Saturday night and turn himself in. If the man in his cell was Ike Paden, he'd eat his boots.

Ten minutes later, Jake strode into the office, waved to Jimmy Ray, who scrambled to his feet behind the desk, then went directly to the last cell in the lockup.

Clearly unconcerned, the man dressed in hunter's camouflage—the man with the brown hair and mustache who clearly was *not* Ike Paden—stared up at him from his comfortable position on the cot. "Good evening, Sheriff," he said with a smug grin.

"That's a matter of opinion, Mr. Blanchard," Jake returned. "Why the masquerade?"

"Partly to see if you had a sense of humor—and partly

because I was sick of being the only man in the county chasing wild geese. Misery does love company.''

"Paden's gone?"

Blanchard nodded. "I thought he'd run to this area because Harper told him about the diamonds. Turns out, he was just passing through. Paden has a sister in Seattle." The bounty hunter shook his head in disgust. "The little twit turned him in, and cheated me out of fifty percent of his bail."

Still keyed up and edgy, Sarah showered, rechecked the doors and alarm, then looked in on Kylie again and went to bed. She'd left a lamp burning downstairs, and a small light on in the bathroom in case Kylie's interrupted sleep patterns caused her to wake again. Thin light from the hall came through her partially open bedroom door.

It was nearly midnight, and sleep wouldn't come. As she lay there in the near dark, things she didn't want to think about floated to the top of her mind.

She was still hurting over Jake's flat, false, offhanded profession of love.

Okay, I love you.

He probably wondered why her heart hadn't sprouted wings.

Even though Jake and Vince were as different as any two men could be, she'd heard that resigned tone often from Vince.

Tonight, Jake had sounded like a man agreeing to do whatever was necessary to get what he wanted. She loved him. She wanted and desired him. But she couldn't wed someone who saw marriage as a means to an end, even though he had "feelings" for her. Feelings? Did the man even know what love was?

Sighing, Sarah looked at the illuminated dial on her

alarm clock. In a little more than six hours, Kylie would be awake and ready to greet the day. Despite her pitiful longing for Jake's love—despite whatever was going on at his office—this was Sarah's life. She was the mother of a spirited young child, and she needed sleep to handle Kylie's energy. So Sarah closed her eyes, willed herself to relax and gave herself over to the dubious peace of dreams.

Something jolted her awake, and Sarah's heart shot into her throat as she sat up in bed. She blinked her eyes, trying to focus. A shadowy figure stood in the dim light outside her door. Knuckles tapped softly against wood.

"Sarah?"

Her heart stopped its furious hammering. "Jake?"

He eased the door open a little wider, and the night-light in the hall outlined his long, powerful frame. He spoke in a hushed tone. "I'm sorry to wake you, but I thought I'd better tell you I'm here so you didn't get alarmed if you heard me in the shower."

Sarah pushed her hair back from her eyes, then inched the sheet up in front of her. The sleeveless cotton nightie she wore was one of her favorites, but it was also much-washed thin.

Her pulse thumped as he slowly crossed the floor and sat on the side of her bed. He took off his hat, held it between the spread of his legs. Movement brought the faint scent of his aftershave to her, and suddenly the room was smaller, warmer.

"The man who showed up at the jail tonight was Blanchard."

She cocked her head curiously. "The bounty hunter?"

Jake nodded. "When he told Jimmy Ray that his name was Ike Paden, I had a fair idea who I'd see in that cell. Paden wouldn't have turned himself in." After a pause, he continued. "The bail bondsman who hired Blanchard to bring Paden in told Blanchard I was looking for him."

"And did he?" Sarah asked hopefully. "Did he bring Paden in?"

"No, Paden's in custody, but Blanchard didn't put him there. Sarah, Paden didn't know anything about the diamonds. He was only passing through on his way to Seattle."

Sarah's heart beat faster. "Then...he wasn't the man who broke in here? What about Blanchard?" she asked quickly. "It could have been him. He knew about the diamonds, didn't he?"

"Yes, but I didn't get the idea that diamonds were on his agenda."

"So there's still someone else out there? Someone else we have to watch for?"

Jake spoke quietly. "I'm sorry. Yes."

A chill moved through her, and Sarah reached for her comforter. Jake pulled it up from the bottom of the bed, then moved up on the mattress and draped it over her shoulders. But when he finished tucking it around her, he stayed where he was, only inches away.

"Don't give up on me, Sarah," he said softly. "We'll resolve this. It'll just take some time."

"I know."

"And now that I've gotten you all riled up," he said with a tight smile, "I'm off to the shower."

Jake eased her back on her pillow, then spread the comforter over her again. "Sleep tight," he murmured.

"You, too. I...guess I'll see you in the morning."

"Guess so." But he didn't move away.

Desire wound around them in the dusky room, fueled by the smell of sleep and the sexy rustle of bedclothes. It was no surprise. It had been simmering between them

since he walked into her room, and all it required to flame
was a soft sigh or an errant move.

Every emotion Sarah felt for him filled her as Jake
inched closer. Need and caring, passion and chemistry…gratitude and tenderness. And love. Even though it
was one-sided, it flared like a Roman candle, lighting
Sarah's heart and propelling her into his arms. He did care
for her. And at this moment, it was enough.

The kiss splintered through her like August lightning.
Because she knew this kiss. She knew that touch.

Sarah slid her hands inside his open jacket to his back.
Coaxed him closer. Brought him with her as she lowered
herself to the pillows again.

"Let me close the door," he rasped.

A moment later, he was stripping away denim and cotton, fumbling with his snaps and zipper, and kicking off
his boots. Then he was under the comforter with her and
slipping her nightie over her head.

"I wanted you so badly when I came home tonight,"
he whispered. "I woke you purposely. I had no intention
of showering this late." Bending over her, he stroked her
hair. "Sarah, I really do—"

"No." She kissed the side of his mouth to stop the
words. "Don't say it." Because if he said it again out of
obligation, or passion, or anything other than complete
honesty, she wouldn't be able to go through with this.

And heaven help her, she needed him.

Chapter 14

Later, sated and pleasantly tired, Jake held Sarah close and spoke in a low, deep murmur. The news he shared warmed Sarah's heart because she knew he had to feel some measure of trust in her in order to finally admit what she'd suspected for some time. There was a smile in his voice.

"When Emily's friend told me that my dad was a Montana rancher named Ross Dalton, I was a basket case. I couldn't wait to get back to the office computer and track him down. It was disappointing to learn that he'd passed away. But it was such a rush to know that I had brothers."

Jake planted a kiss on her forehead. "Know how Kylie's always asking to look through your photo album?"

Nodding against his shoulder, Sarah smiled. "She loves looking at pictures of herself. Terribly narcissistic, our daughter."

"I'd like to see a picture of my dad sometime. Aunt Ruby says I look a lot like him."

"That shouldn't be a problem. All you have to do is talk to Jess and Ross."

"I want to. I'd even planned on doing it tonight, but…"

"Do it," she encouraged. "They like you. They'll accept you. I wasn't so sure about Ross at first," she added with a smile. "But he seemed friendly enough tonight, don't you think?"

Jake's voice lifted curiously. "Yeah. I'm not sure why, but yeah, I noticed."

"I know why," Sarah said smugly.

Jake lifted his head to grin down at her. Once again, Sarah was struck by his raw male beauty. Every corded muscle and sinew invited her touch; every touch he returned took her breath away.

"You and Maggie indulge in a little girl talk this evening?"

Sarah released a long-suffering sigh. "I had to do *some*thing while you were charming the masses. The town council, Maggie's aunt and uncle—our nymphomaniac mayor."

With a silly growl, Jake flopped back down on his pillow and pulled her close. "I don't want to talk about our nympho mayor. What caused the change in Ross?"

"Strangely enough, I think it might've been me."

"You?"

"Mmm-hmm. Maggie senses that he's a little jealous of you—well, maybe not jealous, exactly, but he is a bit insecure where you're concerned."

"Good Lord, why?"

"Because you're the squeaky-clean, straight-arrow sheriff, and Maggie thinks he's making comparisons between himself and you. They nearly broke up because Ross thought he wasn't good enough for a preacher's daughter. He used to be a real hell-raiser.

"But," she added, grinning and sliding her calf along his. "After seeing us together, I guess he's no longer worried about his wife working for such a gorgeous...sexy..."

"Stop that," he grumbled.

"Don't be modest. You *are* gorgeous and sexy. And lean, and exciting, and—"

"What's the matter with him? How could he think I'd try something with my own sister-in-law?"

"He doesn't *know* she's your sister-in-law. You need to let him in on the secret. Jess, too."

A noncommittal grunt issued from his throat. "Speaking of secrets, you told Aunt Ruby about Kylie, didn't you?"

"Uh-oh. Are you upset?"

"No, but I thought you didn't want anyone to know."

"I was scared." She sighed, stroking his chest. "I needed advice from someone I could trust. Know what she said when I told her I was afraid you'd take Kylie away?"

"I'd never do that."

"I know that now. But I didn't then. Anyway...Aunt Ruby said she had a hunch you were a good man."

"She was right," he said, chuckling.

Sarah tugged his chest hair and he yelped. "Seriously, though, Aunt Ruby saw what I was too scared to see—your decency, and honesty, and caring." Sarah tapped a fingertip over his heart. "She saw the man you are in here."

Jake didn't answer, just snuggled her closer in his arms and kissed the top of her head. But as they lay there listening to the comforting sounds of the house creaking and the wind in the trees, Sarah sensed that he was pleased.

She was nearly asleep when she heard him whisper, "Sarah Harper, what am I going to do with you?"

Just love me, she thought, smiling, and drifted off again.

* * *

Two hours later, Jake still hadn't slept. All he wanted was to lie here and hold her, count his blessings and feel his life finally coming together. He was afraid that if he closed his eyes—if he fell asleep—he would have to give back this sense of belonging. And he didn't want to.

Craning his neck, he looked down at her again. Her pale hair spilled over her left eye and cheek, and her hand still lay on his chest. How had he ever gotten so lucky? How could a chance meeting three years ago have ended up bringing him so much happiness?

Trying not to wake her—or, maybe he *was* trying to wake her, he thought sheepishly—Jake scrunched down a little and touched his grateful lips to hers.

Sarah's eyes flew open, and her head came off the pillow.

Seeing his face inches from her own, she expelled a sleepy laugh and lay back down. "You still here?"

"Where else would I be?" he replied.

"In your own bed?"

"Now, why would I want to be there when you're here?"

"Well, let's see," she murmured through a smile. "Maybe because Kylie will be waking soon and you really shouldn't be in my room when she comes in?"

Jake bent to kiss her again, then nuzzled her ear. "The door's closed. We won't let her see anything that she shouldn't."

"I know." But her tone had shifted from playful huskiness to clear concern. "When the door opens and you walk out, though, she's going to have questions."

Jake stilled, and his contented mood slipped a little.

Sarah gentled her voice. "It's just that she's such an indiscriminate chatterbox. She tells every*one* every*thing*. If it's on her mind, it's on her lips."

A knot formed in Jake's throat. Nodding, he slid his arm out from under her neck and rolled to a seated position at the side of the bed. Then he shook his arm to get some circulation back, and reached for his jeans.

He knew she was right. Dead right. Absolutely right. He even knew he was overreacting. But he couldn't seem to stop the feelings of hurt and frustration that were building inside him.

Sarah touched his back. "Jake, I just don't want her carrying tales to my dad. He's coming over this morning to take her out for breakfast and shopping."

"She could carry all the tales she wants if you'd say yes to my proposal." Standing, he stuck his feet into his pant legs and yanked up his jeans. "See? Yet another problem marriage would solve." But then he paused to stare down at her in the faint light of the moon, and his heart softened. "Sarah...let's make an appointment to see Reverend Fremont."

"Jake, please...we've talked about this."

"Okay—" he shrugged after a frozen moment "—your call." Hiding his hurt, he zipped his fly, then snatched up his briefs, shirt, jacket, socks and boots, and loaded them onto one arm. "And you're right," he said at the door. "It'd be disastrous if Kylie blew the whistle on us. How would you tell your dad that you won't marry me, but you don't mind keeping me around for sex?"

He swung the door open and lowered his voice. "I'm gorgeous, sexy, caring, dependable and honest. I'm just not good enough to marry." Then he went to his own room and shut the door.

Fighting tears, Sarah groped around for her nightgown, aching inside and wondering how such a blissful night could deteriorate into such a big, fat mess. Why couldn't he see what was right in front of both of their noses? Didn't he hear the words that came out of his own mouth?

His claim that marriage would solve "yet another problem" made her feel as though he had a checklist in his back pocket. Ten Good Reasons to Get Married. Use all ten, and if that doesn't do the trick, profess a love you don't feel.

Well, Vince had professed to love her, too. He'd ended up bedding any willing female in the county and humiliating Sarah in the process. She couldn't bear it if that happened with Jake. How could she marry him, trusting that she wasn't part of a package, then find out later that his feelings for her weren't deep enough to keep him faithful? She couldn't go into another marriage already fearing divorce.

Sarah stared at his closed door. She also couldn't sleep with him again unless something changed radically between them. Either he had to honestly fall in love with her, which might never happen. Or she had to decide to settle for whatever affection he was able to give and hope real love would grow.

When Kylie woke Sarah a few hours later, Jake was already gone. But his door was ajar, the lingering smell of his soap and aftershave a poignant reminder of the night before.

Trying to ignore the leaden weight in her chest, Sarah lifted Kylie into her arms, unlocked the gate and carried her downstairs. Then she sat her in front of the TV and popped in a video to keep her occupied while she filled a tote bag with toys and snacks to take along in Grandpa's car.

But when Sarah returned a few minutes later, Kylie was sprawled on the floor with the photo album again. A bright smile lit her baby face as Sarah crouched to offer her a children's vitamin and a sip of orange juice.

"Wook! A big fish!"

"Mmm-hmm," Sarah said, not really looking where Kylie's finger was pointing. "Here, honey, chew your vitamin and take a drink. Grandpa will be here in a few minutes, so we have to hurry and get you dressed. You have a big day ahead of you."

Twenty minutes later, when Sarah's father left the driveway, Sarah wandered back into the parlor to pick up Kylie's pajamas and the photo album. But as she was about to close it, she realized that her daughter hadn't been looking at the "Kylie album." She'd dragged out one of the others that were stored on the bottom shelf of the bookcase. One of Miss Lillian's.

She stared at the photo of the "big fish."

For years, it had hung in the mudroom off the kitchen, right across from Vince's tangled collection of fishing poles. The day he'd caught that fish, he'd bragged that it was the biggest cutthroat trout he'd ever seen—probably even a state record. They were dating then, and she'd still had stars in her eyes. Of course, it hadn't been a state record, but he was so proud of the slimy thing, he'd had it mounted, anyway.

Vince's pride and joy...a fish mounted to a big hunk of driftwood. He'd even admired it the night he'd come back to the house—tried to make her admit they'd had fun that day. Tried to soften her enough to be...willing.

Funny. She hadn't thought about Vince doing anything even remotely wholesome for a very long time. Maybe because he'd become such a low, untrustworthy liar in their later years.

Sarah stood motionless for a long moment. *He'd ad-*

mired it the night he came back? The night he'd hidden the diamonds?

Suddenly, a powerful feeling of intuition came over her, and gooseflesh prickled every square inch of her skin. Sarah's gaze came back to that fish.

She'd gotten rid of the fish, too. It had left the same morning the trash collector had taken the rest of Vince's stuff. *But the fish had left with her father.*

She hadn't been able to tell him about the near rape; she'd been too ashamed. But when she'd told him that Vince was there the night before and was his usual obnoxious self, he understood why she'd rid herself of everything that reminded her of him.

"Missed the trout," he'd said, nodding at the mudroom wall. That's when she'd told him to get it out of her house…and when he'd complimented the mount and said, *"It's not the fish's fault that Vince is a jerk. Do you mind if I—"*

"—take it to the camp," Sarah said in a whisper. She hadn't cared. She'd never spent time at her dad's cabin in the mountains, anyway. That was his retreat. To her knowledge, even her mother had only been there a few times.

Sarah's heart beat faster. Could it be? It wasn't *totally* beyond the realm of possibility that Vince had hidden the diamonds inside the trout. He'd certainly had the time and the opportunity to do it.

Or was she just talking herself into this because she needed closure? Without a doubt, she'd be enormously relieved to recover the diamonds; she and Kylie could go back to feeling safe and secure. She'd never have to worry about intruders again.

But then…there'd be no reason for Jake to live with them any longer. Would there?

Still, after last night, he was undoubtedly thinking of moving out, anyway—arrest or no arrest. It was best if she started taking control of her life again. Since Jake had moved in with them, she'd been leaving decisions that *she* should have been making to him.

Sarah climbed the stairs and headed for the shower. Her dad wouldn't be bringing Kylie home until late afternoon. She'd leave him a note, then stop by his house for the extra key to the camp and drive up there herself.

Jake hit the Jeep's loud siren and flashing light, then grimly directed Pete into the nearly deserted, snow-blown parking lot beside Dusty's Roadhouse. He felt the thick animosity coming from the truck before he reached the open window. All right, they didn't like each other, but this had nothing to do with that.

"May I see your license and registration, Mr. Jessup?" he asked in a polite tone. He wouldn't give Jessup a reason to run crying to Sarah. He'd do everything by the book.

Pete scowled, and when he spoke, his breath clouded the crisp morning air. "Ain't you tired of hasslin' me yet?"

Jake sent him a dry look. "License and registration," he repeated. "Failure to stop for a stop sign, and one of your taillights is out."

Pete grew thoughtful, though the hatred in his eyes didn't dim. "Don't have 'em."

"Where are they?"

"Home. In my wallet."

Jake studied the man. He could write him up, or he could give him a chance to produce the items. He thought of Sarah, and decided upon the latter. "Bring them into the office by noon. Otherwise, I'll have to cite you for that *and* the stop sign. And get that taillight fixed."

With a nod and a cold look, Pete rolled up the window and left.

Sarah pulled on her warm hooded parka, grabbed her gloves, then paused for a second in the foyer trying to decide if she'd forgotten anything. Her note to her father—or Jake, she thought, feeling her heart squeeze—was taped to the staircase's thick newel post right in front of the door. She'd armed the security alarm, and they'd have to turn it off quickly upon entering the house. She would get the camp key on her way.

"That's it," she murmured. Then she closed the door and hurried out to the driveway and her waiting Blazer.

As she approached Pete's house, she was startled to see him loading a suitcase and two heavy black trash bags into the back of his truck. A box full of tools followed. Curious, she pulled into his driveway, bumping over tire-packed snow. He looked rushed and angry, and there was something odd about the way he held himself. At first, she thought he favored his left arm, but that wasn't it.

Rolling down her window, she called, "Hi, Pete! Going somewhere?"

With a sharp glance, he pulled the sides of his open parka together, then fastened a few buttons. "For a while," he said gruffly. "Got a sister down south. Think I'll wait out the winter there."

Sarah blinked in surprise. This was the first time Pete had ever mentioned family, *or* expressed an interest to leave.

A little awkwardly, he threw a spare tire through the cab's door. "Where *you* headin'?"

Sarah considered the adventure ahead of her and realized how harebrained her answer would sound. "Uh-uh, you'd laugh. You'd think I was crazy if I told you."

"Try me," he growled. His salt-and-pepper hair stuck out at all angles as he pulled off his red knit cap and came to her window. "I could use a good laugh."

"All right," she said, wincing. "Remember the diamonds that Vince supposedly hid in my house? Well, that might've been true. And I might've given them away."

Pete's shocked expression lingered through her whole story. Then a determined look touched his thick, whiskery features. "Well you can't go up there alone. I won't hear of it. Them mountain passes can be treacherous." He paused. "Or will the sheriff be meetin' you at your daddy's camp?"

Sarah was unprepared for the hard lump that rose in her throat when she answered. "No," she said, unable to hide her regret. "Jake's a busy man. I doubt he'd appreciate my calling him away from his work for something that could be a wild-goose chase."

To Sarah's surprise, Pete lumbered to the passenger side of her Blazer, climbed inside and settled himself in. "Like I said, you can't go alone. Little thing like you should have a man along in case she runs into trouble."

Though she cringed at the sexist remark, Sarah didn't comment. Obviously, Pete hadn't meant to be anything but chivalrous. Still, she suspected that she could finish more quickly without him. "But—aren't you packing?"

"I can finish when we get back. Way you described it, it ain't that far." He threw the red cap in the back seat. "Friends gotta be there for friends. Right?"

"Yes, but—"

"Besides," he said in an ornery tone, "I'll miss you when I take off. You're the only person in this town t'ever give me the time of day twice."

And with those words, Sarah had no choice but to welcome him. "Buckle up," she said, smiling. "We'll be stopping at my dad's for the key first."

Jake raced at breakneck speed over the road, passed the trees bordering Sarah's home, then hit the brake just short of Pete Jessup's old clapboard house and slid the department's Jeep into the driveway. He came to a stop directly behind Pete's truck. A suitcase, bags and tools were clearly visible through the rusted white cab's open door. It looked like Pete—*or whoever the hell he was*—was thinking about leaving.

Because there was no Pete Jessup.

Unsnapping the holster at his hip, Jake climbed the un-shoveled steps and banged at the door. He banged again, then opened it, shouted inside and let himself in.

Signs of flight from a man the computer said never existed gave Jake "probable cause" as far as Jake was concerned, but he had a bad feeling that Jessup had already skipped. A quick walk through his rooms proved Jake right. But where would he have gone in the middle of packing? Clothes he'd obviously intended to take were piled on a beat-up sofa. Why would he leave his vehicle? Where would he go on foot?

Jake felt the quick jolt-and-sting of adrenaline. In two minutes he was bounding onto Sarah's porch. He tried the door, then used his key. The note was the first thing he spotted on entering. Quickly, he turned off the alarm, then reread the note.

A sick feeling pooled in the pit of his stomach as thoughts converged to form a possible scenario. Sarah had gone to look for the diamonds. Jessup had stopped packing in the middle of leaving for a good reason—even though he'd known that if he didn't produce a valid driver's license by noon, he'd be found out. So why wouldn't he just finish and run? Had he expected Jake to wait until noon to run a check on him—which hadn't happened? And believing he had time, might he have discovered Sarah's plan and gone with her?

Too many maybes. But they were maybes that Jake couldn't ignore.

Jake strode to the kitchen and tapped in a number from memory, his intuition building.

"Courthouse," Elvira Parsons said.

"Is Judge Quinn in, Elvira?" Jake asked quickly.

"I'll see."

The next voice he heard was Roy Quinn's. "What can I do for you, Jake?"

"I need a warrant to search Pete Jessup's house, and directions to Bill Malloy's fishing camp, and I need them both an hour ago."

"Something bad going on at Bill's place?" Quinn asked anxiously.

"I hope not," Jake said. "I'll send Joe over for the warrant—we can justify it, I promise you. Now, how do I get to Malloy's cabin?"

A half hour later, Sarah fishtailed the Blazer up the snow-covered grade, feeling faintly anxious. Pete had been stern and silent for some time now, except for turning up the heater and saying he'd like to live someplace warm.

"Maybe a place like where your ex lived," he suddenly added out of the blue. "With an orange tree in the back-yard."

Sarah's uneasiness grew. The only way Pete could've known about the orange tree was if he'd spoken to Vince when he'd run back to Comfort to elude federal agents. "I didn't realize you and Vince were friends. He never mentioned it." In fact, Vince, like most people in town, had never had much good to say about Pete—which was the reason Sarah had kept her distance for so long, too.

"We weren't friends," Pete said with a scowl. "Your husband was a snot-faced braggart who liked to put me down."

"I'm sorry. Vince could be cruel."

The Blazer's tires shuddered through a series of snow-filled ruts. More snow clung to tall pines and Douglas firs, heaped the ditches at the sides of the narrow road. They were alone up here, Sarah realized. There were no tracks on the road except their own.

"We just about there?"

"Next driveway," she said. "Hold on. It's probably plugged solid."

Sarah braced herself, then made a sharp right and hit the gas. The Blazer roared through a two-foot-deep snow-drift, spun tires and ended up barely off the road. But she was afraid to go farther and risk getting the car hung up. "I'll go the rest of the way on foot," Sarah said, feeling her excitement build.

"No, *we'll* go the rest of the way on foot," Pete corrected her and pushed open his door.

Sarah looked at him, concerned. "Pete, the snow's deep. I'll know in a minute if the diamonds are in the fish."

"Come on, missy," he said, chuckling, yellowed teeth showing. "Y'can't cut me out of the fun now that we're here." He jumped down into knee-high snow. "When am I gonna get another chance to hunt for diamonds?"

It took several minutes to make it to the porch of the small wood-frame camp and dig the snow away from the door. Then they were stamping inside the cold, one-room dwelling, and Sarah was staring at Vince's glossy, var-nished trout, hanging over a small stone fireplace.

"There she is," Pete said huskily, and before Sarah

could act, rushed to take it down. He carried it to the painted table and the light of the window.

Long screws went through the back of the bumpy drift-wood and into the fish's body. "You look it over, missy," Pete said excitedly. "I'll see if I can find a screwdriver."

Sarah shoved a chair out of the way so she could get closer to the window. There wasn't a mark on it—not around the glass eyes or the mouth, not around the gills.

Then she squinted down between the fish and the wood. To her utter astonishment, she saw a half-dollar-size plug in the cutthroat's middle, secured with cellophane tape!

Pulse hammering, Sarah slid a finger between the trout and wood to run her fingers over it. Yes, it was definitely a plug! A circular piece of foam had been cut out, then returned to the hole.

"Pete, I think I've found them!"

"Here," he said shakily, handing her a hunting knife. "I couldn't find a screwdriver, but you can probably get them screws out with this."

Sarah worked quickly, the thick blade doing its job. In a moment the fish was free of the driftwood and ornamental greenery the taxidermist had added. She turned it over and pulled out the plug.

Diamonds gleamed and sparkled through the clear plastic bag that contained them.

"Oh, my," Sarah breathed reverently, and lifted the stones from the hollowed-out belly. "Oh, my." With a bright smile, she turned swiftly and gushed, "Pete, have you ever seen such—"

Sarah's smile vanished as, in one glance, she took in the cloth sling beneath Pete's unbuttoned parka that had served as a holster—and the sawed-off shotgun pointed at her face.

"Sit down, missy," Pete said coldly, locking the door. "And kindly put *my* diamonds back on that table."

Chapter 15

Trying to keep his panic in check, Jake pushed the Jeep as fast as conditions would allow up the mountain pass, following the fresh tire tracks in the snow. Blood roared like a freight train in his ears.

Dammit, he should have followed his instincts and checked Jessup out long before this. But thankfully, those instincts had pushed him to check the man out hours before noon.

Pete Jessup had never been printed, never had a social security card, never served in the armed forces, never applied for a driver's license. The "nevers" went on and on. Maggie was still trying to track down his identity, and Joe was searching Jessup's place even now. Judge Quinn's parting comment still rang in his ears. *I'll issue the warrant, Sheriff, but you'd better find something. I'm not ready to retire yet, and I don't want the ACLU picketing my house!*

There would be no picketers, because Joe *would* find

something to justify the warrant. Warning bells were clanging so loudly in his head, Jake knew he had to trust them. A man who kept to himself and used an alias generally had a damn good reason for doing so.

He swerved to avoid a series of ruts. Why hadn't those warning bells clanged when Sarah told him her friendship with Pete had only begun *after* she'd "had some trouble."

Well, people were entitled to turn over a new leaf. But with Ike Paden in jail and Blanchard heading for home, gut instinct said Jessup was the man they were looking for. His instincts also told him that if Jessup offered friendship three years ago, he'd been looking for the diamonds nearly that long. He'd done Sarah's yard work, and she'd trusted him. Pete damn near had the run of the place. Given Sarah's penchant for hiding keys outside the house...

Maggie hailed him on the car's radio. Jake snatched the microphone as the rear fender of Sarah's Blazer came into view. "Yeah, Maggie, what do you have?"

"His name's not Jessup, it's Jenkins," she said quickly. "Joe found some old papers at his place."

"Outstanding warrants?"

"Two 1989 homicides—one in Indiana, one in Iowa—both committed during bank robberies. He still had some of the money left in a closet. Jake, the murders were messy. His weapon of choice is a sawed-off shotgun."

Fear ricocheted off every nerve in his body. "Better send some backup."

"Joe's already on his way."

A minute later, the Jeep was parked ten yards below Sarah's Blazer, and Jake was lunging through deep snow and underbrush, and cutting through the woods to the right of the camp.

Maybe things were okay in there. If the gems *weren't*

in the trout Sarah mentioned in her note, Pete would have no reason to disclose his identity. But if they *were* there…

The wind blew and gusted, pelting him with grainy snow as Jake plunged across the yard, keeping to the windowless side of the dark wood camp. He paused near the right front corner to listen, but the only sound he heard was the wind in the pines and snow hitting the sides of the cabin.

Drawing his gun, barely breathing, Jake moved in a low crouch across the snow-covered porch. Two windows fronted the cabin, one on either side of the door. He paused below the first. Now Jessup's voice carried to him clearly. Removing his Stetson, Jake raised his head cautiously and peered through the bottom of the window.

The only thing stronger than Jake's fear was his rage. Sarah was in a chair, hands bound behind her. Pete stood over her, holding a knife at his side. He muttered something Jake couldn't make out.

Sarah trembled as she stared into the uncaring gaze of the man who'd become a stranger—the man who'd just admitted he had no more use for her than he had for her ex-husband. Feverishly, she tugged at the rope binding her wrists. Suddenly she was afraid that he wouldn't let her live when he left here today.

"What—what do you mean, I gave you the key?"

"Missy, hidin' a key in a flowerpot's so stupid, you might as well have put it in my hand."

With a sneering smile, the thickset man leaned closer, his breath clouding the air as he opened his hands to display the twenty-eight perfect diamonds. He pushed them around with the tip of the knife, and they sparkled brilliantly in the daylight coming through the window.

"I been huntin' these little honeys for three years. Three

years of stayin' calm, puttin' up with your smiley-faced charity—never leavin' a *trace* until the new sheriff started sniffin' around.''

Chills drizzled through her.

''When he kept showin' up, I knew I was runnin' out of time. I *damn well* knew I was runnin' out of patience! Three visits in one day! Three visits!''

Straining and stretching, Sarah bent her fingers at an awkward angle, trying to loosen the knots. But, oh God, they were so tight! ''Is that what happened the night you ransacked my house? You ran out of patience?''

''No, I ran outta sense,'' he growled. ''Drank too much.'' He chuckled coldly. ''Ironic that you came to me for help, wasn't it?'' Returning to the table, he pulled a red bandanna from his hip pocket. ''I figured you had 'em. Maybe kept movin' 'em around. That's what I woulda done.''

''I—I still don't understand how you could've known the diamonds had actually been in the house. The FBI said—''

''The FBI didn't know squat!'' Pete clattered the heavy knife on the table and the sound went straight through Sarah. ''I got that news from your idiot husband. Fool never could hold his whiskey. The night you threw him out, he bragged about leavin' somethin' real special back at his granny's house—and, missy, he didn't mean you.

''Thought it was money, the way he was throwin' it around that night at Dusty's,'' Pete muttered, knotting the gems in the bandanna. ''If there was a dumber crook in the country, I don't know who it coulda been. Only a man who *wants* t'be caught goes to his own house, then stops at his favorite bar.''

Pete tucked the kerchief into the breast pocket of his tan

parka and buttoned the flap. "Now, *I* coulda give him lessons on gettin' lost."

What did that mean? Was Pete a fugitive? Sarah's glance bounced nervously around the room. It halted in shock when it touched Jake's face in the window to the left of the door.

The quick, intense shake of his head stopped Sarah's startled reaction. Then he put a finger to his lips, motioned toward the door and disappeared again.

Oh, God, he was going to try the door, and it was locked! Pete would hear it, and the shotgun lying on the table would hop into his hands in a heartbeat.

Sarah saw the faint movement of the latch—felt her terror build. "I don't know why you locked the door," she blurted out. "Obviously, I'm not going anywhere in the next few minutes." She was terrified to look at the door, terrified that Jake hadn't heard her.

"Missy, you ain't goin' nowhere, period." His stony gaze rested on hers. "You know, for ten years, I kept my nose clean. Had enough money from my other 'endeavors' to last me the rest of my life, and didn't want no more trouble. But your big-shot ex, and his big, fat mouth dragged me back into it. Always pokin' at my pride, always thinkin' he was so much smarter. Well, if he'd known who he was dealin' with, he'da had more respect." Pete patted his pocket. "'Cause, looky who's got the diamonds now."

Slowly, he wrapped his meaty hand around the shotgun, cracked it open and took two shells from his pocket.

Sarah's nerves rioted and her heart banged against her ribs. He meant to kill her! He meant to kill her, and she could have gotten away! The gun hadn't even been loaded!

The loud snap of the gun closing echoed in the sparsely furnished cabin. "I turned him in, you know."

"*You* turned him in?" Keep him talking. Keep him talking and he won't shoot. "The authorities said someone made an anonymous call—"

"I knew he was on the run. He as much as told me while he was braggin' on how rich he was gonna be. So I followed that pile of manure down to Babylon, saw him go into the shack with the girl and made the call."

Another cold chuckle rustled in his throat. "Don't let anybody fool you, missy. There *ain't* no honor among thieves."

Pete backed toward the door, one hand reaching behind him for the latch, the other slowly raising the barrel of the shotgun. Sarah's fear became cold, stark terror.

"Don't you worry," he said, cocking the hammer. "Your daddy'll raise Kylie just fine withou—"

Sarah screamed.

Jake crashed through the door in an explosion of wood shards and splintering boards, knocking Pete to the floor. The shotgun discharged like thunder and bounced away. Pete scrambled to retrieve it. But Jake was on him in an instant, his pistol at Pete's temple, his voice arctic-cold and shaking with fury, his finger needy on the trigger.

"Jenkins, if you value your sorry ass, you'll put both hands behind your back. And I mean *right now*." He complied, and Jake cuffed his wrists. Then, with a helpless look at Sarah that promised he'd be right back, he shoved Pete through the ruined doorway onto the porch while his prisoner spewed expletives and raged. He didn't want this piece of human garbage anywhere near Sarah.

Jake had just finished chanting out the Miranda warnings when Joe came lunging through the snow. "Everybody okay?" he called.

Jake nodded, still enraged that a man Sarah considered a friend had nearly ended her life. "You take him. He'll be safer away from me. And radio Maggie. Tell her to try to find Sarah's dad.'' Then he hurried back inside, grabbed the hunting knife and quickly cut Sarah's bonds.

They were in each other's arms in a heartbeat.

"Dear God, Sarah," Jake rasped, wrapping her tightly. "Dear God. If he'd hurt you, I don't know what I would've done. He's going to pay for this, I swear!"

She was crying so hard she could barely speak. "When he said my dad would be raising Kylie—"

"I know," Jake murmured, rocking her, kissing her face and her ear and her hair. "But he was wrong. You'll be holding her again soon." He let her cry for several more moments, holding back his own tears of relief. But then he had to ease her away. "Come on. Let's get you back to town."

Clutching hands, they plowed through the deep snow to the Jeep and followed Joe Talbot down the pass.

He never let go of her hand all the way down, and Sarah wondered if she were completely insane for trying to see the good in what had happened. The overwhelming relief in his eyes every time they met hers gave her hope. Maybe the ordeal they'd just come through had chased away, once and for all, his mistrust in love.

It was nearly three o'clock when they got back to town to another emotional scene at the jail. Sarah started to cry again when she walked into the office and saw her father and Kylie waiting. Releasing Jake's hand, she ran to them. Her father never left her side except to take Kylie aside when parts of Sarah's statement might have upset her. From time to time, Sarah saw Jake walk by to make a phone call in his office or do something that she assumed related to processing his prisoner.

When it was time to go, Sarah left her father and Kylie for a moment to look into Jake's office. She found him sitting at his desk, his handsome face utterly beleaguered, his mind obviously somewhere else. When he saw her, his expression softened, and he came around the desk to hold her fast again.

"Are you all right? Do you need to speak to someone about this?"

Sarah clung to him, breathed in his scent as he held her in a near-suffocating embrace. "No, no, I'm fine," she murmured. "I have everything I'll ever need right here. Right now."

His voice was a low rasp. "I just keep reliving—"

"Don't do that," she whispered. "I'm all right." Tears filled her eyes and she gazed up at him. "Thanks to you."

He didn't reply, simply pulled her close again for another crushing hug. Then he eased her away from him, regret in his eyes. "I'm waiting on a call from an insurance investigator. He was ecstatic when I told him we recovered the diamonds. He'll be catching a plane within the hour, and he'll want to talk when he gets here. Because of the diamonds, the feds think they need to come, too. And—" he sighed "—Pete's wanted in two other states, so between Iowa, Illinois and Montana, we'll be tossing the dice to see who gets to prosecute him first."

"I understand." Heart swelling, Sarah touched his tanned cheek, kissed his lips softly. "You're busy, and I understand. I'll see you at home later."

He didn't say anything for a moment. Then he backed away. The matching look of retreat in his eyes struck fear deep into her heart. Something had changed.

"You should take Kylie home," he said. "This had to have been a confusing day for her. In fact, maybe you should stay with your dad tonight."

"No." Sarah felt her throat tighten as she stared at him. "No, I'm not staying at dad's. Kylie and I both need the security of having our own things around us tonight. What's going on, Jake? Why do I feel as though—"

"Sarah, it's going to be late when I get out of here."

"I'll wait up."

"No, don't do that. I—" He paused, his gaze becoming even more troubled. "I might not be back tonight at all. I have a lot of thinking to do…some things to get settled in my mind." He moistened his lips, had a hard time meeting her eyes. "Okay?"

Sarah murmured an assent, wondering how she could speak and breathe without a beating heart. After their nightmare in the mountains—after his fierce embrace at Pete's camp—she'd hoped…

But she'd been right about his feelings for her all along. He *didn't* love her. He cared for her, and he was relieved that no harm had come to her. But in the cold light of day, he hadn't been able to say something he didn't feel. Apparently, tender lies were easier said in the darkness.

Feeling his eyes on her back, Sarah walked out of the office, gathered her family and left.

She was still numb hours later as she sat curled on the sofa, an afghan pulled tightly around her. The clock in the foyer began to chime. Nine o'clock and not a word from him.

It was time for a decision.

Since she'd returned home, she'd gone back and forth a hundred times between ending it and accepting his marriage proposal—between saying goodbye or saying I do. Assuming that he still *wanted* to marry her. After the withdrawal she'd seen in his eyes, she couldn't count on it. But no matter how badly she wanted him, she kept coming back to the same heart-wrenching answer. It would hurt too much to go on living under the same roof with a man who might never love her the way she loved him.

Rising, Sarah returned the afghan to the back of the sofa, then, at loose ends, went to the pantry to inventory her stock for an upcoming reception. It would be hours before she slept. She might as well do something useful.

When Jake finally returned, she would tell him to find another place to live.

Jake rang the bell at the Dalton homestead at nine o'clock that night, his belly churning, his palms sweating despite the cold. He mustered a smile when Jess opened the door to him and motioned him inside.

But the phone call he'd made an hour ago asking to meet the whole family at the homestead seemed to have left Jess with a puzzled, even wary look in his eyes. "Maggie said you had some excitement today," he said. He waited while Jake wiped his boots on the mat, then showed him into the den off the foyer. "Is Sarah all right?"

"I think so." But he didn't know for sure because he hadn't seen her for hours. Jake removed his hat and smiled at Maggie as he stepped inside. She smiled back, but there were questions in her eyes, too. Ross sat beside her on the black leather sofa, his gaze unreadable.

As Jess motioned him into a chair and took a seat behind the desk, Casey entered. She set a coffee tray on a nearby table.

"Can I pour you a cup?" she asked, the house's somber mood touching her, too. "Maggie said you and Sarah had a difficult day."

"Thanks, maybe later." *If the invitation still stood when he dropped his bombshell.* "I think it'd be best if we just talked for now."

When she was behind the desk and perched on her husband's thigh, they all looked at him expectantly.

"You sounded serious on the phone," Jess said. "What's up?"

Taking a deep breath, Jake met each of their faces. "I guess there's no right way to tell you this, so I'm just going to say it outright."

Ross leaned forward on the sofa. "You're going to say what outright?"

"I'm your brother."

It was nearly eleven o'clock by the time Jake used his key to enter the dimly lit house, turned off the porch light and relocked the door. He glanced into the parlor. Sarah had left a lamp on, clicked to its lowest setting.

The Dalton reunion hadn't gone badly. There were shocked expressions, and an understandable trace of disbelief. But there had also been a few smiles. It would take his brothers a while to get used to the idea of him, but he accepted that.

On the other hand, his sisters-in-law had been warm and welcoming. One thing had led to another then, and the question of the day had come up; he'd admitted that he was Kylie's father. Kylie, who looked so much like Jess's daughter, Lexi.

Water running upstairs jolted him from his thoughts, and with a sigh, Jake took the steps slowly. *One confession down, one to go.*

Sarah came out of the bathroom just as he stepped over the gate. She was dressed in a flannel nightgown, and her blond hair was wet from her shower. Jake inhaled the combination of citrus and wildflowers coming through the open door—toothpaste, too. Normal, everyday "Sarah smells" that he'd never be able to get enough of. His heart swelled with longing.

"Hi," he said softly. "You okay?"

"I'm all right," she answered, not meeting his eyes. She combed a hand back through her wet hair. "It's late."

"I know. I had some things to do."

"So you said."

After another silent moment, Jake settled a hip against the wall. "The insurance guy's got his gems, and it looks like we'll be extraditing Pete." He paused. "The feds are smiling."

"God's in his heaven, and all's right with the world?"

"Not just yet, but it's getting there." He paused again. "I drummed up the courage to go out to Brokenstraw tonight."

Jake felt a spark of hope when she broke into a genuine smile. "That's wonderful. How did your family take the news?"

"They need some time to get used to the idea, I think. I told them that I wasn't looking for—or expecting—anything. That I just had to get it off my chest. So, they'll either accept me or they won't. Right now, there's something else I need to get off my chest. I have something to say to you."

Sarah's smile wobbled. "I have something to tell you, too. Let's talk about it downstairs."

When they were both seated on the sofa in the parlor, he suggested that she go first.

"All right," she said, studying her clasped hands. "I think it's time you started looking for an apartment. Now that Kylie and I don't have to worry about any more break-ins, it would probably be best if you found a room somewhere else."

"I see."

She jerked her head up, obviously startled. "Then you'll do it?"

"If you want me to. Ever since I moved in, I've been

giving orders and making demands. It's time I cooperated.
If that's what you want, I'll be gone in the morning.''

"Oh," she said, looking a little uncertain. "Well. Thank
you. I mean—" She didn't seem to know what to say.
Standing, she looked around the room for a moment, anywhere, he noticed, except at him. Then she murmured,
"All right, then I guess I'll say good-night.''

"Wait." He stood and caught her hand. "I haven't had
my turn yet." Her cheeks grew pink, and Jake's heart ex-
panded even more.

"I'm sorry. What did you want to say?"

"I love you."

Sarah yanked her hand from his and bolted for the dark
foyer. Jake went after her and pulled her into his arms. He
said it again. "I love you."

"Stop saying that!"

"I can't," he said, holding her fast. "And I'm going to
keep on saying it until you believe it. Sarah, I love you
with every breath in my body, and that's been true for a
long time."

"You're just reacting to what happened with Pete."

"No, I'm not. But I was afraid that I *could* be, and that's
why I needed some time away from you tonight. To see
if I still felt this way after the adrenaline wore off. *I did.*"

Tears slid over Sarah's cheeks, and she shook her head.

"I've proposed to you twice," he continued, tipping her
face up to him. "And I did an asinine job of it both times.
I made it sound like a business deal. I didn't tell you then
that every time I look at you, I thank God we met that
night at Cotton Creek. And I thank God for Kylie, and I
thank God for the goodness in you that let me fall in
love...for the first time in my life."

Now there was no stopping the tears or the racking sobs.

"I never loved Heather," he continued. "I talked myself into it because after living in flophouses, and foster homes, and apartments, I wanted a *real home* so badly. But as deceitful as she was, I wasn't much better because I saw her as the means to having that home.''

He cupped her face, wiped her tears with his thumbs. ''I cared about her, and it hurt when we broke up. But what I felt for her was *nothing* compared to what I feel for you. Sarah, I don't know how to say it any other way. *I love you.* Not because you're Kylie's mother, and not because you're safe from Pete, but because without you...I don't think I'll ever be able to breathe again without hurting.''

That did it. With a sharp sob, Sarah flung her arms around his neck, and Jake crushed her to him. ''I love you, too,'' she whispered. ''Jake, I love you, too.''

''For better or worse? For richer or poorer? In sickness and in health?''

''Yes,'' she said, tipping her teary face up to him. ''Oh, yes.''

Then they came together in a kiss that was everything they were and felt—fire and commitment, trust and joy. More than that, it was a pledge to never let what they had at this moment ever slip away.

Floating on the richness of her love for him, Sarah was only minimally aware of Jake fumbling with something behind her back. Then he found her left hand and brought it up between them. The weight of the ring on her finger made Sarah ease from the kiss.

They both laughed softly.

Sarah stretched out a hand to snap on the foyer light, a grin replacing her tears as she twirled his signet ring on her finger. ''I don't know what to say. It's lovely.''

''No, it's temporary. We're going to the jewelry store

the second it opens tomorrow. But if you don't mind, I'd rather not buy you a diamond.''

"After everything that's happened, I don't *want* a diamond. In fact," she said, her voice dropping to a murmur, "all I want is a simple gold band. And you."

They stayed there at the bottom of the steps for a while, kissing, tasting, their hands slowly rediscovering each other. Then abruptly, Jake scooped her into his arms and smiled. "Why are we standing down here when there are four perfectly good beds upstairs?"

Sarah wrapped her arms around him and nuzzled his neck. "I can't imagine." He started up the stairs. "Wait," she said, laughing. "We didn't turn out the lights." He kept climbing the stairs. "Jake? Jake, we really should—"

"No, we shouldn't."

"But it's so—"

Chuckling warmly, he breezed into their bedroom and shut the door with his foot. His voice turned to velvet as he slid her down his length in the darkness. "Send me the electric bill," he whispered. "You know where I live."

Epilogue

Jake and Sarah held each other close as they gazed out their bedroom window at dawn's glittering snow below. It blanketed everything in sight, all the way to the jagged peaks in the distance. Brokenstraw lay at the base of that second deep cleft in the mountains.

Reverend Fremont had married them there last night. They'd been surrounded by family, a few close friends, and more flowers, candles and satin ribbons than Jake had ever seen outside a church. Jess and Maggie had stood for them, and Kylie and Lexi had twirled and giggled in their flower girl dresses. When Bill Malloy put Sarah's hand in his, her quiet beauty in the off-white gown had made him feel like a king.

Then they'd had their first traditional Thanksgiving dinner as a whole family.

"You're smiling," Sarah said softly, kissing his chest while her fingers played with the waistband at the back of his navy shorts. "I guess that means you don't regret our decision to bring Kylie back with us last night."

"Not at all. It was nice of your dad to offer to keep her, but... We'll have our time next week when we fly to the islands. After just being elected, the town might frown on their sheriff slipping away so quickly." He bent to nip her ear. "Will you wear a grass skirt for me?"

"No, sir, I won't," she teased. "If I can't be naked with you all week, I'm not going."

Raising a questioning brow, Jake left her to move their rocking chair over to the window. Then Sarah curled in his lap, and he moved a lazy hand over the satin-covered curve of her hip as they watched the morning sun appear.

"You realize that I'm probably pregnant, don't you?"

Jake grinned. "If you're not, you never will be."

"Then I really hope that I am. Kylie needs playmates."

He made a low rumble of pleasure in his throat as she nibbled his earlobe, and found more nice things to do with her hands. "How many playmates?"

"Three, I think. Heaven knows we have the room since you tore down the sign out front. People think they're no longer welcome here."

"People are right," he said with a chuckle.

He couldn't believe that once he'd been terrified of loving her—so sure that if he let down his guard, he'd end up regretting it. It shamed him to remember that one brief instant in the attic when he'd even feared her love for Kylie—thought there would never be enough left over for him. Now he could see that love was self-propagating. The more you loved, the more there was to go around.

The sound they'd been waiting for squeaked and sighed in the baby monitor, and after sharing a grin, they turned the chair around to face their open doorway. In a moment, they heard Kylie's running steps, then saw her peek into their room.

Like a little tornado, she ran across the room to launch herself onto the chair with them, and they gathered her close for silly hugs and kisses.

Then with a lump forming in his throat, Jake smiled down into his daughter's blue eyes and they repeated the greeting they'd begun the day he'd put the sapphire engagement ring on Sarah's finger.

"Good morning, sweetheart," he said, feeling his heart swell with love. And as Sarah clutched his hand tightly, Kylie answered with a beaming smile, "G'morning, Daddy."

* * * * *

INTIMATE MOMENTS®

Silhouette®

MEN
OF THE
BAR. H.

The Henderson brothers are back!

Men of the Bar H: *Though most of the Henderson brothers have roamed, all of them know…there's no place like home!*

Don't miss
MISTAKEN IDENTITY (IM #987),
Merline Lovelace's next installment of her
Men of the Bar H series—on sale in February 2000,
only from Silhouette Intimate Moments.

And coming in April 2000, the *Men of the Bar H*
are back! Be sure not to miss Evan Henderson's
story in **THE HARDER THEY FALL**—
only from Silhouette Intimate Moments.

Available at your favorite retail outlet.

Silhouette®

Where love comes alive™

If you enjoyed what you just read,
then we've got an offer you can't resist!

Take 2 bestselling
love stories FREE!

Plus get a FREE surprise gift!

Look Who's Celebrating Our 20ᵗʰ Anniversary:

Celebrate 20 YEARS

"Working with Silhouette has always been a privilege—I've known the nicest people, and I've been delighted by the way the books have grown and changed with time. I've had the opportunity to take chances…and I'm grateful for the books I've done with the company. Bravo! And onward, Silhouette, to the new millennium."

—*New York Times* bestselling author
Heather Graham Pozzessere

"Twenty years of laughter and love… It's not hard to imagine Silhouette Books celebrating twenty years of quality publishing, but it is hard to imagine a publishing world without it. Congratulations…"

—International bestselling author
Emilie Richards

INTIMATE MOMENTS®
Silhouette®

INTIMATE MOMENTS®

Silhouette®

Welcome to

MATERNITY ROW

The street where little miracles are born!

SILHOUETTE BOOKS
and
PAULA DETMER RIGGS

are proud to present two brand-new stories
in this popular miniseries:

DADDY BY CHOICE
IM #998
and
Family by Fate

available in **A BOUQUET OF BABIES**,
a romantic anthology in honor of Mother's Day.

Look for both on sale in April 2000

Available at your favorite retail outlet.

Silhouette®

Where love comes alive™

SILHOUETTE'S 20TH ANNIVERSARY CONTEST
OFFICIAL RULES
NO PURCHASE NECESSARY TO ENTER

1. To enter, follow directions published in the offer to which you are responding. Contest begins 1/1/00 and ends on 8/24/00 (the "Promotion Period"). Method of entry may vary. Mailed entries must be postmarked by 8/24/00, and received by 8/31/00.

2. During the Promotion Period, the Contest may be presented via the Internet. Entry via the Internet may be restricted to residents of certain geographic areas that are disclosed on the Web site. To enter via the Internet, if you are a resident of a geographic area in which Internet entry is permissible, follow the directions displayed on-line, including typing your essay of 100 words or fewer telling us "Where In The World Your Love Will Come Alive." On-line entries must be received by 11:59 p.m. Eastern Standard time on 8/24/00. Limit one e-mail entry per person, household and e-mail address per day, per presentation. If you are a resident of a geographic area in which entry via the Internet is permissible, you may, in lieu of submitting an entry on-line, enter by mail, by hand-printing your name, address, telephone number and contest number/name on an 8"x 11" plain piece of paper and telling us in 100 words or fewer "Where In The World Your Love Will Come Alive," and mailing via first-class mail to: Silhouette 20th Anniversary Contest, (in the U.S.) P.O. Box 9069, Buffalo, NY 14269-9069; (In Canada) P.O. Box 637, Fort Erie, Ontario, Canada L2A 5X3. Limit one 8"x 11" mailed entry per person, household and e-mail address per day. On-line and/or 8"x 11" mailed entries received from persons residing in geographic areas in which Internet entry is not permissible will be disqualified. No liability is assumed for lost, late, incomplete, inaccurate, nondelivered or misdirected mail, or misdirected e-mail, for technical, hardware or software failures of any kind, lost or unavailable network connection, or failed, incomplete, garbled or delayed computer transmission or any human error which may occur in the receipt or processing of the entries in the contest.

3. Essays will be judged by a panel of members of the Silhouette editorial and marketing staff based on the following criteria:

   Sincerity (believability, credibility)—50%
   Originality (freshness, creativity)—30%
   Aptness (appropriateness to contest ideas)—20%

   Purchase or acceptance of a product offer does not improve your chances of winning. In the event of a tie, duplicate prizes will be awarded.

4. All entries become the property of Harlequin Enterprises Ltd., and will not be returned. Winner will be determined no later than 10/31/00 and will be notified by mail. Grand Prize winner will be required to sign and return Affidavit of Eligibility within 15 days of receipt of notification. Noncompliance within the time period may result in disqualification and an alternative winner may be selected. All municipal, provincial, federal, state and local laws and regulations apply. Contest open only to residents of the U.S. and Canada who are 18 years of age or older, and is void wherever prohibited by law. Internet entry is restricted solely to residents of those geographical areas in which Internet entry is permissible. Employees of Torstar Corp., their affiliates, agents and members of their immediate families are not eligible. Taxes on the prizes are the sole responsibility of winners. Entry and acceptance of any prize offered constitutes permission to use winner's name, photograph or other likeness for the purposes of advertising, trade and promotion on behalf of Torstar Corp. without further compensation to the winner, unless prohibited by law. Torstar Corp and D.L. Blair, Inc., their parents, affiliates and subsidiaries, are not responsible for errors in printing or electronic presentation of contest or entries. In the event of printing or other errors which may result in unintended prize values or duplication of prizes, all affected contest materials or entries shall be null and void. If for any reason the Internet portion of the contest is not capable of running as planned, including infection by computer virus, bugs, tampering, unauthorized intervention, fraud, technical failures, or any other causes beyond the control of Torstar Corp. which corrupt or affect the administration, secrecy, fairness, integrity or proper conduct of the contest, Torstar Corp. reserves the right, at its sole discretion, to disqualify any individual who tampers with the entry process and to cancel, terminate, modify or suspend the contest or the Internet portion thereof. In the event of a dispute regarding an on-line entry, the entry will be deemed submitted by the authorized holder of the e-mail account submitted at the time of entry. Authorized account holder is defined as the natural person who is assigned to an e-mail address by an Internet access provider, on-line service provider or other organization that is responsible for arranging e-mail address for the domain associated with the submitted e-mail address.

5. Prizes: Grand Prize—a $10,000 vacation to anywhere in the world. Travelers (at least one must be 18 years of age or older) or parent or guardian if one traveler is a minor, must sign and return a Release of Liability prior to departure. Travel must be completed by December 31, 2001, and is subject to space and accommodations availability. Two hundred (200) Second Prizes—a two-book limited edition autographed collector set from one of the Silhouette Anniversary authors: Nora Roberts, Diana Palmer, Linda Howard or Annette Broadrick (value $10.00 each set). All prizes are valued in U.S. dollars.

6. For a list of winners (available after 10/31/00), send a self-addressed, stamped envelope to: Harlequin Silhouette 20th Anniversary Winners, P.O. Box 4200, Blair, NE 68009-4200.

Contest sponsored by Torstar Corp., P.O. Box 9042, Buffalo, NY 14269-9042.

ENTER FOR
A CHANCE TO WIN*

Silhouette's 20th Anniversary Contest

Tell Us Where in the World
You Would Like *Your* Love To Come Alive...
And We'll Send the Lucky Winner There!

Silhouette wants to take you wherever
your happy ending can come true.

Here's how to enter: Tell us, in 100 words or less,
where you want to go to make your love come alive!

In addition to the grand prize, there will be 200
runner-up prizes, collector's-edition book sets
autographed by one of the Silhouette anniversary
authors: **Nora Roberts, Diana Palmer,
Linda Howard** or **Annette Broadrick**.

DON'T MISS YOUR CHANCE TO WIN!
ENTER NOW! No Purchase Necessary

Silhouette®
Where love comes alive™

Name: _____

Address: _____

City: _____ State/Province: _____

Zip/Postal Code: _____

Mail to Harlequin Books: **In the U.S.**: P.O. Box 9069, Buffalo, NY
14269-9069; **In Canada**: P.O. Box 637, Fort Erie, Ontario, L4A 5X3

*No purchase necessary—for contest details send a self-addressed stamped envelope to:
Silhouette's 20th Anniversary Contest, P.O. Box 9069, Buffalo, NY, 14269-9069 (include
contest name on self-addressed envelope). Residents of Washington and Vermont may
omit postage. Open to Cdn. (excluding Quebec) and U.S. residents who are 18 or over.
Void where prohibited. Contest ends August 31, 2000.

PS20CON_R